SOUL HARVEST

BR KINGSOLVER

Soul Harvest

Book 3 of The Rift Chronicles

By BR Kingsolver

brkingsolver.com

Cover art by Heather Hamilton-Senter
www.bookcoverartistry.com

LICENSE NOTES

Get updates on new book releases, promotions, contests and giveaways!
Sign up for my newsletter.

BOOKS BY BR KINGSOLVER

The Rift Chronicles

Magitek

War Song

Soul Harvest

Rosie O'Grady's Paranormal Bar and Grill

Shadow Hunter

Night Stalker

Dark Dancer

Well of Magic

Knights Magica

The Dark Streets Series

Gods and Demons

Dragon's Egg

Witches' Brew

The Chameleon Assassin Series

Chameleon's Challenge

Chameleon's Death Dance

Diamonds and Blood

The Telepathic Clans Saga

The Succubus Gift

Succubus Unleashed

Broken Dolls

To Mason

You great, lumbering, adorable clown. I hope there is a rainbow bridge, and that you find your Marta and the rest of the pack on the other side. I miss all of you so much.

CHAPTER 1

The rumor was that a new demon lord had come across the Rift and taken control of the Metroplex. That, the rumors said, was why the demons had stopped fighting on the side of the Akiyama Family in the Magi's civil war. The new lord was more interested in consolidating his rule than in sacrificing his minions to the machinations of human mages.

I had no ideas if the rumors were true. I heard three different versions of the story from three different vampires. I hadn't tried to look up a demon to ask. In spite of most people's opinions about me, I was in favor of self-preservation.

I was on my way over to Enchantments—my roommate Kirsten's shop—when a demon stepped out of a doorway and confronted me. He was tall, even taller than an elf, and his face was dominated by horns that grew out of his forehead and swept to the side and back, curling like a mountain sheep's. His skin was red, which often indicated a fire demon, but not always. He was dressed in a tailored purple suit, and his grin showed teeth that could easily tear the flesh from my bones.

"Danica James," he said, his voice a rumbling growl. "I am Besevial. You have something that belongs to me."

"I don't think so, but what do you think I have?" I took a step back and placed my hand on my Raider, prepared to draw.

"An avatar of Akashrian."

"I don't know who or what that is."

His eyes narrowed and he leaned closer. "Take care, daughter of Lucas James. You play with the fires of hell."

And then he was gone. Besevial. That was the name of the rumored new demon lord of the Mid-Atlantic region. And I had a very bad feeling that I knew who Akashrian was as well.

I continued to Enchantments and got there as Kirsten was showing her last customer out the door. Her likeness on the store's sign—a painting of her wearing a pointed hat and riding a broomstick sidesaddle in a miniskirt—had been joined by Santa and his reindeer flying next to her. Colorful lights outlined the windows and the door, and the window displays showed cheerful winter scenes.

"Good day?" I asked.

"Business is picking up. The more they clean up the neighborhood, the more comfortable people feel coming down here. If you can just convince the Rifters to riot and pillage a little less frequently, all the merchants down here would be very grateful."

After a short-lived war between factions of the Magi, life was, to a certain extent, getting back to normal. Construction crews —many of them including mages—were starting to clean up the debris and the wreckage. Stores and restaurants that hadn't been destroyed were reopening and putting up Christmas decorations. Trucks delivered food to restaurants and grocery stores.

Kids went back to school. And shoppers and tourists filtered back into Baltimore's Inner Harbor neighborhoods.

"I'll make sure that I mention it to the new demon lord next time I see him," I said.

Her head snapped up from where she was totaling her day's receipts. "You saw him?"

"On my way over here. He wants the avatar of Akashrian. Says it belongs to him."

"The avatar of who?" Kirsten bit her lip as the import of what I said sunk in. "That little statuette?"

"I guess so. That's the only thing I have that I got from a demon, other than a few scars."

"How does he know you have it?"

"Beats me, but it's someplace he'll never find it. I'm in the mood for oysters, and Jack's has reopened. Hungry?"

Walking over to Jack's, we passed an old church. I wasn't sure if it was being used before our little war, but I didn't remember the scorch marks around the windows and doors. Someone was obviously working on the place, however. Two large construction dumpsters sat outside partially filled with debris. I stopped and checked the city permit posted on the door.

"Harvesting Souls Church," I read.

"Sounds creepy," Kirsten said. "It had a different name before it was trashed during the Rifter riots last fall. I figured after it burned, they'd tear it down."

"Nope. This permit is for demolition, but also for renovation. Looks like they're going to keep the shell and rebuild the inside."

We continued to Jack's, where we gorged on oysters and steamed shrimp, drank a couple of beers, and then went home.

I didn't think anything more about the old church until a couple of days later when I passed it again. My partner, Detective Sergeant Carmelita Domingo, and I were on our way to grab a quick lunch. Tiny Carmelita hadn't been my partner very long. The granddaughter of the head of a top Ten Magi Family, she was sharp and fearless, and I enjoyed working with her.

"Pretty strange crew to have working on a church," Carmelita said.

I glanced in that direction and stopped in my tracks. Every being I could see who was working around the church was a demon.

"Burn 'em down so you can build 'em up? I'm sure your family loves that business model," I said.

"Oh, yeah. My father would have a stroke if he saw that." Carmelita's family was one of the largest financial conglomerates in the world and had taken heavy losses on their insurance portfolio due to the recent fighting.

"Hey, at least they're employed."

"What do they need money for? Food? Most of them just hang around the bars late at night and eat drunken college students."

"If it keeps the students from driving drunk, that might be considered a public service."

Carmelita snorted. "You're terrible."

On our way back, I made a point to take a look inside the church. All the workmen were demons, and the building was practically gutted. It sort of made sense. Demons were far stronger than humans, or even vampires, and they were very good at destroying things. I wondered who would be doing the construction.

Kirsten had a date that night, and my boyfriend was out of town, so when I got off work, I took the opportunity to go Christmas shopping. Kirsten, of course, was a pagan, as were most witches. I had no idea about Aleks's views on religion. I had slept at his apartment on Saturday nights, and he had never mentioned anything about church on Sunday mornings. Since I had been raised by my half-elf mother, practically all my knowledge of human religions was secondhand. My grandmother and most of my Findlay relatives went to church on Easter and Christmas but didn't seem to spend much effort on their religion at other times.

That didn't mean the pagans, elves, and almost everyone else in my life didn't want presents. Some celebrated Christmas, others celebrated Solstice, and the Elves celebrated Yule—which was on the same day as Solstice.

I knew that other people gave gifts at New Year. At least my list wasn't terribly long—Mom, my grandfather Joren, my grandmother Olivia, Kirsten, and Aleks. I had bought gifts for my grandmother and Mom from Kirsten. But what do you buy for a four-hundred-year-old elf? And Kirsten? I knew what she really wanted was a marriage proposal from Mychal Novak, but I didn't have enough money to buy that.

And then there was Aleks. It had been more than ten years since I had a boyfriend at Christmas. It had been never that I had a boyfriend who was the filthy rich scion of a Hundred Family. Kirsten had suggested buying a sexy elf costume, putting it on, and tying a bow in my hair. Then she laughed at the expression on my face. I let her live but still wasn't happy that she didn't have a better suggestion.

I had finally fallen back on making Aleks a present—a combination enhancer-converter magitek device for his car. He'd never have to plug it in or add fuel. It cost me about seventeen credits in materials and had a retail price of ten thousand, so I hoped he'd like it.

So, presents for my grandfather and Kirsten were still on my list.

I took a run up to my mom's place at Loch Raven Reservoir to tell her and my grandfather about Besevial and his request for the statuette.

Several elves were hanging around as Mom's house was the center of the community Joren had established when he came to protect Mom and me during the war. They seemed to have set up some sort of marketplace, with little booths displaying things they had made and were willing to exchange or sell. I waved hello and parked my bike in Mom's garage, plugging it in to recharge the battery.

"This is a surprise," Mom said as I walked into her kitchen. As always, it smelled like heaven. She was baking *elitriel*—an elven pastry using *eli*—a grain from the elven home world—and filled with a mixture of apricots and raspberries. She told me that in the home world she would have used redfruit, but only a few of those bushes grew in our world.

"I could smell what you're baking all the way downtown," I lied, and received a laugh and a hug in return.

I told Mom about my gift dilemma.

"Can you afford one of those demon-killer pistols you carry?" she asked. A Raider .50 caliber fired magically enhanced explosive-incendiary rounds. Cops often called it a hand cannon.

"Yeah, but why? Joren has enough magik to kill a demon in his little finger."

"Because sometimes you don't want to use magik. And your grandfather will love it because it came from you. Remember, he's a warrior mage. He'd much rather have a weapon than a fishing pole."

Especially since he could catch a whole boatload of fish with magik if he wanted to. I could get an employee's discount on weaponry from Whittaker Arms, so I could take care of that the next time I went to work.

Mom didn't have any good suggestions for a gift for Kirsten. What to get for the girl who has everything except a ring on her finger? We tossed ideas around for a while but didn't hit on anything we both liked.

My grandfather came in a little later and gave me a hug, and the three of us sat down with tea and those lovely pastries.

I told them about my encounter with Besevial.

"An avatar?" Joren asked.

"That was what he said. He called it an avatar of Akashrian. Have you ever heard of her?" Mom and Joren had watched me stash the statuette in a cabinet in my workshop in the back of the house.

He shook his head. "No, but I can contact someone in Ireland who has spent far more time studying demons than I have. It could either be some sort of demon queen or one from their pantheon. They do have a large number of gods and goddesses. To my knowledge, no one has ever been able to determine whether their gods are corporeal or not."

"You mean a real god walking around?"

Joren shrugged. "What is a god? How long do demons live? We don't know if the being symbolized by that figurine is two feet tall or two hundred feet tall. I've never seen a dragon, but our history says the largest of those who came through a rift into Alfheim were a hundred feet from nose to tail. Maybe they have dragons in the demons' world."

"You should write fantasy novels," Mom said. "You could make a fortune."

He chuckled. "I know someone who's doing that. Taking historical tales from Alfheim and publishing them as fiction. But back to reality. You take care, Danica. The artifact is safely warded, but don't trust that demon to act rationally. He might decide to eat you out of spite."

We talked for a while longer, and then they accompanied me out to my car. I paused to take a longer look at the goods the elves were selling. One guy had a sort of display set up with what looked like wood carvings. Curious, I wandered over to see them.

Elves don't use sharp tools to work. They use magik. I found myself looking at some incredible sculptures by a master artist.

"These are fabulous! Do you sell them?" I asked.

He preened. "Of course. You like them?"

One in particular caught my eye. It looked like an abstract sculpture of a woman. "What do you call this?"

"It's a depiction of the Goddess," he said. "I'm asking two hundred for it."

"Sold. Can I bring the money for it later this week?"

"Sure. I'll give it to Amelie to hold for you. Just give her the money when you come." He picked it up and handed it to my mother.

Solstice present for Kristen solved with a day to spare. Life was good.

Mom walked me over to get my bike.

"Where do they get money?" I asked.

Mom grinned. "From people like you. I've introduced them to that farmers' market in Baltimore on Sundays, and there's a craft market in Towson, and one in York on Saturdays. Some of the merchants who buy my wines have taken some things on consignment. Between themselves, they barter labor or services or food for money if they need it. Elves developed trade and capitalism while humans were still living in caves.

"They seem to be settling in here. Do they plan to go back to Iceland when this war is over?" I asked.

She shook her head. "I don't think so. They like the trees. Joren brought two hundred warriors with him, but there are more than five hundred elves here now. I've spoken to your grandmother, and Olivia will help us bargain with the Council for the land surrounding the reservoir. By next winter, there will be a permanent town here."

CHAPTER 2

The type of assassinations that presaged the Council War —as the latest spat between Magi Families was being called—continued in the Metroplex. Members of Magi Families —even the youngest, least consequential members—were learning to travel with security guards and shields.

And then there was the sabotage. While the war's overt fighting was in a lull, there continued to be bombings—both mundane and magikal—of buildings and facilities on both sides. Magikal sabotage of electrical, hydrologic, and mechanical equipment—not to mention occasional other nasty tricks— were ongoing.

So, while the soldiers employed by the various Families had time to drink, brawl, and whore, cops were knocking down overtime like crazy.

Unfortunately, captains didn't get overtime. We got something called "compensatory time." That meant we could take extra time off some time after hell finished freezing over to make up for working twenty hours a day while we were still young enough to walk.

Out of curiosity, I kept an eye on the old church. The demons finished gutting it, and the place stood idle—or so it appeared at first. Then, one morning, I noticed progress on new construction—someone had been working at night.

That evening, after dinner with Aleks, I talked him into taking a detour from our normal route between the restaurant and his apartment. It was about ten o'clock, and we could see red light leaking through the cracks around the boarded-up windows.

I swerved off the sidewalk and up the steps to the front door.

"Where are you going?" Aleks asked.

"I want to try and peek in. I'm curious as to what's going on in there."

He shrugged. "Whatever vampires do at night when nobody's watching."

"Vampires?"

"Sure. Can't you feel them?" Aleks was a spirit mage, the first one I had ever been close with, and I was still learning about his abilities.

"No, I can't. You can feel whether there's a vampire or a demon or a mage in there? Through solid walls?"

"Two demons." He hesitated. "Twenty-three vampires, no mages."

"I'll be damned. Can you tell the difference between a crook and an honest man?"

He chuckled. "Wouldn't that be great? No, and I've never heard of anyone who can. Even truthsayers can be fooled."

My curiosity still wasn't satisfied. I climbed the front steps and put my eye to a place where the crack between the stone wall and the plywood covering the doorway was widest. I couldn't see a whole lot, but it appeared as though the people inside were engaged in construction work. I leaned back and turned to Aleks, who had come up behind me.

"Can you feel humans?"

"Sure, but there aren't any humans in there."

As we continued down the street, I thought about that. Vampires weren't known as construction workers in the Mid-Atlantic, but I wasn't sure about other places. I did know that they had cities and towns in their home dimension. They were somewhat civilized, by human standards. They had brought some of their animals across the Rift and were breeding herds in places such as the Russian steppes and the Argentine Pampas.

"Who would hire vampires to do construction?" I asked.

"Maybe they work cheap," Aleks said.

Maybe. But a church? Rifters were forbidden under the Compact to allow humans to worship in any Rifter religion. Some humans did, of course, but covertly. Sort of like being Catholics in sixteenth-century England, although I couldn't see the attraction for demon worship.

The following morning, I did a datanet search for vampire construction companies. I found two that said they employed vampires, although I had to do some digging to determine that. What they actually said was that vampires were encouraged to apply for jobs. Figuring out who owned those companies was even more difficult.

Another hour of digging turned up that one was owned by the Rudolf Family, and the other by a partnership of Rudolf and Moncrieff. Karl Rudolf and David Moncrieff were both dead. David's wife, Courtney Findlay-Moncrieff, was officially a wanted criminal, and her daughters were in Scotland in the protective custody of my grandmother, Olivia Findlay-James.

I tried to call both companies, but their listed phone numbers had been disconnected. A check with the construction licensing authorities showed that both companies were in good standing in spite of the listed owners being deceased. Curiouser and curiouser.

I spoke to my second-in-command, Lieutenant Mychal Novak, and to Carmelita, about the church, asking them to keep an eye on the place. But I didn't have time to do much else as dispatch sent me an urgent message about a Magi murder.

☙❧

It was snowing outside, but little was sticking to the ground. The wind was the worst part, and the snow wasn't falling so much as blowing sideways. The drive from Police Headquarters had been a joy, with streets more suited to ice skates than tires. It didn't help that I wasn't completely comfortable with the new car the department had given me. I decided I should add another set of stabilizers to the magitek devices I had already installed.

I drove while Carmelita filled me in on the information she found on her laptop concerning the address that dispatch had given us.

The Danner Family was one of the Hundred. Their headquarters was in Denver, but they had offices in the Baltimore-Washington Metroplex, just as most Magi Families did. They were loosely allied with Findlay, my grandmother's Family, which put them on the side of the Western Alliance, which ruled what was left of the Magi Council.

The Danners' local trade representative, Fredrick Danner, lived in the Roland Park area of Baltimore, amidst other rich Magi. He was a younger brother of the Family head, married, with three children. The mansion was modest by the neighborhood standards, the grounds surrounded by a brick wall topped with spiked wrought iron.

On one side of the large main house was a long, one-story building with multiple doors. A six-car garage was on the other side. The doors of what I assumed were servants' apartments were all open in spite of the weather.

The uniformed sergeant who met Carmelita and me at the front door said, "This is a strange one, Captain. I know we're not supposed to jump to conclusions, but it looks like the whole damned family was poisoned."

He first led us to the kitchen, where the air was filled with the stench of burned bread mixed with the smells of sickness and death. A window was open, and the room was decidedly chilly. An open oven had half a dozen lumps of charcoal in blackened baking tins. A portly woman lay on the floor, her head in a puddle of vomit, and brown stains showing on the back of her dress.

"She was baking bread," the sergeant said. "Got sick, passed out, and the bread burned. Damned lucky the house didn't catch on fire."

"Who called it in?" I asked.

"The chauffeur. His room is over the garage. Said he was out with friends last night and didn't eat here. The building next door has five small apartments for the servants. A body in each, one man and four women."

I sent Carmelita out to the servants' quarters, while the uniformed cop led me upstairs to the third floor. "The family is up here."

"What about the security guards?" I asked.

"Night shift didn't see anyone. They took over at eleven last night, and the evening shift went home. All of them denied seeing any of the family after they came on shift."

Mr. Danner was in bed, and his wife was in the attached bathroom. Both showed signs of vomiting and diarrhea, and they were very dead. Down the hall, we found a man and a woman in separate rooms. Both looked to be university age and exhibited the same symptoms.

In the woman's room, I found Kelly Quinn, the Arcane Division medical examiner, crouched over the victim, who was half-sprawled onto the floor.

"Initial impressions?" I asked.

"Thallium sulfate poisoning. Possibly magikally enhanced," Kelly said. "Dani, it would have been extremely painful."

"Time of poisoning? Time of death?"

Kelly shook her head. "Time of death, between midnight and three or four o'clock this morning for all the victims. I have some people going through the trash, cupboards, and refrigerators trying to identify any food that might have been consumed yesterday. I'm assuming the poison was delivered in either food or drink."

The servants' quarters were visible from the bedroom window. "I haven't seen the bodies outside," I said. "Same symptoms?"

"Identical."

"Then I would look at food. The servants wouldn't be drinking the same wine as the family, but they would be eating some of the same food."

She nodded. "I'll be able to tell you more once I can examine stomach contents."

"Looks like you won't have to cut them open to do that," I said, as I backed out of the room. All of the victims I had seen were violently sick before their deaths. It didn't take a genius to understand why no one had called a doctor. Dealing with a phone while puking your guts out wouldn't be easy for anyone.

The sergeant and I headed out to the garage. "Tell me about the security guards," I asked him as we walked.

"Eight in total—contracted from Whittaker. Jeff Collins is their captain. Decent electronic security system, but mostly automated. The guards don't live here, and their captain told me the night-shift guys bring their lunch or have it delivered sometimes."

"I'll want to talk to their captain, and to each of them. Keep them separated from each other."

We entered the garage through a side door. One of the six slots for cars was empty, the others held a limo, a European sports car, and three expensive sedans. We took a set of stairs to the second floor.

The chauffeur was younger than I expected. Mid-twenties and vid-star handsome.

"Captain Danica James," I said, flashing my ID.

"Colin Murphy," the chauffeur said. I noticed a hint of an Irish accent.

I looked around. He had a small but comfortable apartment. Sitting room, kitchen with a table and chairs, bathroom, and bedroom.

I took a seat on the couch. "Tell me what you did yesterday, where you were, who you were with, and what you found when you came home."

Murphy sat down in a chair across from me. The uniformed sergeant remained standing by the door.

"Yesterday was my normal day off. I drove over to Delmarva to see a friend. We stayed the night at a hotel, and I drove back this morning. I discovered Martha's body when I went into the kitchen about eight o'clock. The room was full of smoke. I opened the window and turned off the oven." He closed his eyes and took a deep breath. "I called out, didn't get any answer. When I checked upstairs, Lord Danner's door was unlocked. I went in, and then I called the police."

"Did you touch anything? Any of the bodies?" I asked.

He shook his head. "Only the window and the oven, and I opened the front door. The smoke was all over the house."

"What about the security guards?"

"I found Jeff after I called the cops. He went inside, but I stayed outside after that. I checked on the other staff and found them in their rooms."

"Who is your friend in Delmarva? And where in Delmarva?" The Delmarva Peninsula was a big place, and his description was rather vague.

"I'd rather not say."

Considering the morning I was having, I wasn't terribly sympathetic. I smiled and batted my eyes at him. "Sergeant, arrest Mr. Murphy on suspicion of murder."

"Wait! Look, her husband..." Murphy's calm demeanor evaporated. Shaking his head, he leaned forward and said, "She won't back my story."

I stood. "Sergeant, please have Mr. Murphy escorted downtown."

The look on Murphy's face was priceless.

CHAPTER 3

"You arrested the chauffeur?" Carmelita asked. "What? They didn't pay him enough or something?"

I shook my head. "I don't think he did it, but he's being uncooperative, and I'm not in the mood. I wanted to deliver a message not to screw with me. He gave me that tired old line, 'I can't corroborate my alibi because of her husband.'"

Carmelita snorted.

"At the very least, I can charge him with obstructing our investigation if he continues to piss me off," I said. "Have we figured out where the other daughter is?"

It was her turn to shake her head. "Julia? Nope. Bed not slept in. Guards say she left yesterday around noon and hasn't come back. That was about an hour after the chauffeur left in his own car. I put out an all-points bulletin on the missing car."

She cocked her head and studied me. "This doesn't feel like either the HLA or one of Akiyama's assassinations."

The Human Liberation Army had carried out a series of terrorist bombings and assassinations in North America and Europe, but we had done a pretty good job of breaking up their network in the Metroplex. And the Akiyama Family and its allies had carefully targeted their covert assassination efforts. Killing women and children—not to mention servants—was something both sides in the war had avoided. No one wanted their own families harmed, or the war to turn into one with magitek-enhanced bombs decimating population centers. The war was over profits and control, and there wasn't any profit to be made from a wasteland.

"Yeah, I agree. I want you and Novak to tap into your country-club contacts and find out if anyone had a personal grudge. This strikes me as amateurish. No pro would plan this kind of collateral damage. And how would someone from outside manage to plant the poison?"

"Deliveries of food," Carmelita said.

That made sense. "Call Luanne and have her come over here. We need to go through the household computer records with a fine-toothed comb."

Luanne Armstrong was my administrative assistant—a smart, young uniformed cop with good computer skills. I knew I could hack the Danners' systems and give her access.

I spent the next two hours questioning the guards and their captain. Except for incompetence and laziness, I couldn't identify anything in their answers that aroused my suspicions. But no one could contact the evening-shift guards. I told dispatch to send uniforms to their homes.

"Captain James?"

As the guard captain was leaving, Kelly Quinn showed up at the door of the room I was using for my inquiries. She held a metal cylinder in her hands.

"Hi, Kelly. Come on in." I raised an eyebrow at the canister she put on the table. "What have we here?"

"Salt," Kelly said as she sat down, "heavily laced with thallium sulfate. White powder, odorless, tasteless. It's slow acting, so in high doses, it usually takes three to four hours for symptoms to manifest."

I didn't open the can. My natural curiosity didn't extend to sampling causes of death.

"Do you carry a mass spectrometer with you in the field?" I asked.

She gave me a faint smile and wiggled her fingers. "After a manner of speaking. Shall we say that my magik is a lot more suited to being a pathologist in a police department than being a pediatrician."

"So, a cook could add salt to the soup, taste it, and then add some more when it wasn't as salty as she expected. How much would it take to kill someone?"

"And the person eating the soup might add a little more at the table. The salt in the shakers for the table contained thallium, too. A lethal dose is between one and three grams, depending on a person's size. Half a teaspoon would kill all the victims, and I probably have ten or twenty times that much in this salt can."

"Fingerprints?"

"The cook's and two of the dead servants. None on the shakers. They've been polished along with the rest of the silver."

I sighed. "So, anyone in the house could have done it. Family, staff, guards. Or a delivery driver."

Kelly nodded. "Or any visitors who wandered into the kitchen. But my guess is, it was done yesterday. We're not talking about a slow poisoning over time."

While we were talking, Luanne showed up. As always, she looked sharp, her uniform creased and immaculate, and her short afro gave her a military-like appearance. I had snatched her from Dispatch, where I was sure her smart mouth and offbeat attitude would have eventually landed her in trouble.

I waved her in and pointed to the computer sitting on Fredrick Danner's desk.

"I need you to go through all the orders and deliveries for the past week. Pay attention to salt or any other white powder."

"Like sugar, flour, etcetera?" she asked.

"Any white powder," Kelly said. "We're looking for thallium sulfate, which is sometimes used as rat poison, so deliveries to the gardener as well as the kitchen."

Luanne nodded. "Got it."

"Also," I said, "when you finish with that, look through Mr. Danner's business files and correspondence for any disputes, financial issues, or threats. After that, look at the emails of the rest of the family and staff. Any of the guards being blackmailed?" I took a deep breath. "Hell, Luanne, I'm grasping at straws. Even if you find a delivery of fifty pounds of thallium sulfate, I don't have a motive for why someone poisoned an entire family."

By late afternoon, we learned from the security guards that a food delivery had been made the previous morning. However, when we asked Mid-Atlantic Produce, the company denied making a delivery that day. None of the empty wine bottles we found tested positive for thallium. The landscaping company that maintained the grounds denied ever using thallium, but we did find that vermin control companies in the Metroplex used it, mostly in areas near the Waste—where rats grew as large as small dogs—and in warehouses near the harbor. In other words, it wasn't hard to acquire.

Dispatch called.

"Captain?"

"Yeah, what have you got?"

"Uniforms called in. They say they checked the apartment for those security guards, but no one answers."

I sighed. "Their supervisor says that neither of them is answering his phone. One of them has a white compact car, about ten years old." I gave her the license number and waited.

"Captain? They say the car is there."

I had a bad feeling. "Tell them to try not to break anything too badly, but go in. On my authority."

"Yes, ma'am."

I waited some more. When the dispatcher came back on the line, she was significantly more subdued.

"Captain, they found them. Both dead. Said they looked like they'd been sick."

"Ok, thanks. Call forensics and have them go out there."

I hung up and went looking for Carmelita. I found her talking to Kelly Quinn. "You can add the evening-shift guards to the casualties," I told them. "Evidently, they talked the cook into feeding them. It's been a long day. Catch a ride back to headquarters, and I'll see you downtown in the morning."

"What about Murphy? The chauffeur?" Carmelita asked.

"He'll be a lot more willing to talk after spending the night in a cell," I replied.

Home was closer than the office, but I drove in to Police Headquarters. I had received several calls throughout the day, and one incident in particular concerned me. I called Mychal when I left the Danner residence and asked him to meet me.

"So, what happened?" I asked as Mychal handed me a take-out cup of coffee.

"Joel Romero left his office about twelve-fifteen to meet his wife for lunch," Mychal said. "Between the front door and his limo—about ten steps—someone blew his head off with a high-powered rifle." Romero was a Hundred Family and an ally of Findlay.

"Sniper."

"Yeah."

"Any idea why?"

Mychal shrugged. "His wife says he doesn't have any personal enemies that she knows of. But Joel was the younger brother of the Family head, who is in poor health."

"Sounds like an Akiyama-Moncrieff assassination," I said. "They want to sow chaos among the Families that support the Magi Council."

"Yeah. It was definitely a professional hit. Do you really want me to spend time investigating it? I'm not real hot on driving up to Wilmington and asking Akiyama Hiroku if one of his assassins ventured down to Columbia today."

I shook my head. "Back burner. What else is going on?"

"A couple of drug dealers—humans—have turned up dead this week. Rumors are that a new big boss is consolidating her power."

"Her?"

He chuckled. "Reina de LaCosta. One of our informants describes her as mid-twenties, medium height, a bit chubby, with blonde hair, and magik."

"Susan Reed," I said.

"That was my first thought."

Reed had been an HLA activist we captured and imprisoned at the arcane prison in Gettysburg, northwest of Baltimore. She had escaped with a man who had once been the Magi crime kingpin of the east coast. Shortly thereafter, she killed him and disappeared. Her new name, translated as Queen of the Coast, fit with her profile. Susan was one of those people who thought she was a lot smarter than everyone else. I had to admit, she usually was one step ahead of everyone else, including me.

"I don't suppose your source has an idea about where she hangs out?" I asked.

"Not a clue. Very mysterious."

"Stay on it. I'll have Carmelita check with her sources as well."

I dreamed about the dragon lady that night. Akashrian. I cowered in the corner of a room lit with the red light that demons favored. She towered over me, bloody red. The saliva that dripped from her mouth hissed when it burned holes in the floor. Her glowing eyes pinned me like a butterfly, helpless before her. In one hand, she held a human leg dripping blood, and every so often, she would take a bite from it. Human screams came from somewhere beyond my sight. The screams sounded like my father's voice.

The dream seemed to last forever. I woke up in a cold sweat, with the first light of dawn showing through my window.

CHAPTER 4

Colin Murphy had lost a lot of his casual arrogance by the time Carmelita and I sat down with him in the interrogation room at Police Headquarters. A night in jail does that to a lot of people.

"Good morning," I said, taking a sip of my take-out coffee. Murphy stared longingly at the cup, but I didn't offer him anything to drink. Jailhouse coffee might have been considered a form of torture. "With a little more time to reflect, do you have anything new to tell me today?"

"I didn't kill anyone."

"Where were you on Thursday, and who were you with?"

He shook his head. "Her husband will kill me."

"If he does, I'll lock him up."

Murphy took a deep breath. "Ivanka Johansson."

That was a name I hadn't expected. My Aunt Courtney's best friend and certainly no friend of the Danners. Also, a fan of

Ronald Rump, a gigolo hairdresser who hung out with Court-ney's crowd.

"Out of curiosity, how much did she pay you for your little assignation?" I asked.

He told me, and Carmelita snorted. Murphy was younger and better looking than Rump, and his fee was half as much, but Rump would have done Ivanka's hair as part of the service. It still boggled me how much people were willing to pay to get laid.

"Tell me about Julia Danner," I said, switching gears. Julia was the youngest Danner daughter, and she still hadn't turned up.

Murphy's demeanor changed again. He began to fidget, shifting uneasily in his chair. His gaze darted around the room, looking anywhere but at me or Carmelita.

My partner leaned forward. "What are you so worried about? You were doing her? A sixteen-year-old kid? Her daddy's dead, and you're out of a job and a place to live. What do you have to lose by being honest with us?"

Murphy started to say something, an indignant expression on his face. Carmelita held up her hand. "Yes, I know. Don't tell me sixteen is legal age. That doesn't change the fact that you're disgusting and will probably never work in this town again. So, tell us about her."

"Who told you that?" he practically shouted.

"You did, honey," Carmelita said. "It's written all over your face. You're in so deep that oxygen is getting scarce. Your only hope is to cooperate with us. Don't worry, we're homicide, not vice. But unless you want us to charge you with hindering our inves-tigation, I suggest you start answering our questions. Truthfully."

After spending a minute or two trying to imitate a cornered rat, Murphy deflated.

"I didn't seduce her. She came after me. Smart kid. Too smart. She thinks she's an adult, but her father didn't see it that way. Graduated high school early, set to start at Hopkins in the spring. She's a lot younger than her brother and sister, and that caused problems. She wanted to do the things they do—go out to bars, sleep around, that sort of thing. She accused Sara—her older sister—of ratting on her to their parents and trying to control her. Accused Sara of being jealous because Julia is prettier and smarter."

"Was she banging anyone else?" Carmelita asked.

"Probably. She got caught sneaking out at night, and it wasn't to see me."

"Any idea where she is?" I asked. "Friends, places she likes to hang out?"

He gave us a couple of names, along with a pub where Johns Hopkins students hung out. "She used to go over to the library at Hopkins," he said. "She might have met some people there."

"The library?" Skepticism dripped from Carmelita's voice.

"I said she was smart. She loves chemistry the way most kids love video games."

"Do you know anything about her magik?" I asked.

"Oh, yeah. Air and water. Inherited from her mother and father."

I thanked him for his cooperation and terminated the interview. As Carmelita and I gathered our things and got ready to leave, Murphy asked, "Am I free to go?"

I grinned at him. "Oh, no. That was a pretty story, but you're still a suspect, and we might need to ask you more questions. Besides, if you're innocent, you don't want to leave us. You're a material witness, and someone might want to finish killing the rest of the staff. You'll be safer here."

As soon as we were outside the room, Carmelita giggled. "Did you see his face?"

"Yeah. I want you to go up to Hopkins and snoop around the library. I'm going to go visit Julia's friends."

"You think she did it? Poisoned her whole family?"

"Murphy seems to think so. Or maybe he's just trying to point us in any direction except him. If she didn't do it, then she's in danger, and she may know who did it. Let's follow up his leads, and maybe tomorrow we can figure out what else he might be able to tell us about the Danner family. Right now, I'm not sure what questions to ask him."

❈

Before I left the building, I went downstairs to the morgue in the basement. I found Kelly Quinn supervising one of her assistants who was conducting an autopsy on a man with half a head.

"Joel Romero?" I asked.

"Correct," Kelly said. "I should have the cause of death sometime today." She winked at me, and I could see the grin wrinkles around her mask.

"Anything on the bullet?"

"Either a soft-point high-velocity round, or an explosive. We didn't recover anything except tiny fragments. I'm leaning toward the soft-point." She put her finger on a small round hole above Romero's left eye. "I would expect an explosive to leave a much larger entrance wound." I agreed. An explosive round from my Raider 50 probably would have blown his head off.

"Have you done the Danner family yet?"

She nodded. "As I suspected, thallium sulfate poisoning."

"You said that it might have been magikally enhanced."

"It's not only enhanced, but it was bound to the salt. Not a true chemical reaction, so it would have to be a magikal binding. I thought at first I'd probably find thallium only in the top of the can, but none of the salt was clean."

"Thanks. Anything else?"

"We found a jar with traces of sodium chloride and thallium sulfate in the trash outside. No fingerprints."

I looked up the friends of Julia Danner that Murphy identified. One was a freshman at Johns Hopkins, the other was still in high school. As far as I could tell, both lived with their parents. Interestingly, while both families were Magi, neither were members of the Hundred.

The Hundred were an insular group, mostly socializing and doing business with each other. I ran a quick check on the girls' families. Katie Starling was a scholarship student at Hopkins. Her parents owned a construction company in West Virginia. Darlene Marberry's father worked for a Danner-owned company. Her place at Julia's prep school was through a Danner-supplied scholarship.

The girls' class schedules weren't public information, but for a magitek hacker, accessing them was like taking candy from a baby. By the time I reviewed the available public and secure information, I felt like I had a handle on where and when I could corral Julia's friends for private conversations.

But I wanted a more expansive picture of Julia, so I went to her school early to speak with the headmistress, planning on talking to Darlene Marberry after she finished her classes for the day.

As I walked into the building for the first time in almost twenty years, that old feeling of trepidation came over me. The place where I had been bullied so relentlessly hadn't changed at all. I felt like I could have closed my eyes and walked straight to the headmistress's office.

"Captain James, Metropolitan Police," I said to the receptionist, showing my ID. "I'd like to speak to Dr. Stolnikova, please."

She spoke over an intercom, "Dr. Stolnikova, a policewoman is here to see you."

There was an audible sigh. "Send her in."

Galina Stolnikova had gone to university with my father, and my grandmother told me once they had a relationship for a while. Tall, blonde, busty, and immaculately tailored, she hadn't changed much in the twenty-some years since I saw her last.

"Captain James," I said, holding up my ID as I walked through the door.

"You!"

I smiled. "It's a real pleasure to see you again, too." I sat in a chair in front of her desk without being invited. "I'd like to talk to you about one of your students, and then I need to meet with another one. I assume you heard about the Danner family?"

Stolnikova attempted to recover from the shock of seeing me. "Yes, I heard. Dreadful. But none of their children are students here."

"Oh? I thought that Julia attended here."

"She did, but she graduated and moved on."

That didn't completely tally with what I'd found online. "I thought she wasn't due to graduate until the end of the term. Another two weeks, I believe."

"Well, officially. But she's finished all of her requirements, so there wasn't any need for her to continue attending classes."

Gee, that sounded familiar. The headmistress had ushered me out the door before the end of a term.

"What did she do?" I asked. "Blow up the chemistry lab?"

Stolnikova looked uncomfortable, but when I continued to wait for an answer, she finally said, "She didn't blow anything up, but she was conducting forbidden experiments. Mixing magik with chemical reactions. Why? You don't think she had anything to do with her family's deaths, do you?"

"What can you tell me about her? Socially? Academically? Emotionally?"

The woman across from me took a deep breath. "Well, I guess now that she's dead, I'm not breaking any confidentiality. She was a bright girl—extremely bright—and took top marks in all of her courses. Funny you should mention emotionally. Very emotional, very quick to take offense, unstable temperament. She didn't have many friends, and didn't seem to care. I guess the easiest way to describe her was a nerd—smart, socially awkward, but pretty and athletic."

That sounded like both me and Dr. Stolnikova.

"And her friends?"

"Only a couple, and very much like her. They had their own little clique. The only one left now is Darlene Marberry."

"I'll need to talk with her. And, by the way, to our knowledge, Julia is still alive. She wasn't home when the rest of her family died. She is missing, though, and we're trying to find her."

CHAPTER 5

D arlene Marberry was the sort of girl that no one noticed. She was pretty, but not in a way that caught a person's attention. Brown hair, brown eyes, average build and figure for a seventeen-year-old girl, especially when wearing a school uniform.

She shuffled into the small conference room where I awaited her, acting for all the world like an unappreciated teenager. I introduced myself and invited her to sit. She eyed me with suspicion, and I debated with myself as to how to approach her.

"Darlene, I've been told that you're friends with Julia Danner."

After a moment, she nodded. "Yeah?"

"I'm investigating her family's deaths. You've heard about it?"

She nodded again, staring down at the table.

"Do you know where Julia is?"

Her head snapped up and she stared at me, her eyes wide. "She's —I mean, I thought—"

"We didn't find Julia's body. We think she's still alive."

The relief on Darlene's face couldn't have been faked.

"The information we have," I continued, "is that she left her home around noon on the day before the deaths were reported. No one has seen her since, and she isn't answering her phone. Darlene, I'm worried about her. Whoever caused her family's deaths may want to finish the job, or she might have been kidnapped. Whatever happened, I need to find her. Do you have any idea where she might have gone? Does she have a lover, or another friend she might be hiding with?" I leaned forward and made sure she met my eyes with hers. "Her parents are dead, Darlene. Nothing you tell me is going to get her in any trouble."

"There's a guy. Freddy, but I don't know his last name. I think he's a university student, but I don't know where he goes to school. I never met him. I do know that her parents found out about him, and she got in trouble. She stayed out all night and they grounded her."

"Does he go to school here in town?"

Darlene shrugged. "Somewhere in the Metroplex. Her dad took her car away for a while, but she still went to meet Freddy using the train."

"Any idea where she originally met him?"

"At a party, I think. Katie might know."

"Katie Starling?"

Darlene nodded.

"Does Julia have any other friends that you know of? Besides you and Katie and Freddy?"

Darlene shook her head. "We're not exactly part of the in-crowd. Me, especially. My parents aren't members of the country club, and I don't get invited to all the cool kids' parties." She said it matter-of-factly, but a little bitterness snuck in there.

"What can you tell me about Julia's magik?" I asked.

"Whhoo. She's bad. Air and water, and pretty strong. Nobody here messes with her. A couple of girls—older girls—tried to bully her when she first came here, and she kicked their butts. That's how we got to be friends. A few girls were being mean to me, and Julia stepped in. She and Katie. Everyone gives them a wide berth."

"What's Katie's magik?"

"She's an electrokinetic."

"And yours?"

"Fire."

"Is Julia an illusionist?"

She hesitated, and I waited. Reluctantly, she nodded. "Yeah. She's pretty good at it. That's how she's able to sneak out without her parents catching her."

I thanked her, gave her my card, and told her I might need to speak with her again. Checking my chrono, I saw that I had just enough time to catch Katie Starling when she finished her last class of the day.

⚜

I had a picture of Katherine 'Katie' Starling, a tall slender Native American with long black hair and a model's face. I almost didn't recognize her when she came out of the classroom building at the university. She was as flashy and flamboyant as Darlene was nondescript. Her hair was purple on one side and lime green on the other. Her makeup was also far from demure and made it hard to tell what she actually looked like.

"Katie Starling?" I asked as I stepped in front of her, holding out my ID. "I'm Captain Danica James, Metropolitan Police. I need to ask you a few questions."

She reacted the way young, rich drug users normally reacted. Having spent some time on the drug squad, I knew it well. Shock, paranoia, then complete denial flashed across her face. She smelled of weed, but since that was legal, I wondered what else she experimented with.

"I don't know nothin'."

"Including grammar? Dr. Stolnikova would be mortified," I said. "I've been told that you do know Julia Danner. And if you give a damn about her, you'll help me find her. I think she's in mortal danger."

A different kind of shock played across her face. "Julia?"

"You know her entire family has been murdered, don't you?"

"Uh, yeah. I saw it on the news."

"She escaped. I need to find her. Got time for a cup of coffee?"

Katie licked her lips, her eyes searching my face. "Yeah, okay."

I suggested a popular café just off campus, and she nodded. We set off in that direction.

"I spoke with Darlene," I said. "Just to bring you up to date, Julia's entire family and all their servants were killed. Julia wasn't there for supper, and she didn't come home that night.

What I'm concerned about is, whoever killed her family is probably looking for her. Do you see what I mean? She escaped. She's our only link to who did this, and they surely don't want her to talk to the cops."

"Uh, yeah. That makes sense."

We walked to the café, where I ordered coffee and Katie ordered a milkshake.

"Darlene told me that Julia's been seeing a guy named Freddy," I said. "Do you know him?"

"Yeah, I know him, but I don't know where to find him. He's a student, I think, but not here. Maybe one of the UM campuses?"

When a girl's best friends knew nothing about her boyfriend, it was because she had something to hide. I was getting an increasingly uneasy feeling about Julia.

"Do you know his last name?"

She shook her head. "Some people call him Fast Freddy, and I heard someone call him Freaky Freddy once."

"He's in the scene?"

Katie hesitated. "Uh, yeah, I guess you could say that."

"Is he a dealer?"

I hoped the girl never tried to play poker. Her face showed the inner struggle she was having, even through the weird makeup.

I leaned forward, my elbows on the table. "Katie, we're talking life and death. Someone went to a lot of trouble to wipe out Julia's entire family. I don't know why, but if anyone has the answer, it's Julia. But I'm afraid that if I don't find her soon, we won't find her alive. I'm not the drug squad. I work for the Magi Council."

"Yeah, he's a dealer. Downers, uppers, *astropene*, *quararg*, *nesforl*, as well as magikally enhanced weed. He's like a one-stop shop."

"And Julia's doing all that?"

Katie shook her head emphatically. "No, just the weed. She's smarter than to get into that other shit."

"I hope you are, too."

"I don't get my weed from Freddy. I don't trust him." She gestured toward the window. "I get mine legally."

There was a cannabis shop across the street from the café.

I thanked her and paid for our drinks. "If you hear from her, call me," I said, handing her my card. "And if you find out where I can find Freddy, definitely call me."

As I stood to leave, she looked up at me. "You really think she's in danger?"

"Yes. I hope she's still alive, and if she is, she's definitely in danger."

CHAPTER 6

I went back to the office and put Luanne to work searching for any and all male college students in the Metroplex with a first or middle name starting with 'Fred.' I knew the list would be extensive, but once I had it, I could parse it into a number of different searches.

While I was talking to Luanne, Carmelita came in and stood there waiting until Luanne and I finished.

"Any luck at the library?" I asked her.

"I showed Julia's picture around and people recognized her. One of the librarians said Julia regularly flirted with boys, but she didn't recall her meeting with or being with one particular boy. The last time Julia was there was the day before the murders."

I filled her in on what I discovered talking with Julia's friends. As we talked, I realized the coffee I had with Katie hadn't filled the void in my stomach.

"I'm hungry. Did you have lunch?" I asked.

"Nope."

On our way to a sandwich shop around the corner, Carmelita said, "Oh, by the way, I think they're getting ready to open that church you were curious about."

"So soon? The place was totally gutted."

"There's a sign out front inviting people to come worship this Sunday."

"Does it say what kind of church it is?"

Carmelita shrugged. "I asked Uncle Rodrigo, and he said it wasn't Catholic. With a name like that, he said it was probably some Protestant evangelical sect."

"Uncle Rodrigo?"

"Yeah, he's the archbishop of the Baltimore diocese."

"And a mage?"

"Of course. Magik and religion aren't mutually exclusive. I mean, the existence of demons is a provable fact."

She had me there.

On the way back from lunch, we took a tour by the church. It certainly looked a lot better. The scorch marks were all gone, and the stonework looked brighter than it had. New wood framed the stained-glass windows and the doors, one of which stood open.

We climbed the steps and peered inside. The place smelled of new wood and paint. Shiny wooden pews marched from the rear up to the altar rail. Arched wooden trusses soared from the floor to the peak of the roof.

A man wearing a long black cassock with a white surplice over it stood there. Catching sight of us, he smiled.

"Curious?" he called in a cheery voice. "Come on in and take a look around."

He hastened toward us. As he drew nearer, I saw that he was a large man—as tall as I was—and rotund. His dark hair was receding, he wore dark-framed glasses, and his ruddy face was split in a large smile.

"Come in, come in. Welcome to Harvesting Souls Church. I'm Reverend Charles Wilding."

"Good afternoon," I said. "We saw that the church had been renovated and were a little curious."

"Yes. Luckily for us, the previous owners just wanted to be rid of the place, so the church was able to buy it for a good price. Donations from the very welcoming community have enabled us to restore it, and once again, it's a house of the Lord."

From somewhere in his clothes, he produced a pair of brochures. "Here is a little something telling you about the church and our philosophy, and a schedule of services and events. I hope you'll be able to join us this Sunday as we give thanks to the Lord and pray for his continued blessings."

He was very friendly and gave us a tour of the sanctuary, showing us the stained glass, and bubbling on about the place. I wanted desperately to ask him about the demons and vampires but refrained. It just didn't seem polite. It took us about fifteen minutes to finally work our way out the door and back onto the street.

"Whoa!" Carmelita said. "Is he enthusiastic, or what?"

I agreed. The last person I met who was that excited about something was the realtor who sold Kirsten and me our house.

We went on back to work to discover that another Magi Family leader had been killed by a sniper. Caught up in the chaos that always engulfed Police Headquarters, I didn't think anything more about the Reverend Wilding.

❀❀❀

"I sent the Fred list to you," Louanne said when I showed up at the office the next morning. "The ones that have any kind of police record—even a parking ticket—are highlighted. I also split the list, with all the men under thirty separated from the older guys, and the ones enrolled at a college or university are also marked."

"You're wonderful," I said.

"I know." She winked at me. "Try to remember that when it's time for my next raise."

I called up the files on my computer and first looked at the students with a police record. Only one hundred seventy-six. Who knew the name Fred was so popular?

I printed out their pictures and then checked Katie's class schedule. She finished her classes that day at two o'clock, so I had plenty of time to drive over to the scene of the most recent assassination. I grabbed Carmelita and Novak, and we took my car.

Noah Carpenter had recently lost his son to an HLA assassin. We had caught that murderer and broken up the violent HLA radical cells in the Metroplex. Now his widow had to deal with losing her husband as well as her son.

Carpenter had left his office in downtown Baltimore to meet some business associates for lunch across the street. The sniper had taken him out while he waited for the light to change.

Standing on the corner where Carpenter had stood, I looked around at all the tall buildings surrounding us. Some of the older and shorter ones—relics of the nineteenth and early twentieth centuries—had windows that opened. The more modern buildings didn't. A group of uniformed cops milled around on the sidewalk across the street.

"Any idea where the sniper was?" I asked.

"I had a dozen men searching through the older buildings," Mychal said, "but we didn't find anything. There are at least four or five empty office spaces that overlook this corner. No one heard the shot."

"Silenced, probably," I said. "Same bullet as used in the Romero killing?"

Mychal shrugged. "Possibly. Remember that we didn't find much of the bullet that killed Romero, but Kelly thinks it's possible. Soft-nosed high-velocity bullet. Shot him in the chest."

My phone rang. "James."

"We have a major problem," Police Commissioner Whittaker said. "Meet me at Trombino's as soon as you can get there."

"I'm standing across the street from it. That's where Noah Carpenter was going when he was shot." Trombino's was *the* upscale Italian restaurant in downtown Baltimore. I had been there a couple of times, most recently with Aleks. There were three cops standing in front of the place talking to some civilians.

"I'll be there in ten minutes," Whittaker said and hung up.

We walked across the street. One of the cops noticed me and came over.

"Captain. A couple of employees showed up for work—the place opens at eleven for lunch—but everything's locked up. They tried calling the owner and the manager, but no one answers."

He motioned me to follow him to a window. I looked in and saw a pair of legs on the floor in the doorway to the kitchen.

"I need some authorization before I go busting into the place, ma'am," the cop said.

He followed me back to the door where I used my magik on the lock. As soon as I stepped inside, the smells of the Danner house assailed my nose. A quick search of the place turned up four bodies.

I assigned Carmelita and Mychal each to one of the four employees who had been outside, and I took the other two employees aside.

"Who were these people?" I asked the middle-aged man, who turned out to be one of the lunch cooks.

"Joseph was the night manager, and the others were the cook, a dishwasher, and the head waitress on the night shift," he said. "They would have been cleaning up after dinner. The place closes at eleven."

"How many more people on the night shift?" I asked.

He took me to their break room and pointed to a schedule posted on the wall. Between him and one of the waitresses, they identified all the people on the schedule.

"Where are the rest of the people who are supposed to be working today?" I asked. I had four employees who had been waiting outside, but the schedule showed eight people, plus the day manager, who hadn't shown up.

"I don't know," the waitress said. "All of us were off yesterday."

With a sudden feeling of fear, I took another look at the schedule. None of the people who worked the previous day had come to work. The employees we were talking to said that none of the people who had worked the previous day were answering their phones.

About that time, Commissioner Whittaker walked through the door. I went to meet him.

"We have at least five calls of deaths that mirror what you saw at the Danner house," he said, "and six more people in the ER are being treated for thallium poisoning. Two people have died. All of them either work here, or ate here yesterday."

CHAPTER 7

Kelly Quinn went straight to the kitchen and searched out every salt container. After checking them all, she raised her head and looked across the room at me, then nodded.

"Is the magikal binding the same?" I asked.

"Yeah, it is."

Carmelita came out of the restaurant's office. "What the hell?"

I had a sinking feeling. "It looks as though the Danner murders were a testing ground. A dress rehearsal. I need a list of every reservation, every payment from yesterday. Send cops around to every employee's home, and send someone to every hospital." I shook my head, then turned to the waitress. "How many people come in here on a normal Wednesday?"

Before she could answer, the cook said, "Wednesday lunch we usually serve about two hundred meals. Wednesday dinner about the same. Half of that for Saturday lunch, and double on Friday and Saturday evenings."

It made sense. Weekdays they got the people working downtown for lunch. The area was a ghost town during the day on weekends. The tourists spent their time and money closer to the harbor.

We had already determined that the lunch shift came in at ten o'clock and the doors opened at eleven. The restaurant closed at two-thirty to clean up for dinner, and the evening workers started between three and four-thirty, depending on their jobs. As was common in restaurant work, an employee got a shift meal. And considering restaurant wages, I doubted anyone turned down food prepared by Trombino's chefs.

The state of the employees' washrooms made me glad that I wasn't responsible for cleaning them. Several people had been violently sick in both employees' washrooms and in the customers' washrooms as well.

The computer in the office revealed that several employees had clocked out early the previous evening. The first to leave was one of the cooks, who bailed out at eight o'clock.

"I've never seen anything like this," Whittaker said, falling in beside me when I went outside to get some fresh air.

"I have Carmelita and Luanne in the office trying to figure out who all yesterday's customers were," I said. "But when one person pays for the table, and the people eating together aren't related..."

"We'll find some of them only after they're dead," he finished.

"Oh, I imagine most of them are already dead," I told him. "The ones who made it to hospital were mostly yesterday's lunch crowd. They got sick and their families called an ambulance or took them in. If you ate here last night and left at eight or nine, you'd be dead between midnight and two or three o'clock. And if you took the whole family out to dinner, and you all got sick, it would be a scene like the Danner family."

He shook his head. "We'll be finding bodies for days. Maybe weeks. What kind of monster would do such a thing?"

"Whoever it was, they targeted a place frequented by the Magi. You practically have to get a credit check just to walk into the place. I think we need to warn the Council."

"We need to crack down on sources of supply," he responded. "Every place that sells thallium needs to be identified, and every place that uses it."

"There are other poisons," I said. "A talented chemist with the right set of magikal talents could make something far worse."

"But, why?"

"Akiyama or Moncrieff could be doing it to weaken their enemies," I said, "or the HLA could be trying a new tactic, or we could see a ransom demand. Pay us, or shut down every restaurant in the Metroplex. I'm sure there are more possibilities, but those are the ones that come most readily to mind."

"Could it be a copycat?"

"If it is, we have even larger problems." I turned so that he looked at my face. "We haven't released the Danners' cause of death. All we've said is that we suspect foul play. No one outside my team and Kelly's team knows it was thallium poisoning."

I broke away from the horror show at Trombino's and took the pictures of all the Freddys up to Johns Hopkins. When Katie came out of her class, she spotted me immediately. We stood staring at each other for a moment, then she deflated, and trudged over to where I was standing.

"May I help you?"

"I certainly hope so. I have some pictures I need you to look at, and I'll pay in milkshakes."

"It's been a crappy week, and I'm eighteen. How about a beer?"

"It's been a crappy day. You're on. Where?"

She took me to a place near campus advertising one hundred twenty beers from all around the world. I ordered an Irish porter, and she ordered a Belgian ale. We sat by the front window where the light was best.

"I'm hoping one of these guys is Julia's Freddy," I said, pushing the stack of photos across the table.

"What did you do, get a picture of every Fred in town?"

I grinned and batted my eyes. With a sigh, she took a pull on her beer and started going through the pictures. Two-thirds of the way through, she stopped.

"That's him."

"You're sure?"

She turned the picture around and pushed it toward me so I could see it. "If he hit on you, would you forget his face?"

I had to admit, she had a point. Wild dark hair, straggly beard, acne, a lazy eye, and what looked like a permanent sneer weren't what I would consider attractive. But twelve years on the police force had taught me that my personal tastes were my personal tastes.

"She's in love with that?"

Katie's chuckle was dry as a desert. "Drugs and a big dick. At least, that's what I figure. He's smart, manipulative, and a hero of the revolution. What more could a girl want?"

"He's political?"

"Hell, I don't know. He talks a big game, but I always figured he was playing the dashing revolutionary to get chicks. You know what I mean?"

"HLA."

Her eyes sparkled. "Yeah. You know the type?"

"Unfortunately. Julia was into that?"

"Oh, yeah. The Magi versus the downtrodden masses. Easy for her to say—her family is richer than shit. But Julia is smart, ya know? Super smart. She's scared to death of becoming a trophy wife like her mom."

"Your family isn't exactly poor."

She shook her head. "No, we're not. But have you ever been to Charleston, West Virginia? Would you like to get stuck there for the next two hundred years? If I go into the family business —which is what my parents want—that's my future. My brother feels the same way."

She stopped and seemed to think about something. Maybe a way to make me see her viewpoint. Then she reached into her bag and pulled out a sketch pad. Flipping it open, she shoved it across the table to me. It was a picture of a sunset as seen from the Hopkins campus. It was done with colored pencils, and it was incredibly realistic. I flipped through the sketches. Male and female nudes. Landscapes. Portraits. Still lifes. They were gorgeous.

"What's your preferred medium?" I asked.

"Acrylics and oils. I want to be an artist, Captain James, not build cookie-cutter houses for middle-class norms."

"And Julia?"

"She wants to be a chemist. She wants to do research that combines chemistry and magik. You're a magitek, aren't you? So you understand that?"

"Yeah. I'm also a James. I understand the problems that can occur when magik interacts with the real world."

Katie nodded. "Yeah. How well did you understand that when you were seventeen? Or did you dwell on the unfairness of the world and how you were mistreated?"

"Do you feel mistreated, Katie?"

She drained her glass and grinned. "Oh, poor me. The weight of the world is on my shoulders, and I suffer for my art. Do I get a second round? I'm not driving."

I ordered two more beers.

CHAPTER 8

"Alfred Wallace. Parents' address listed in Arbutus. Student at the University of Maryland, Catonsville campus," I said, tossing his picture down in front of Carmelita and Luanne. "Let's go find him."

"Me, too?" Luanne asked.

"You did the scut work to find him, don't you want to be in on the takedown?"

"Yes, ma'am!"

"We don't even know if he's done anything," Carmelita said as we rode the elevator down to the parking garage.

"According to our informant, he deals cross-Rift drugs to college kids," I responded. "Have you ever known a street dealer who didn't carry his dope around with him?"

"True."

It was a twenty-minute drive to Freddy's parents' house. The area was lower-middle class, the homes mostly small and more than a hundred years old.

"Is this guy a mage?" I bothered to ask, silently cursing myself for not checking.

"Witch," Luanne answered. "His mother's a witch, nothing in the databases about his father."

That could be good or bad. A witch as powerful as Kirsten would be bad.

We left Luanne in the car, not wanting her uniform to make anyone in the house jumpy. A middle-aged woman with salt-and-pepper hair answered the door. Judging from the flour on her apron, we had interrupted her baking.

"I'm Captain Danica James," I said, holding up my ID. "We're looking for Alfred Wallace."

The woman took a deep breath, and her shoulders slumped. "Oh, Goddess. I'm not even going to ask what he's done. But he doesn't live here."

"Do you have an address for him?" I asked.

She rattled off an address a few blocks away, which was closer to the university campus. I thanked her, and we trooped back to the car. I glanced back and saw his mother watching us through a gap in the curtains.

"We'd better hurry," I said, "in case she calls him."

We rushed back to the car, jumped in, and I drove as fast as I safely could in a residential neighborhood. The location she gave us had a lot more cars parked on the street, many of the houses needed a coat of paint, and I saw a few 'For Rent' signs.

"Student ghetto," Carmelita remarked.

I drove past the house with Freddy's address. It was one of the largest houses on the block, with at least six cars parked in front, in the driveway, and in the yard. It had two stories, the paint was in terrible shape, quite a few roof shingles were missing, and the front porch sagged.

"Pretty obvious why Julia would rather live here than at her parents' mansion," Carmelita said.

"You can watch the cockroach races when you're stoned," Luanne said. "Hard to find that kind of entertainment in Roland Park."

"Ah, I didn't think of that."

I parked down the street and turned off the car. Turning to my companions, I said, "We don't know if she's here, or if she ever was. Keep an eye out for her, or any other underage kids, but our main objective is to bag Fast Freddy. Luanne, go through the alley to the back of the house. If the place is full of druggies, they'll be bailing out the back along with the cockroaches. Carmelita, you take the point. Knock on the door and ask for Freddy. I'll hang close to back you up."

Carmelita didn't look much older than Julia, even though ten years separated them. Both she and Luanne were aeromancers, able to shield themselves if bullets or magik started flying, while I didn't have that talent.

We gave Luanne time to get into position, then Carmelita left the car, walked up the street to Freddy's, and knocked on the door. A minute or so later, the door opened. I listened through a magitek device she carried as she asked someone inside for Freddy.

"Hey, Freddy! Some chick looking for you!"

A pause, then another man's voice. "Yeah?"

"Are you Fast Freddy?" Carmelita asked.

"Who wants to know?"

"I'm Dolores," she said, putting a sexy purr into her voice. "Katie said you might be able to help me."

"You're a friend of Katie's? Sure, come on in."

I rolled my eyes. The idiocy of drug dealers never ceased to amaze me. Send a hot girl in, and they opened the door.

"Is Julia here?" I heard Carmelita say as the door closed.

"Yeah. Come on up to my room. She's up there. What are you looking for?"

"Do you have any *quararg*?"

"Yeah, some good stuff," Freddy replied, practically panting. "You can try a taste before you buy."

I chuckled as I got out of the car and strolled toward the house. Carmelita was on the ball. *Quararg* was a drug from the vampire world with some aphrodisiac properties. A drug for those who wanted to live fast and leave a wasted-looking corpse. Addicts usually didn't live more than a year or two.

"Luanne, get ready," I told her, using my implant to communicate with her phone. "Both Freddy and Julia are in there, plus at least one other male."

"There's no fence on the alley," she replied, "so I threw an airshield across the back door. No one's leaving."

I reflected on how enjoyable it was to work with competent people. Stepping onto the front porch, I drew my weapon and palmed the magitek electrical box my father had made for me, then knocked on the door.

The guy who answered the door was as tall as I was, and half-again as broad. Half his head was shaved, the other half was plaited into a braid that fell across his shoulder. He wasn't old enough to grow a beard.

Shoving the muzzle of my Raider in his face, I grinned and said, "Shhh. Loud noises make my finger twitchy."

He backed away, and I followed him inside.

"How many people in the house?" I asked in a quasi-whisper.

"Uh, five." His eyes flicked toward the stairs. "Six."

"Where?"

"Two in the kitchen, three upstairs."

A voice from the back of the house called, "Who is it, Jase?"

"Let's go meet them," I said, gesturing in the direction of the voice. He turned, and I prodded him forward with the gun against his back.

Two other men, a little older than the doorman, sat at the kitchen table. They were stuffing weed from a pile in the center of the table into small bags and weighing them. Since the weed was pink instead of green, I knew immediately that it wasn't legal. *Nesforl.*

There was a pink haze in the air over the table. The men weren't wearing masks, so I knew they wouldn't move very quickly. And the last thing I wanted to do was get too close to the drug.

"Everyone put your hands in the air," I ordered, pushing Jase toward his buddies and stepping to the side so I could cover all three of them. Through my implant, I said, "Luanne, come on in. I need someone to help cuff some drug dealers. And either shield or put on a mask."

The three guys stared at me, or maybe at the Raider, then slowly raised their hands. Then the back door exploded inward, causing me to jump as startled as the three men. Luanne strode through the door with her Raider in her hand. She took stock of the situation, then pulled a pair of handcuffs from a pouch on her belt.

"Nice entrance," I said. "Not a chance now that I'll catch the people upstairs by surprise."

I could tell she blushed, even with her dark skin. "Sorry."

The guy farthest from me decided we might be distracted. Flame shot from his hand toward Luanne. It splashed harmlessly against her shield. I countered by directing a miniature lightning bolt from the box in my left hand toward him. It knocked him from his chair and left him senseless on the floor.

"Anyone else want to fight?" Luanne asked. She pulled the arms of the man still sitting in a chair behind his back and cuffed him, threading the cuffs through the opening in the back of the chair. Pulling out another pair of handcuffs, she cuffed Jase and forced him to sit on the floor.

"Keep an eye on these guys," I said, handing her another set of cuffs. "Carmelita is upstairs with Freddy and Julia."

Whirling around, I raced through the house and took the stairs three at a time. From the upstairs landing, I was presented with five closed doors.

"Dolores?" I shouted.

"Here!" Carmelita's voice came from the end of the hall.

I used the magitek box to blow the door open. That was accompanied by the sound of breaking glass. I rushed into the room to see an open window with shards of glass still hanging from the frame. Carmelita approached the window with her Raider in her hand. Julia—half dressed—sat on the bed on the opposite side of the room.

Carmelita looked out the window and started laughing. I joined her and looked down. Freddy lay there—bleeding from cuts on his arms, face, and head—holding one of his legs that was unnaturally twisted, and whimpering in pain.

"As far as dramatic escapes go, I would call that an epic fail," Carmelita said.

CHAPTER 9

My heart sank when I took a quick look around Freddy's bedroom. HLA posters on the walls—along with a couple of nude models—and HLA propaganda on the desk. Carmelita noticed it, too.

I waved my hand in Julia's direction. "Encase her in an airshield. I don't want her going anywhere. She has air and water."

Then I called the local station and went downstairs to discuss things with Freddy.

"Landed wrong, huh?" I said standing over him. "I hate when that happens."

"I think I broke my leg," he said through gritted teeth.

"Yeah, I think so, too."

"Aren't you going to do something?"

I squatted down beside him. "Like what?" Grabbing his foot, I shook it. He screamed. "I called an ambulance, but I'm not quite sure what else you want me to do. Maybe we could chat while we wait. Tell me about the HLA."

"I don't know nothin."

"I hear that a lot lately. Terrible grammar they teach kids nowadays." I shook his foot again, and he screamed again. "Or maybe you'd rather tell me where you're getting Rifter drugs."

He glared at me but didn't say anything.

"You probably think that it's smart to be more scared of your local demon dealer than of me. That's a lousy bet. At the moment, I have you pegged for a lifetime of misery in Antarctica. And the only way you're going to avoid it is by cooperating."

I heard sirens out in front of the house. Soon we were joined by two drug detectives, three uniforms, and an ambulance.

The drug cops, the uniformed sergeant, and I had a chat. "The guy with the broken leg," I said. "I need a guard on him twenty-four seven. He's a suspect in the mass murder of a Magi family." I turned slightly so I was facing the drug cops squarely. "I also suspect that all of these guys are either HLA or sympathizers, so keep that in mind when you interrogate them. Any information on that front I want reported to me immediately."

They all nodded. After bombing a cop bar in Baltimore, the HLA didn't have any friends on the police force.

"What about the girl?" one cop asked.

"She's coming with me. She's from a Hundred Family."

The uniformed sergeant snorted. "So she gets a slap on the wrist."

I batted my eyes at him. "It was her family that Mr. Broken Leg is suspected of slaughtering. I'm not sure if she's a victim or an accomplice, but I'm going to find out."

The cynical grin disappeared from his face.

The EMTs were getting ready to load Freddy in the ambulance. I called them over and said, "I don't have any idea what kind of drugs that guy is on, but it's probably a bad idea to give him any painkillers. Tell the doctors at the hospital, okay?"

"Got it, Captain."

Freddy watched me as I approached him, and stiffened when I laid my hand on his foot.

"I'll be around to talk with you later, Freddy. Think about what I want to hear. Your choices will have a direct bearing on your future."

"I want a lawyer."

"Freddy, Freddy. Don't you know that too many drugs and watching too much screen will rot your brain? I'm Arcane Division, Freddy. I work for the Magi Council. Your chances of seeing a lawyer this side of heaven are pretty slim."

"I didn't know there were any lawyers in heaven," one of the drug cops said.

I grinned at him. "Yeah. Freddy's chances of seeing heaven are pretty slim, too."

When I went back inside, Luanne approached me.

"You need to see the basement."

As I started down the stairs, she put a hand on my shoulder.

"Captain, I'm not sure it's safe down there. Stay in contact with me, and I can wrap you in my airshield."

I nodded and took the stairs more cautiously. When I reached the bottom, I understood. I'd seen plenty of illicit chemistry labs when I worked in the drug division. What was scary about the one in Freddy's basement was that we hadn't found any meth or other home-concocted drugs. But we were investigating poisons.

"Oh, crap." I turned back and took the stairs going up two at a time, pushing Luanne before me. When I got to the top, I went looking for the drug cops.

"There's a lab in the basement," I told them. "And I think they were making poison, not drugs."

One cop stared at me, his eyes almost popping out of his head. The older one rolled his eyes and reached for his phone.

"I'll call the meth lab guys," he said. "They'll treat it like a toxic-substance spill."

❧❧❧

We found Julia's clothes, most of which were in a small designer suitcase, and got her dressed. Carmelita walked her downstairs and put her in the back of my car, then sat with her until I was ready to leave.

When we arrived at Police Headquarters, we placed her in a cell in the Arcane Division jail in the sub-basement. Leaving Carmelita and Luanne to write up our report, I took the elevator up to the top floor to report to Commissioner Whittaker.

"So, you found her," he said as I dropped into the chair in front of his desk, holding the cup of coffee he handed me. "What does she have to say?"

"Not much. I'm waiting for the drugs to flush out of her system before I talk to her. She's pretty out of it. But her boyfriend had HLA posters and literature scattered about. That's been my concern about these poisonings."

"And not the sniper attacks?"

"Judging by the HLA members we've busted so far, hiring a professional assassin doesn't seem to be their *modus operandi*. They're amateurs, and they think like penniless college students."

"How about the boyfriend? Is he going to talk?"

"He's even higher than his girlfriend. I'm hoping that after they set his broken leg and the drugs wear off, he'll think about what kind of trouble he's in."

I finished my coffee and went back downstairs. Carmelita was sorting through the boxes of paper and personal belongings we'd taken from Freddy's house, and Luanne was writing up our collective report.

"Take a look at this," Carmelita said, holding out what looked like a professionally printed color brochure.

Harvesting Souls Church. It was the brochure that Reverend Wilding had given Carmelita and me. It had pictures of smiling, singing worshipers—most of them young and good-looking—and a rousing explanation of the church's philosophy.

"I know that Wilding hands these things out wholesale," she said, "but I thought it was interesting that Freddy kept it instead of just tossing it as soon as he was out of sight. There was one in Julia's suitcase, too, and it had a couple of services and events circled."

"Interesting. Why would Wilding's church spark an interest in a pair of druggies on the run?"

"Perhaps they feared for their immortal souls."

I searched her face and saw not a hint of irony. "Perhaps." A thought struck me. "How much money did we recover?"

Carmelita laughed. "Practically none. The total amount from all of them was about six hundred creds. I've already checked all of their bank accounts, and there isn't enough there to pay their rent."

That made no sense to me. "How much were the drugs worth?"

"Mychal said probably ten grand wholesale, three or four times that on the street." Novak had been with the drug squad a lot more recently than I had, and we all respected his expertise.

I thought about what needed to be done. "First thing in the morning, I'm going back over to that house. Call Kevin Goodman and tell him I need one of his magik detectors to meet me there."

"What are you thinking?" I heard Mychal say from the doorway. I glanced over and saw him leaning against the jamb.

"How does someone like Fast Freddy get hold of ten grand worth of drugs? Rifter drugs?" I asked. Holding up my hand, I ticked the options off my fingers. "He stole them from someone with access to those kinds of drugs who is even stupider than he is." I held up a second finger. "He bought them. But no one spends every penny they have to buy drugs hoping to sell them. And if he did, where did he get the money?" Third finger. "Someone who is really, really stupid fronted them to him. I find that hardest to believe. Now, that means there is more money or more drugs, or both, somewhere."

◈◈◈

My phone rang, and my immediate reaction was, *What now?* But for a change, it wasn't a disaster clamoring for my attention.

"James."

"Hello," Aleks said. "How's your day going?"

"It could be worse, I guess. No one's nuked us yet, and it's more than halfway through the day.

He chuckled. "You always have to look on the bright side. Are you going to have time for dinner?"

"You mean go out? Uh, how would you like to come to my house for dinner with Kirsten and Mychal?"

"Sure, that would be okay," sounding a bit reluctant.

"Did you hear about Trombino's?" I asked.

The restaurant was permanently closed, with the owner and both managers dead, along with the head chef and most of the staff. So far, the victims we had identified included thirty-four people associated with the restaurant and more than two hundred of their customers. We suspected there were more. Whittaker said it was the largest mass murder he'd ever been involved with.

"No, why?" Aleks asked.

"I'll tell you about it tonight. Shall we say that I'm not planning on eating out any time soon. Come by about five-thirty, and we'll take my car."

67

That reminded me to call Kirsten and tell her to check all the food she bought. The warning brought a chuckle from her.

"Dani, I always check everything. You do know that most pesticides cause cancer, don't you? And while the Magi think magik users are immune from viruses, they definitely aren't immune to bacteria that cause food poisoning." Another chuckle. "Or to thallium sulfate, I guess. Dani, you're never going to see a hearth witch poisoned. I mean, what good is magik if you don't use it? Shrimp all right for dinner?"

CHAPTER 10

The following morning after I dropped Aleks off at his apartment, I picked up Marsha, the magik detector, at my office, and we drove to Freddy's house in Arbutus. I had worked with the woman before, and had a lot of confidence in her abilities.

While she wandered around the house and yard looking for magik, I wandered around looking for electronic or mechanical locks or other mechanisms that might help to hide a stash. Neither of us was successful. There was a loose floorboard in Freddy's closet that revealed a small area where someone might have hidden something, but the space was empty.

Frustrated, we drove back to Police Headquarters. When I walked into the office, Luanne waved me over to her desk.

"Trombino's computer has a record of two deliveries yesterday morning from Mid-Atlantic Produce. But when I called the company, they said they made only one delivery."

"I think we have a pattern," I said. She nodded. "Call the company and tell them that they are now required to put the license number of their trucks on their invoices. Order of Commissioner Whittaker. Also tell them that they need to notify all of their customers to record the license number of all the trucks when they take a delivery."

Luanne's forehead wrinkled. "You think that will do anything?"

"It might, if everyone complies. If we can identify the fake delivery truck, we might be able to find it. First, call downstairs and have Julia Danner brought up to interview room two."

I asked Carmelita to join me, and we took the stairs down one level. Julia awaited us in the interview room.

"Good morning, Julia. How are you feeling?" I put on my most cheerful demeanor because the girl looked so miserable. She was obviously hung over and needed a shower and a hairbrush. Probably a toothbrush as well.

"Why am I here? Am I under arrest?"

"Possibly. We found you in a house full of illegal drugs. Tell me about thallium sulfate."

She stiffened, and a trace of panic flitted across her face. "I want a lawyer. I want to call my father."

"Ms. Stolnikova told me that you were conducting experiments combining chemistry and magik. Is that correct?"

Julia pouted, staring at me with an ugly expression. I sighed.

"Girl, let me explain your situation. No lawyers, and no courts. Do you know what a Magisterial Tribunal is? Your father is dead, along with your mother, brother, and sister. You are suspected of murdering them, which is a crime against the Hundred. A life sentence in Antarctica. Understand? You'd better use what's left of your brain and start talking to me."

At first, she showed no reaction to what I said. Carmelita and I sat silently and watched her. After a minute or two, her mind started working.

"What do you mean, my family is dead?"

"Poisoned. Now, tell me what you know about thallium sulfate."

She fainted. I rushed around the table and caught her as she fell out of her chair, and laid her gently on the floor.

"Well, that was certainly an interesting reaction," Carmelita said. "I guess she hadn't heard the news."

"We've been keeping it quiet. It certainly seems as though she didn't know. Call medical and let's transfer her to a more psychologically comforting environment. I'll call Ruth Harrison to evaluate her."

When Julia woke from her faint, she was shaky and dazed. A couple of EMTs came and got her, taking her to a holding area used for people with psych problems.

"What now?" Carmelita asked.

"Let's go talk to Freddy."

University Hospital was a short walk from Police Headquarters. It had a wing devoted to holding prisoners, including a special section in the basement for holding magikal prisoners.

"Broken fibula and tibia," the doctor on duty told us. "Multiple lacerations requiring stitches, and some bruises. Nothing life threatening."

"Has he received any medication?" I asked.

He shook his head. "Nothing for the pain. As high as he was when he came in here, I'm not sure he could feel much at all."

"Hi, Freddy," I said when we entered the room. His panicked expression told me that he remembered Carmelita and me. I found that rather gratifying.

His left leg was in a cast up to his crotch, and he had several bandages visible on his head, face, and arms. His long hair and beard were gone. I assumed they had to shave him to stitch him up.

"That was quite a stash of drugs we found," I said as I pulled up a chair and sat down. "*Astropene*, *quararg*, *nesforl*, magikally enhanced cannabis, methamphetamine. You're a regular supermarket. You probably make pretty good money selling all that crap at the various universities here in town. But that's over now. You're going away for a long stretch. The only questions are how long and where. So, ready to tell me where you're getting the Rifter drugs?"

He didn't respond.

"Okay, let's try another topic. Tell me about thallium sulfate."

That got a reaction. He still didn't say anything, but he looked ready to jump out of another window. Not an option in a basement.

"Was it your idea to poison Julia's family? Or was it hers?"

"I didn't poison anyone. Neither did she."

"Really? It's just a coincidence that she whipped up a batch of magikally camouflaged poison, and her whole family happened to swallow it the day she ran away to play kissy face with you? Freddy, Freddy. Come on. Tell me something I might believe."

Carmelita had been standing in the background. She sauntered over, leaned forward, and said, "If you really are innocent, then you won't mind accompanying Julia when her uncle comes to collect her. I'm sure the Danner Family head will be fascinated by tales of your adventures with his niece."

It took a few moments for what she said to filter through his addled mind, but watching his face, I could tell when it did.

I heaved myself to my feet. "Screw this. I'll bring a truthsayer and some *visolin* tonight and find out what he knows. He's not using his brain anyway."

Visolin was another cross-rift drug that demons used as a mild sedative. But no human would use it for pleasure. It was illegal for all uses, since it basically turned a human brain into jelly and the person into a mindless husk. I didn't even know where to find any, and the chances that Whittaker or the Council would okay me administering it to Freddy were zero. But he didn't know that.

We started to walk out. Carmelita was already in the hall when Freddy called out. "Wait!"

I turned around. "For what? You're boring me, and I have things to do."

"She had nothing to do with it."

I shrugged. "And how do you know that? Because you did?"

"No! It wasn't like that."

"Oh? Then perhaps you should tell me what it was like."

He shook his head violently and blurted, "Reina will kill me."

I smiled. "I assume you mean Reina de LaCosta? Don't worry about her. She and I are old friends, but I promise not to tell her where I picked up any juicy gossip you tell me."

"And if you don't tell us," Carmelita said, "you still won't have to worry about her. Even Reina can't reach you in Antarctica. Or wherever Ralph Danner buries you."

His eyes flicked wildly back and forth between the two of us. I wondered if he'd been smarter before all the drugs. He seemed to make a decision, and let his breath out in a whoosh.

"Look, Julia made the stuff, but it was just a chemistry experiment at school. She gave me some of it to get rid of the rats at my house. Worked like a charm." He took a deep breath. "I happened to mention it to a friend, and he told Reina. She showed up at a party we were at one night and pulled Julia outside to talk. Afterward, she told me that she would trade dope for a quantity of the stuff."

Interesting. "How much quantity? And that still doesn't tell me how it got into the food at Julia's house."

"I dunno. Honest, I had nothing to do with that. I didn't even know her parents got poisoned. Reina gave us the lab equipment, and I traded her twenty-five pounds. Ten kilos."

"But you knew Julia's family were dead."

"Yeah, but not how. The media report I saw didn't say."

"Who was the HLA friend you told about the poison?"

Freddy didn't miss a beat or deny his friend was HLA. "Mark Clifford. He lives in Tacoma Park." Freddy rolled his eyes up to the ceiling. "Shit, how am I going to explain this to Julia?"

I shook my head. "Don't worry about it. You're never going to see her again. You'll be going from here to a Magisterial Tribunal, and then to prison. I'll put in a good word for you, so it'll probably be the Yukon instead of Antarctica. Enjoy."

CHAPTER 11

"Susan Reed." Carmelita spat out the name like a curse. "Damn that woman. I swear, if I get her in my sights again, I'm pulling the trigger."

We walked back to Police Headquarters, and the instant I stepped into the office, Luanne jumped up and came toward us.

"You know that Mid-Atlantic Produce truck you wanted to identify? The company reported one of their trucks stolen."

"When?" I asked.

"A few weeks ago. It was making deliveries out in the Gettysburg area. Truck disappeared, and the driver was found dead."

Carmelita and I looked at each other.

"That explains how Crozier and Susan got from Gettysburg back to the Metroplex," Carmelita said.

"Yeah, but it doesn't make it any easier to find the truck. I doubt it still has the same license plate," I said. "That license plate is probably on a truck from a completely different company. Luanne, who owns Mid-Atlantic Produce?"

"The Benning Family."

One of the Hundred, and a Family with recent tragedy of its own. Justus Benning, the Family head, had recently been assassinated and his wife wounded. Before that, their daughter had been kidnapped and sold into slavery. My investigation into her disappearance had set off the events leading to the Council War.

I stepped out into the bullpen and called Mychal, who kept far better track of the affairs of the Magi than I did.

"Who inherited at Benning?"

"Devon Benning, a younger brother, but word is that Justus's widow is the one actually in charge. Devon is about our age."

Diana Benning wasn't much older. But I knew her, and she had a brain, unlike so many of the Magi's trophy wives. She was also an empath, which probably helped in business negotiations.

"Has she recovered?" I asked.

Mychal shrugged. "I haven't seen her, but I heard that she's back in public."

I mused for a few moments. "I'll stop by and see her on my way home tonight. Maybe we can figure out a way to identify that missing truck. For now, though, I want to go see how Julia Danner is doing. Carmelita, see if you can locate a Mark Clifford in Tacoma Park."

Before I visited Julia, I called Dr. Ruth Harrison, police psychiatrist and magik detector.

"How's she doing?" I asked.

"Fairly disoriented," was Ruth's reply. "She's been smoking magikally enhanced cannabis—rather heavily—for some time now. And the news that her family is all dead hit her hard. She's having a hard time distinguishing reality from whatever fantasyland she's been living in."

"Is there any point in me talking to her?" I asked. "I really do need to know some things about the poison she concocted, and if she's played with any more exotics. Ruth, that stuff fell into absolutely the wrong hands."

After a couple of moments of silence, I heard a sigh. "I'll be right over."

While I waited for Ruth to drive downtown, I looked over Carmelita's shoulder while she searched for Mark Clifford on the computer. He wasn't hard to find. Our records showed that he was a sociology instructor at the University of Maryland, teaching classes at both the College Park and Catonsville campuses. Some quick cross-referencing revealed that Susan Reed and Alfred Wallace had both taken a class with him, although at different times.

Among his academic publications I noted one on Marxism, another one on the HLA, and another one on wealth inequality since the Rift War.

"Magik?" I asked.

Carmelita shook her head. "Nothing in the databases."

I pointed to a line on the screen. "Can't always trust what's in the computer. Especially for people born that long ago."

"Oh. Right."

According to the computer, Mark Clifford was one hundred thirty-six years old. He was born before the Rift War. In fact, he had graduated university before the Rift War. To my knowledge, only magik users lived that long.

Ruth came up to my office, and I called the jail to have Julia Danner taken to an interview room.

"Have you had enough time with her to do an initial evaluation?" I asked Ruth as we took the stairs down.

"Not really. Between the drugs and the trauma, she's not really here. What do you know about her before all this happened?"

I filled Ruth in on what we had pieced together from our interviews.

"So, you had her in your sights as the possible murderer?" she asked when I finished.

"Yeah. I mean, there are a lot of chemicals she could experiment with. Why a compound known as the poisoner's poison? It's not that easy to get hold of. I'm still waiting on our forensics team to see what else she was playing with in that lab."

Ruth shook her head. "She's barely seventeen, very sheltered and naïve. I'm not seeing it. I mean, the first thing she did when you pulled her in was ask for her daddy."

"I'm not saying she's a ruthless murderer, but how many teenagers—at one time or another—wished their parents were dead? They think with their emotions more often than with their brains."

"True."

Julia was waiting for us. She looked much better than the last time I saw her. Her dark hair had been washed and brushed.

Her dark eyes were prominent in her pale face. A pretty girl. Even without any makeup, she would turn heads. But at the moment, she simply looked like a scared little child.

"Julia, I'm Captain James, Arcane Division. I'm investigating the deaths of your family. Are you aware of what happened to them?" I figured it was a good idea to reintroduce myself, since I had no idea what she understood or remembered from our previous meetings.

Her voice was quiet, almost inaudible. "You said they were poisoned."

"Yes. Your parents, brother and sister, all of the servants, and two of the security guards."

"The servants?"

"Yes. Everyone who ate at your house that day—the day when you took off with Freddy."

Julia sat quietly, her expression unchanged. I waited. Gradually, I saw something change in her eyes. And then a tear broke free and trailed down her cheek.

"We found a can of salt in the kitchen pantry," I said. "Salt magikally bound to thallium sulfate. The cook used it in the food, everyone ate it, everyone died. Now, we found traces of thallium sulfate in that lab in Freddy's basement, and Headmistress Stolnikova told me that you had conducted unsanctioned experiments using magik with chemistry. So, what I want to know is, why you wanted to kill your family."

"There has to be some kind of mistake," she wailed. "You're lying. Why are you doing this?"

"What else were you playing with? Potassium cyanide? Ricin? The HLA are not a bunch of selfless revolutionaries. They're ruthless thugs. You made them a batch of poison, and they tested it on your family. And if you had stuck around for lunch instead of running off to get high, you'd be dead as well."

Ruth reached out and touched my arm, shaking her head, and I realized I'd pushed too hard.

"Freddy said he was selling it to a guy who owns a pest-control company," Julia sobbed. "They wanted it for rats from the Waste. I never would have done it if I knew they were going to use it on people."

I relented and let Ruth take Julia back to her room. I had what I needed. The girl had been foolish, and the drugs hadn't helped her make good decisions. But from my point of view, her actions were only borderline criminal. Counseling and restrictions were probably enough to turn her around. I wouldn't be recommending any prison time. Her Family would take care of her.

CHAPTER 12

M ark Clifford's age bothered me. He was old enough to have fought in the Rift War, and he'd survived. I called my boss, another survivor of that war.

"Do you know a man named Mark Clifford? He's an instructor at UM, and our databases don't have much on him, but he's about your age."

"Hang on," Whittaker said. "Let me pull up his picture."

I waited, hearing typing in the background.

"Ah, yes, but not under that name. I know him as Jonas Clifford. Pyromancer, and a strong one. He was against the formation of the Magi Council. Thought we should have a democracy, with everyone over eighteen having a vote. Needless to say, that didn't make him too popular among other mages."

"What was his position back then?"

"A high level field commander who led the defense of Atlanta. He was a university professor before the Rift War, and I guess he returned to it afterward."

More typing in the background.

"Here it is," Whittaker said. "Full name is Jonas Marcus Clifford. I'll send you the link to where I found it. Old database. Why do you want to know?"

"Because I think he's HLA, in league with Susan Reed, and behind the thallium poisonings."

Whittaker cursed. "You'd better take some serious firepower with you if you try to arrest him. When I say he's a pyromancer, that's like saying your grandmother is an electrokinetic. Factual, but understating his power."

"Wonderful."

"Take Jim Conway's SWAT team with you," Whittaker said. "And tell him you need his spirit mages."

I suddenly felt numb and cold. In the past, I had worked with Captain Conway's team and the three spirit mages the police department employed. If Whittaker was that concerned about Clifford, I knew enough to be afraid.

It was mid-afternoon, and I knew coordinating the SWAT team and other people I needed would take time. I called Conway and arranged a meeting with him the following morning. Then I called Mychal. Carmelita was a strong aeromancer, but Mychal was stronger and older.

Mage power tended to grow with age, then plateau at each person's peak power when they were about a hundred fifty years old. That meant neither my grandmother nor Tom Whittaker nor Mark Clifford had reached their peak yet. And if Whittaker considered Clifford to be impressive seventy years before, the only way his powers could have diminished was through alcohol, drugs, or injury. Even lack of use wouldn't cause a serious deterioration.

Figuring the following day was going to be a doozy, I took off a little early and walked over to Kirsten's shop. On the way, I stopped by a fish monger's shop and picked up a whole flounder for dinner.

The wood sculpture of the elven goddess sat in Kirsten's front window, as breath-taking and beautiful as the first time I saw it.

"Hey, you're off early," Kirsten said when I entered the shop. "Slow day for crime?"

"Slow day for results." I held up the wrapped fish. "Think you can do something with a flounder and a pound of crab meat?"

She grinned. "I'll figure out something. Are we having company?"

"I hope so, but I haven't called Aleks yet."

I put the fish in the fridge in her back room, then called Aleks and invited him to dinner. I had seen his refrigerator and knew he wasn't much of a cook. That worried me since I didn't trust any of the fancy restaurants he tended to frequent. I doubted the HLA would target crab shacks, pubs, and diners outside the richer neighborhoods.

I also called Diana Benning. When she answered, I said, "Diana, this is Danica James. I was wondering if you have a little time for me this afternoon."

"Of course, I do, Danica. Stop by the house."

Telling Kirsten I would see her at our home, I drove up to the Benning residence in Roland Park. I hadn't seen Diana since the ambush that took her husband's life and put her in the hospital with major injuries to her head and face.

Security guards checked my ID at the gate to the Benning estate. A human butler answered the door. I noticed a bulge in his coat where a person would wear a shoulder holster. It appeared that Diana had bolstered her security. Neither of those things were evident the last time I visited the house.

The butler showed me to a cozy parlor with a fire in the fireplace. A tea service and biscuits sat on a low table between two comfortable chairs facing the fire. Diana rose to greet me.

"Danica. It's been a while." She pulled me into a quick hug and motioned for me to sit. I did and watched her pour tea.

"So, what can I do for you?"

I told her what we had discovered about her missing truck and how we suspected the HLA was using it.

"Each of our trucks is numbered," she said when I finished. "I can send an email out to all of our customers, but I can't guarantee they'll read it."

"And we can't guarantee that there aren't any HLA radicals among your customers' employees," I said, "but it's better than nothing. Tell them to simply set aside anything delivered by that truck and call my office." I handed Diana a card with Luanne's phone number. If she wasn't at her desk, the call would route to the main Arcane Division receptionist.

"And how are you doing?" I asked. I could see a couple of faint scars—one on her forehead and on her left cheek.

"Fairly well. The hospital and doctor's bills were fairly staggering. I now know how the Silverman Family ranks in the Hundred. I'm still not used to being alone. I miss Justus far more than I expected I would. I find myself wanting to tell him something, and then realize he won't be coming home. It's the worst at night. I sit here alone, and then get in a cold bed. Danica, I've always considered myself a strong woman, but I've discovered I need a man in my life. We got married right after I graduated university, so I've never really been alone."

Diana was much younger than her husband, and perfectly fit the image of a trophy wife. But I knew she was far more intelligent and capable than the average arm candy.

After I cleared the dinner dishes and Aleks opened the second bottle of wine he'd brought, I told my friends about Mark Clifford.

"I'm not sure what the best approach is," I said. "The homes in his neighborhood are close together like we are here. We can try to intercept him when he's out somewhere, but I don't know if he drives or takes the train to work. And trying to arrest him at the university has its own problems with the number of people around."

"I've been meaning to ask why so many houses on your street are for sale," Aleks said with a raised eyebrow.

"We had a minor demon problem," Kirsten said. "The neighbors' insurance companies were a pain in the ass."

"That's why I'm pulling as many aeromancers on the force as I can for this operation tomorrow," I said. "If Clifford resists arrest, we'll need as much shielding as we can muster."

"And what are *you* going to do?" Aleks asked.

"Make Mychal hold my hand."

"Why don't you make a magitek device to shield you?" Kirsten asked.

With Mychal and Aleks jumping in to second her, that is what I spent the rest of my evening doing.

In my workshop behind our house, I had a supply of the silver boxes that magiteks used to capture and store magik, as well as manipulate mechanical and electrical devices.

I set up one of the boxes, then asked Mychal to cast a shield spell at the box. Instead of the box being shielded, it sucked up the magik. After an hour or so working on it and fine-tuning it, I had a box that would project four different magikal shields of various strengths. The strongest of the shields used Mychal's air magik enhanced by Aleks's spirit magik. My testing showed that it worked, but none of my friends was trying to toast me with steel-melting fireballs.

When we finished, Kirsten asked, "Isn't there any way to make one of those boxes multi-functional? I mean, you have that electrical box, and an airshield box, and converters and enhancers, and what all else. It seems you're carrying a lot of little boxes around."

I shrugged. "I've built some multi-function boxes, such as the ones that run your greenhouses, but the various spells need to be kept separated from each other. If I were to load several different kinds of magik in one box, differentiating them would be impossible. Too chaotic. Besides, several small boxes are easier to carry than one the size of a soccer ball."

CHAPTER 13

Jim Conway, Mychal, and Janice Clarington—a spirit mage I had worked with before—met in my office at eight o'clock in the morning. I told them about my concerns of arresting Mark Clifford, then sat back and listened. Even though I was in charge of the operation, Conway had a lot more experience than I did, while Mychal and Janice had talents that might help mitigate any resistance from Clifford.

We brainstormed several possible scenarios, and in the end, everyone sort of threw up their hands, turned to me, and asked, "So, how do you want to handle this?"

I decided that participatory democracy was highly overrated.

"We know where he'll be today at noon," I said. "Walking out of his class on the Catonsville campus. We encase him in an airshield and haul him off in a containment van."

"Sounds good to me," Conway said, and the others nodded.

A containment van had null-magik spells built into its walls, just as the cells in our jails and prisons did. Even the strongest mages and witches were powerless inside.

I laid out the plan for the rest of my team, and we headed out to Catonsville.

There hadn't been any official announcement of Freddy's arrest or Julia's recovery, but I suspected the word about our bust had probably filtered out. To have Freddy and three other drug dealers just disappear was bound to attract somebody's notice. And who knew how many people living on their street might have known them or noticed all the cop cars and the ambulance?

So I wasn't surprised when our plan went sideways almost immediately. Most buildings have at least four sides. Conway and I had seven aeromancers and three spirit mages, so it left us a little thin trying to cover all of the exits. Clifford also let his class out early. That shouldn't have been a problem if everyone had been focused and vigilant. But a little bit of wandering attention meant that Clifford made it out of a side door of the building in the midst of a crowd of students.

"Captain, subject in sight, but he's in a crowd," Carmelita said when I answered my phone.

"Surround him at a distance and move with him," I responded. "I'll have reinforcements there in a minute."

I contacted Conway, and he began directing people. Mychal, Janice, and I were standing across the street from the main entrance, and we took off toward the side Carmelita was covering.

When we rounded the corner of the building, we ran into a crowd of students. They were armed with signs supporting the HLA, and a fierce determination.

My phone rang again. "Captain, we seem to have walked into the middle of an HLA demonstration."

Looking around, I saw several large groups scattered around the area, carrying protest signs.

"Where is Clifford?" I asked.

"Headed in the direction of the student center. It looks like they plan to use the front porch for delivering speeches. I can see some loudspeakers and a microphone stand."

"Don't let him out of your sight."

Mychal was on his phone as we trotted along. We reached an open plaza along with several hundred students. They milled around, some seemed curious, some boisterous, a few had serious expressions. Those carrying placards appeared excited. I hadn't been around many campus demonstrations when I was a student. Engineering students usually didn't have time for such frivolity. We were too afraid of flunking out.

"This demonstration was announced this morning," Mychal said as he put his phone away. "The university hasn't granted them a permit, so technically it's an unlawful gathering."

"Right. Somehow, I can't see anyone being stupid enough to start arresting people. I'm sure the campus cops don't want a riot any more than we do." I called Carmelita. "Where is he?"

"Standing at the front with a mic in his hand."

Mychal and I made our way through the crowd and took up positions to the right of the makeshift stage in front of the building entrance.

"Conway," I said into my direct connection to him, "keep the uniforms back. I don't want to spook him." It was bad enough that Mychal and I stood out—Mychal due to his suit, and both of us due to our ages. But as I looked around, I saw others in the crowd as old or older than we were.

What followed were speeches by Clifford and three other people denouncing the Magi, demons, and Rifters in general, and the unfairness of life under the current system. Their complaints primarily targeted the oppression of the Magi, and the economic control the Families held over the far more numerous normal humans.

I kept my focus on Clifford—who he stood with, and who he spoke with when he didn't have the mic in his hand, as much as what he said and his body language when he addressed the crowd. His thick hair was salt-and-pepper, his face strong and handsome, and he looked fit enough to hold his own in a fight. He looked the part of a distinguished professor—tweed jacket, necktie, swaggering confidence. I wondered why he was still at an instructor's rank. He certainly had the seniority and credentials.

I mentioned that speculation to Mychal.

"His politics," Mychal said. "His views. No one is going to promote someone who is anti-Magi and make it look like the university endorses his radical views."

I didn't reply. A lot of the HLA's views coincided with mine. The Thousand controlled ninety percent of the world's resources and wealth. They horded when millions were starving. They accrued power and lorded it over everyone else, and I intimately knew that many of them were personally worthless, with the intelligence, morals, and ethics of alley rats.

But I couldn't condone the HLA's methods. Lawlessness and slaughter weren't the way to change the world.

One of the speakers excoriated the Magi for their deal with the demons that ended the Rift War. He said we had sold out humanity. It was a common gripe, but one that ignored reality. The magik users—mages and witches—weren't numerous enough or powerful enough to truly defeat the demons. And there was no way to repair the Rift. No matter what we did, demons would continue to come across, and since the Rift constantly and randomly moved around, there was no way to construct viable defenses.

"He's moving," I said, elbowing Mychal in the ribs. Clifford was edging away from the center of the speaker's stage. He climbed down from the tables that had been pushed together and stood there, looking around.

Mychal spoke into his collar mic, "Subject is moving. Everyone stand by."

Gradually, Clifford began sidling away from the center of attention, reaching the edge of the crowd, and then slipping in amongst them.

"Let's go," I said and stepped forward. I halted when Mychal put a hand on my shoulder.

"Cast your shield."

"Oh, right." Without taking my eyes off Clifford, I reached in my pockets and pulled out both my lightning box and the new airshield box.

It actually would have been difficult to miss Clifford in a crowd. The man was huge, a head taller than anyone around him and built like an armored car. I tracked him, keeping my distance, until he reached the fringes of the crowd. Then I moved in, Mychal and Janice close behind me.

"Mark Clifford?" I asked, standing about ten feet in front of him. "Jonas Marcus Clifford?"

He stopped, but I couldn't detect any surprise or question in his face. I realized that he probably recognized me. I had been on the news in connection with several high profile cases, and especially those involving the HLA.

"I need to ask you some questions," I continued.

His reaction was to point a finger at me. A white-hot jet of pencil-thin flame shot out. If I hadn't been shielded, it would have burned a hole completely through me.

I responded with a lightning bolt from my box. It hit and rocked him, and he staggered. But it didn't knock him down. His response was to kindle a wall of flame around himself. I felt the heat for a moment, and then it shut off, even though the flames were still there. Mychal and Janice had cast a shield over Clifford.

The people around us backed off, some running, stumbling, tripping over each other. A girl screamed. A man shouted. I vaguely heard someone else shouting over the loud speakers.

The plaza was turning into a madhouse. Another voice over a different loud speaker system called for calm. A quick glance around me showed the campus police and Conway's SWAT unit moving in. And although most people near us were trying to get away from us, other people in the crowd were moving toward us.

"Get that containment van in here, now!" I said into my comm device.

A fireball arced out of the crowd toward us. Something hit my shield at the same time as I heard a gunshot, followed by a volley of automatic weapons fire. I prayed the fool who pulled the trigger was aiming in the air.

The demonstration morphed into the riot I feared. A lot of people were trying to escape the plaza, but the cops and SWAT members stood in their way. Demonstrators attacked the cops, the cops fought back.

"Conway! Pull your men back! If people want to leave, let them! And for God's sake, tell your men not to shoot anyone!"

"On it," was his response. I hoped he was able to do something. News-media drones hovered over the scene, attracted by the demonstration. I shuddered to think of what Whittaker was going to say.

The flame surrounding Clifford died. He stood there, staring at me and swaying. Then he collapsed, falling to his knees, and then onto his face."

"We cut off his oxygen," Mychal said.

For the first time, I focused on what the guy with a microphone was spouting through the loud speakers. "...and this is why we must challenge the entrenched hierarchies. The demons and the Magi conspire together to silence our voices, but we will not be silenced!"

"Mychal, can you let Janice handle Clifford while you shut that loudmouth up?"

He grinned. "It will be a pleasure."

It took another ten minutes to get the van to where we were. We loaded Clifford and two other protest organizers into the van, and it drove away. Then I spent the next hour in the office of the university chancellor trying to calm him down. Luckily, no one had been shot, no one died, and only two people had to go to the hospital for treatment of their injuries.

Compared to what could have happened, I considered the operation a rousing success. The chancellor didn't see it that way, and neither did Commissioner Whittaker when I reported back to my office.

CHAPTER 14

Mark Clifford was powerful and antagonistic enough that Whittaker forbade anyone being in the same room with him. That made Clifford's interrogation a unique experience. I sat in a room with a truthsayer and an illusionist, while Clifford sat in another room facing an image of me the illusionist projected.

"What am I being charged with?" he asked as my image sat down across the table from him.

"Assault on a police officer and resisting arrest. Both of which you could have avoided by simply agreeing to talk with me instead of trying to kill me."

He snorted. "I'm well aware of how you storm troopers deal with peaceful protests. I was just defending myself."

"We have an informant who is willing to testify in court that you brokered a deal for ten kilos of magikally enhanced thallium sulfate."

"I don't admit to doing that, and I wasn't aware that thallium was illegal. It's used quite commonly."

"Do you know a woman named Susan Reed?"

"She was a student of mine."

"When did you last see her?"

"I don't recall."

We spent three hours going around and around without him ever admitting to anything or answering any of my questions. He refused to tell me anything about Susan. Eventually, I got tired.

"Well, I guess that's it," I said. "I thought you might be able to help me. But since you can't, I'll be recommending a life sentence to Antarctica. Attempted murder of a police officer, conspiracy to commit mass murder, and sedition. It really won't make any difference. I'll catch Susan, or Reina if you wish, and she'll join you down there."

As my image started for the door, he called out. "Wait!"

I turned back. "Yes?"

"Antarctica seems a bit harsh. What could I do to mitigate that?"

"One, tell me where Susan is. Two, tell me about the next target."

Clifford shook his head. "I don't know who's being targeted, or the method of attack. But I do know where Susan is. No Antarctica?"

"If you tell me the truth."

I didn't like the smirk on his face. "She's staying with an old lover of mine. Courtney Findlay-Moncrieff."

My Aunt Courtney? It didn't make any sense. Courtney and the HLA? But as I thought about it, Susan and Courtney together did make some sense. Leaving the HLA out of it, both were criminals with a strong drive for power, and both were on the run from the Council. And was there anyone of dubious character who Courtney hadn't slept with?

I glanced at the truthsayer who was physically sitting beside me. "He believes he's telling the truth," she said.

"I'll check it out," I said, nodding to the illusionist who finished removing my image from Clifford's presence.

⚜

I hadn't paid any attention to Aunt Courtney recently. The last time I did, she was locked into the Findlay estate on Worthington Ridge north of Baltimore. The Council didn't want to risk the effort and manpower necessary to assault the heavily fortified estate, and relented on humanitarian grounds to allow food deliveries and for her hair dresser to attend her.

There were a thousand guardians defending the estate, and Courtney's allies—the Akiyama Family—had twenty thousand more fighters at their holdings in Wilmington.

"There have been some additional concessions," Whittaker told me when I reported on Clifford's interrogation. "The Council has allowed traffic along one road into the estate from Wilmington, and she's getting her supplies that way."

"So, is she allowed to come and go?" I asked.

"Yes, although I don't know if she does."

"Which means that Susan Reed can get in and out. She's found a place from which she can run her criminal enterprise with impunity."

"If she leaves, and gets off the safe passage route to Wilmington, you can arrest her," Whittaker said.

"Great. And you'll give me the manpower to watch that route twenty-four seven?"

He gave me a look that wasn't promising. "You can give her picture to the troops I already have guarding that route."

"She's an illusionist."

He shrugged. "Best I can do. If you want to argue with the Council about the situation, be my guest."

For amusing ways to pass the time, arguing with the Council ranked up there with poking a sharp object in my eye. Arguing with Whittaker was bad enough, but he always let me live. I excused myself and went back downstairs.

I briefly toyed with the idea of loading a magitek bomb on a drone and dropping it into the Findlay mansion, but if my grandmother ever found out, she'd skin me alive. I knew that in spite of her being exiled to Scotland, she hoped to return to her home one day. Preferably with Courtney's skin for a pair of new lampshades.

Out of desperation, I called my business partner, another magitek.

"Mary Sue. Do you know any way to monitor magikal or magitek communications?"

"You mean like to eavesdrop? And by the way, I've left a dozen messages for you. Don't you ever return calls?"

"I've been a little busy. Yeah, like a magikal wiretap. I think someone I'm investigating is living at Findlay House. We've got wiretaps on all their mundane communications—phone, radio, wireless—but they use those only to say nasty things about me and the Council. Nothing substantial."

There followed a full minute of silence. "Let me do some research and I'll get back to you. Assuming you bother to answer your phone. And as long as I've got you, we need to talk. Can you meet me at your mom's sometime soon? I've got orders and money and papers that need to be signed and a lot of other piddly stuff."

"Money?"

"Yeah. We're making money. You never did give me any bank account info to pay you. And Olivia wants you to call her. I guess you don't answer her calls, either."

Grandmother Olivia was the third partner in our magitek business. "Okay. Let me see when I can make it, and I'll call you."

While I was mulling over what my grandmother could possibly want, Carmelita knocked on the door and came into my office.

"There are some parents downstairs who say their kids have gone missing. A couple of University of Maryland students."

"Have them fill out the standard complaint. Why are you telling me this?"

"The parents say the last time they saw their kids, they were going to a service at the Harvesting Souls Church. Said the kids had been going there a lot, getting really involved, and then one day they just disappeared."

Alarms went off. "Check with Missing Persons and see if that church is mentioned in any other cases."

"Will do."

A church built by vampires and demons? Why would I possibly be suspicious?

I took a look at my paperwork backlog. I knew other captains spent most of their time in the office. Whittaker spent most of his time in the office, and he did when he was deputy commissioner, also.

I got up and went into the outer office. "Luanne, do you know of anyone—a lieutenant—in the Arcane Division who is obsessed with paperwork? You know, the kind of nerd who is more concerned about getting reports in on time than in catching criminals?"

She laughed. "Yeah. Lieutenant Billie Cargill. She works in the Northwest DC station. Spit and polish. I hear she really is a good cop, but she seems to worship the bureaucratic crap. Why?"

"Because I hate the bureaucratic crap. I've got more bad guys than cops, and more paperwork and reports than time. How do you know Billie?"

"She's my cousin. You know her?"

"Yeah, we went through the Police Academy together. Give her a call and tell her to get her ass up here Friday morning, nine o'clock. And make sure I don't forget."

Luanne stared at me. Her expression wasn't happy. "Am I going to end up reporting to Billie Cargill?"

I grinned. "Possibly, but I'm going to tell her she can't charge any of my officers with insubordination. As long as you do your job and don't slug her, you'll be okay." With a chuckle, I said,

"Which is the same thing Whittaker told *me* about *her* when she made lieutenant."

Dutifully, I went back to my office and slogged through the most urgent tasks demanding my attention. It was about quitting time when Carmelita came back.

"We have reports on a total of seven missing young adults—ages seventeen to twenty-three—that mention the Harvesting Souls Church. And the place has been open for business only a couple of weeks."

CHAPTER 15

Luanne did some in-depth research on the Harvesting Souls Church. It turned out to have physical churches in half a dozen locations, with its headquarters in a huge hundreds-year-old complex north of DC abandoned by another church. We couldn't find any online presence.

Everyone knew the headquarters location, as its tall spires could be seen above the trees miles away. It was evacuated when the first nuke hit DC. It later became a refugee camp and a squatters' slum over the course of the wars that saw DC nuked two more times.

Demons overran the place during the Rift War, were evicted by the Magi, retook it later, and abandoned it when they retreated to the Waste at the end of the war.

The Harvesting Souls Church bought it from the Brown Family for a pittance just before the Council War started. They also took over the burned out church I knew about in downtown Baltimore, a derelict church in Annapolis, one near College Park, one in Delaware, one in Pennsylvania, and one in

Charleston, West Virginia. All of that within a six-week period.

But prior to that activity, Luanne couldn't find any record of the church or any of its officials whatsoever. Reverend Wilding seemed to have been conjured from thin air. Very curious.

What was more than curious was the number of disappearances tied to the church at all its locations. By the time Luanne finished compiling her report, we had twenty-seven missing people—all under thirty—who had attended services at the church or talked about the church to people they knew. As far as I could tell, my office was the only group that had identified that connection—if it was a connection.

I grabbed my coat. "Carmelita, with me."

"Where are we going?"

I realized she was trotting to keep up with me and slowed down. My legs were twice as long as hers.

"To talk with Reverend Wilding. I want to learn a little more about his church."

She grinned at me. "Worried about your immortal soul?"

"Something like that. Or other people's immortal souls. What's the difference between a church and a cult?"

We got in the elevator, and I punched the button for ground level.

"Probably depends on whether you agree with what the church teaches," she said.

"Or your perception of what the church teaches. From my point of view, a lot of the differences between various churches are pretty trivial."

She nodded. "That's true. Fine points of theology tend to excite the clergy, but not anyone else."

When we got there, a schedule of events was posted outside the church, listing times of services, youth group meetings, Bible study, and prayer groups, along with a pot-luck dinner on Saturday evening. For a church that hadn't been there very long, it seemed impressive. Two Bible study groups were listed at the time we arrived—one for adults and one for early teens.

"Busy place," I said.

"Uh-huh."

The study groups were meeting in rooms off to the side of the nave. We glanced in and saw that both were being led by men in priestly black suits with reversed collars. The man leading the adult group was probably in late thirties to mid-forties, and the youth group leader looked to be in his early twenties. I counted twenty adults of all ages and twelve children.

Wandering deeper into the church, we saw a small sign on a side passageway that said, 'Church Office,' with an arrow. Following that led us to a suite of rooms that looked like any modern business office. A smiling secretary directed us to Reverend Wilding in a spacious office with a large desk and a small conference table.

"Ah, back again?" he said with a smile, getting up and coming around the desk to greet us.

I flashed my ID, carefully watching his face. "Captain Danica James, Metropolitan Police. This is Detective Sergeant Carmelita Domingo. We'd like to ask you a few questions."

The smile didn't alter, nor did the sparkle in his eyes. "Well, I shall try to answer them," he said. "Come, sit. May I get you some coffee or tea?"

"I think we're fine," I said, taking a seat. I pulled out the pictures of the two students reported missing the previous day. "These young people have been reported missing. Their parents said they have been attending your church. I'm hoping you might recognize them."

He studied the pictures, then said, "Robert and Elizabeth. Yes, they attend services here. They have become very devoted, and they've chosen to become more involved. The last time I saw them, I believe they planned to attend one of the services at the cathedral in Kensington."

"And when was that?"

"Sunday morning. They came to our early service, and I spoke to them afterward."

"Their families said that they never came home on Sunday."

Wilding shrugged. "I believe both are of legal age. Sometimes children and their parents disagree, especially when it comes to life choices."

He turned his attention to Carmelita. "I'm sure in your family there have been differences of opinion when someone decides to take holy orders."

She looked surprised, then said, "Yes, sometimes. Are you saying that Robert and Elizabeth were contemplating a more formal relationship with the Church?"

"They have questioned me and Brother Patrick about our choices."

I wondered if Wilding had any Elf in his ancestry. He was very good at answers that didn't directly answer the questions asked.

"If they are at your facility in Kensington," I said, "I would appreciate it if you could ask them to contact my office." I handed him my card. "At this point, we have them officially listed as missing persons, and I would like to clarify their situations."

"I certainly shall. Is there anything else I can help you with?"

"Do you have a seminary in Kensington?" Carmelita asked. "Or something similar?"

"Yes, we do. Training for both the ministry and the superfluity. There are also facilities for those who seek a more contemplative relationship with God."

After he showed us out, I said to Carmelita, "I hope you noticed, Wilding knew who you are, and who your Family is."

"Yeah, I noticed. He's been doing his research."

"What in the hell is a superfluity?"

Carmelita snorted. "A group of nuns. It appears the Harvesting Souls Church has a dichotomy as far as what roles men and women may fill."

"I would think you were familiar with that," I said.

"That doesn't mean I like it. I swore off the idea of a life in the Church when I discovered that nuns weren't ninjas. My father has forbidden me to talk to my uncle the archbishop beyond hello, goodbye, and thank you."

"Feminist."

"Guilty, your honor."

"Let's plan a trip down to Kensington. What else do we have going on?"

"A couple of mass murders, the lovely and charming Queen of the Coast, a war that the Council that pays our salaries seems to think is important, and it's New Year's Eve. Other than that, not much. By the way, unless you have more magikal powers than I've seen so far, I'm off tonight and tomorrow, and I don't plan on answering my phone."

"You're as insubordinate as Luanne."

"It's part of the office culture. We take our cues from the top."

"Got a date tonight?"

"Sizzling."

"See you on Thursday?"

"If I don't get a better offer."

I laughed. "Thursday it is."

She waved and walked away. Pulling out my phone, I noticed that I had at least a dozen messages. Luanne, Whittaker, Kirsten, Aleks, Mary Sue, and my grandmother. At first, I tried to tell myself that it was nice to be wanted. Then I faced reality. I cared only about two of those messages. Out of a sense of duty, I called Kirsten first.

"Where the hell are you and why aren't you answering your phone?"

"Downtown, and I've been busy."

"Nine o'clock at Aleks's apartment. New Year's Eve party. Or have you forgotten?"

"I think I have an engagement at my mom's place."

"That's tomorrow. You forgot what day it is, didn't you?"

I briefly considered lying to her, but she would see through it.

"Yeah."

"You're hopeless. Belvedere. Six o'clock for dinner."

"I thought you said nine at Aleks's."

"That was on your calendar. Something you were supposed to pay attention to. Dinner is something new." I heard her sigh. "I suppose it's too much to ask that you dress girly and sexy for a fancy dinner on New Year's Eve."

I checked my implant. I did have time to go home and change. "I have a message from Aleks. Should I call him?"

Pause. "Oh, hell. Why give him hope? Just try and show up for dinner. Surprise all of us."

Kirsten hung up.

CHAPTER 16

There were times when driving a cop car was useful. As soon as I reached the freeway, I took the car airborne and cut at least half an hour off my trip home. That gave me time to shower, wash my hair, and use the magitek hair dryer I'd given Kirsten some years before.

I never used much makeup, just a little mascara around the eyes and lipstick. Then I took a dive into my closet. It was too bad Courtney had burned all the fancy dresses my grandmother bought for me over the years. I did have a couple of them at my home, but when I tried to put one on, I remembered how old it was. It was a little depressing to realize that in spite of the exercise I did, my ass was larger than it had been twelve years before when Kirsten and I bought the house. On the bright side, my bust was a little larger, too, but on the downside, so was my waist. A long look in the mirror confirmed that while mages aged slower than normal humans, the process had started. At least I didn't get carded at every bar like Carmelita did.

But I did have a couple of nice-looking dresses I'd bought in a moment of madness at a witchy clothes shop run by a friend of Kirsten's. In addition to fitting and looking great, they were also spelled to repel knives and bullets, not to mention demon claws. Since I was going downtown on New Year's Eve, that was probably a good thing.

I debated between heels—my tallest heels were two inches—or flats. I had a lot of pretty flats. Aleks and I were the same height, so I chose a pair of flats. I also chose an ankle-length coat with a magitek heater that my mom had sewn into the collar.

Then I drove back downtown and parked my car at Police Headquarters.

The walk to the Belvedere Hotel was only a mile, and parking near the hotel was almost non-existent. It was dark already, and below freezing, but my coat kept me toasty warm, and I kind of liked the brisk air.

My route took me through one of my favorite parts of the city. Most of the buildings along North Charles Street were hundreds of years old. I passed the Basilica, Walters Museum, and Peabody Institute, through Mount Vernon Place and the Washington Monument, and past historic mansions and townhouses. Although the old homes had been repurposed repeatedly over the years, Kirsten and I had always loved fantasizing about what life in them had been like for their original owners in the nineteenth century.

I wondered if my grandmother and her mother had done the same. They had certainly tried to recreate an aristocratic nineteenth century lifestyle—an incredible mansion, lavish dinners and parties, with hordes of servants catering to their every whim.

Of course, often evening strolls in downtown Baltimore were a little more exciting than a girl walking alone might wish for. Perhaps I was simply being oblivious to my surroundings, but demons had a habit of seeming to appear out of thin air.

Seven feet tall, as broad as a garage door, burgundy red, with claws and teeth as long as my fingers, the naked demon was indisputably male. Whether he cared about my gender, or only about how I might taste, I didn't care to know. I pulled my Raider out of my purse and pointed it at him.

"Metropolitan Police! Stand aside!"

He was either hard of hearing or not the law-abiding sort of demon. He leaped at me, arms and claws outstretched. I stepped to the side even as I pulled the trigger twice. The incendiary-explosive bullets threw his trajectory off, and he sailed past me, landing on the sidewalk and sliding into the feet of another demon who could have been his twin brother.

I didn't wait to see if the second demon was friendly or not, but aimed and put a slug in his head.

Frantically looking around to see if there were more of them, I also reached into my bag, pulled out the airshield box, and activated it.

Sure enough, there was another demon. Besevial. Thankfully, he was dressed. And thankfully, he was about thirty feet away.

"Danica James. I believe Happy New Year is tonight's appropriate greeting. Have you thought about our previous conversation? I still expect you to return my property."

"What makes you think I have something of yours?"

An image of the statuette appeared beside him. Or rather, an image of the creature the statuette was crafted after. She had the body of a woman—a human woman—with the head of a dragon. Sharp ridges ran from the top of her head, between her horns, and down her back to the tip of her tail, which twitched like a cat's.

When she appeared in my dreams, she was huge—Besevial's size. But the image was much smaller, shorter than Besevial, no more than a few inches taller than I was. Her red eyes were hypnotic, holding me frozen like a rabbit. Her snake-like tongue flicked out.

"Akashrian's avatar is not for a human to hold," Besevial said. "She is not pleased that you have touched it."

The image turned its head and appeared to speak to Besevial.

"Her patience is not infinite," he said, "and neither is mine. And although you may be beyond her reach, someone you hold dear is not."

Both the image and the demon lord disappeared. An icy cold feeling passed over me and I shivered. The two demons I had shot were also gone.

Someone I held dear. That could mean my mom or Kirsten, but my thoughts immediately went to my father. Who else was within Akashrian's reach?

It was the first time—other than my dreams—that I had any indication that my father might be still alive. The only other explanation was that I was descending into madness, with my nightmares becoming waking delusions.

I practically trotted the rest of my journey to the Belvedere.

Somehow, I showed up on time. Kirsten and Mychal were waiting by the elevators.

"What's wrong?" Kirsten asked. "You look a little flustered."

"Oh, no big deal. I just had to fight my way through demons to get here."

"Are you okay?" Mychal asked, taking a step past me toward the outer door.

"I'm fine. Just a little shook up. Is Aleks coming?"

"Yes," a voice behind me said. Arms snaked around my waist and pulled me backwards into a body with a familiar smell. He nuzzled my hair. "You look incredible," he whispered into my ear.

We rode up the elevator to the penthouse restaurant on the thirteenth floor. My grandmother said there had been a bar or a restaurant in that space since the hotel was built at the start of the twentieth century. The building was converted to luxury condominiums before the wars, but the front of the building still said, 'Belvedere Hotel.' The restaurant had consistently been considered one of the top five in the Metroplex, with prices to match its reputation. Needless to say, it was not one of Kirsten's and my regular hangouts.

But when you're dating scions of fabulously wealthy Families, I figured it would be rude to mention that the hors d'oeuvres cost more than my monthly motorcycle payment, or that the total bill—including wine and champagne—was more than Kirsten and my monthly mortgage. It did make me uncomfortable, though, and reminded me that the basic HLA gripes about the Magi were well-founded. I knew that the cost never crossed the minds of either Mychal or Aleks.

When our meals came, I looked at Kirsten and raised an eyebrow. She grinned and passed a charm over each of our meals.

"They're clean," she said, tucked the charm back in her bag, and picked up her fork.

After dinner, Aleks called for a limo to take us to his place, and we arrived shortly before the first guests. The caterer had everything ready to go, from booze to canapes to music. At least Aleks hadn't gone completely crazy, and the waiters were robots instead of humans.

At midnight, the champagne corks popped, and the fireworks display over the harbor was clearly visible from the wall of windows on the south side of his living room.

But the grand finale was unlike anything anyone had ever seen. As the sky lit up with the final barrage, a three-hundred-foot high magikal image—projection, hologram, I didn't know what to call it—of a woman with a dragon's head appeared. Her clawed feet seemed to stand on the surface of the water. The image was as clear as though she really existed, and stayed for almost five minutes before fading away.

During that time, there was total silence in the room. Other than a collective intake of breath when she first appeared, no one uttered a sound. We stood and stared, completely entranced, completely frozen in place.

"What in the hell was that?" Aleks broke the silence as the image faded. Kirsten and I shared a wide-eyed look, but neither of us said anything.

CHAPTER 17

In the morning, miracle of all miracles, I didn't have any messages from Whittaker or Dispatch reporting that half of the city had been murdered by Rifters. Mychal and Kirsten had stayed over in one of Aleks's spare bedrooms, so she and I walked to get my car in the morning. Nothing like a brisk early morning winter walk to alleviate a hangover.

We went home and changed from cocktail dresses into something more elven—leggings and tunics sewn and embroidered by my mom—and drove up to my mom's house.

Along the way, I told her about my encounter the evening before.

"And you think that projection over the harbor was aimed at you?" she asked.

"Hard to think of it as being anything else. I got a warning, then a more emphatic warning. I'm sure if Besevial knew where the statuette was, he'd go after it. But the wards we have set on it are blinding him." I hadn't told her about the threat. I never spoke of my father, or my dreams about him, to anyone. But I couldn't interpret the threat against 'someone you hold dear' in any other way.

The elves who had come with my grandfather from Iceland a couple of months before showed no indication they planned to go home. In fact, the military camp surrounding Loch Raven Reservoir was becoming larger and more permanent. I remembered one of the elven warriors telling me that he enjoyed Maryland because of the trees. One thing for sure, there were even some children living in the area.

"I thought elves celebrated Solstice as the beginning of the new year," Kirsten asked my mom after we shed our coats and followed our noses into the kitchen.

"Oh, they do," she replied with a grin. "But never let it be said that an elf squandered an excuse to party. There will be another celebration for the Chinese New Year as well. They are absolutely delighted that humans have so many celebrations."

She enlisted us to help her load up the back of her pickup truck with baked goods, and we drove a couple of miles up the east side of the lake. It took me a few minutes, but I quickly realized we were driving on a dirt road that hadn't existed a couple of months before.

"This is a new road."

"Yes, sort of," Mom replied.

"Sort of?" Kirsten asked.

"Well, it officially doesn't exist. And you can't see it from the air."

I laughed. "And since outsiders for the most part can't get within miles of here anymore..."

Mom laughed. "I always said you were smarter than people give you credit for."

I knew Kirsten couldn't see the village we were driving through. Partly because she didn't know what to look for, and partly because she couldn't see through the elven spells covering the structures and pathways. I didn't have much, if any, elven magik, but I could see through the veils.

"Mom, is there a charm or spell or something you can do so Kirsten can see the village?" I asked.

"Huh?"

"What village?" Kirsten asked.

Mom almost drove off the road, then hit the brakes, and brought the truck to a skidding stop.

"You folks have the whole reservoir area spelled," I said. "I think she can see the people, but that's probably all."

Kirsten looked totally confused. "I see elves walking around, and some of their trucks, but village? You mean like houses and stuff?"

The expression on my mother's face was priceless. For the first time in my life, I was in a position to tell her to use her head, but I bit my tongue.

"Oh, crap." Mom waved her hand and sketched a couple of runes, reached out and touched Kirsten's forehead, then said a Word.

Kirsten stared, her head whipping back and forth. The area to the east of the southern end of the reservoir was thick forest without any roads. But since the elves had moved in, they had created homes, sheds, workshops, and a meeting hall about a hundred yards in front of us that was large enough to hold all five hundred members of their community. Of course, they didn't want their enemies to know they were there at all, so the area around the lake was shrouded behind a veil.

Mom started up the truck again, drove to the meeting hall, and parked. We helped her to unload all the stuff she'd brought, and took it inside. Kirsten still had a gobsmacked expression on her face, staring at the buildings around us.

"Hey," I said, punching her in the arm. "You look like one of the tourists down at the harbor."

"How did they build all this in just a couple of months?" she asked.

I chuckled. "They didn't. They grew it using magik. This building? It's a living organism."

"Actually, twelve living organisms," Mom said. "Twelve trees we planted in two rows. Yews they brought over from England." She hesitated a moment, then said, "They're toxic, by the way. The inside of the hall is spelled, but be careful about touching the outside. Druids used to plant them around their settlements as a first line of defense."

"And you trained them to grow in the shape of a large church? In just a month?" Kirsten gasped. The inside of the hall, with its arched ceiling, did sort of resemble a church.

"Oh, much quicker than that. We used it for Solstice."

I was surprised that Mary Sue showed up. Then I saw her greet the elf who invited her. The way they said hello to each other left little doubt about how friendly they were.

"Hey, Cuz. Got some business to go over with you before you head out of here," she said. "When are you leaving?"

"We're staying the night. Can we do it in the morning?" Driving after an elven party was not something anyone with a survival instinct would contemplate.

"Oh, yeah, that'll work. Do you know Callon?" she asked, indicating the tall elf she was hugging.

"I think we've seen each other around," I answered.

What followed was ten hours of eating, drinking, dancing, singing, and general debauchery. The Magi had nothing on the elves as far as throwing a party. The nicest thing about an elven party, though, was that drunken elves never got mean or aggressive. I caught you kissing my boyfriend? He kisses well, doesn't he? Let's drink to that.

Kirsten, Mom, and I left Mom's truck at the meeting hall and stumbled home together. And I had less of a hangover the following morning than I had after Aleks's party. Probably the difference between elven wine and human champagne.

Mary Sue showed up for breakfast with a portfolio full of papers.

"Can't we just make a rubber stamp with my signature?" I asked.

"Sure," she said. "But don't say I didn't warn you when your bank account turns up empty and I'm nowhere to be found."

Mom and Kirsten thought that was funny.

"But," Mary Sue continued, "you still have to read the stuff I give you to read, and you still need to work on the stuff that needs to be designed. The big thing this week is, we're going to be rich. Someday. Maybe."

She pulled several packets of paper from her bag and spread one of them out. "Whittaker wants us to build magitek-enhanced battle robots."

I scanned the drawings in front of me, then shifted through the rest of the paper in the packet. Schematics, specifications, and descriptions.

"These are ancient," I said. "No one has built battle robots like these since the end of the Rift War."

"Yeah. And robotic science has come a long way since then," she said. "We're going to have to design the new ones from scratch."

The battle robots deployed in the Rift war were often called demon killers. They used tank treads for locomotion, and were armed with magitek-enhanced lightning generators and rail guns firing incendiary-explosive projectiles. I sorted through all three packets, and saw the plans were for three different sizes of machines, ranging from one that was man-sized to one the size of a kitchen table, to one the size of a truck.

"I've spoken to my uncle," Mary Sue said, "and Dressler Robotics will partner with us. We supply the designs and the magitek engineering, and they'll do the manufacturing."

I shook my head. "I hope Whittaker understands this is going to take some time. They'll be lucky if we can produce a proto-type for one model in a year."

"I told them that. I figure two years at least before we can start production. Dani, this contract could be worth billions."

Taking a deep breath, I said, "Dressler needs to provide a couple of robotics engineers to work with me. That's not my area of expertise."

She smiled. "Done. I'll have them contact you, and we'll set up an office for you to work with them near Police Headquarters."

"When do you plan to sleep?" Kirsten asked.

I laughed. "Good question."

When Mary Sue packed up to leave, she said, "Did you hear about the poisonings in Wilmington?"

Since the Port of Wilmington had been occupied by Akiyama's forces early in the current war, our information about what was going on there was limited.

"Poisonings?"

"Yeah. A whole barracks of battle mages at the port got some kind of food poisoning and died. Akiyama is trying to keep it quiet, but word leaked out. Hard to cover up more than two hundred deaths. And then the fanciest restaurant in the city had an incident. Dozens of high-ranking mages and other officials died. The hospital there isn't that big, and they were overwhelmed. I wondered if it might be connected to the incident at Trombino's."

"Interesting. Any idea what they died of?"

"One of my engineers was in a pub near the hospital and heard something about thallium. Ring any bells?"

CHAPTER 18

When I met with Commissioner Whittaker for my weekly briefing, he told me, "Our spies reported that there was some kind of excitement out in Wilmington, but we weren't able to pin down exactly what happened."

"I suggest your spies spend a little more time in the bars," I said.

He gave me a sour expression, then said, "I'll make a note of that. As to your plan to go out to the church in Kensington, I don't think that's a good idea."

Projecting a map onto the wall, he continued, "The northeast Washington area still has extensive demon activity. North of Kensington, the Akiyama forces hold a transport corridor linking their port at Wilmington to the Potomac west of Washington. Southeast of there, the Rift is still open and a lot of the area is held by demons."

"The main church headquarters is in Akiyama-demon territory?"

"Close enough."

"So, what do I do about all these missing people who are tied to the Harvesting Souls Church?"

"Figure out a way to investigate it that doesn't involve putting your ass at risk in a war zone."

I went back to my office and found Mychal dictating a report. Perching myself on the corner of his desk, I filled him in on my conversation with Whittaker and what Carmelita and I had found out about the church.

"I guess I could send Carmelita in undercover," I concluded, "but the priest has met her. She'd have to use an illusion."

Mychal shook his head. "I'd send in a magik detector first. Maybe even a spirit mage. You don't know whether there are spells set that might blow her cover."

"I hadn't thought of that. What kind of church uses protection spells?"

"What kind of church hires demons and vampires to do construction work?" he replied.

The magik detectors who worked for the police were in forensics, and they weren't sworn police officers. Using an untrained person as an undercover operative wasn't a standard procedure. But Aleks had military training. Maybe I could talk him into doing a quick survey of the church. No harm in asking, so I called him.

"Aleks. What are you doing this evening?"

"Sitting around lonely and forlorn, wallowing in self-pity."

I stifled a laugh. "Think you could take a break long enough to eat? I'm buying."

I heard a theatrical sigh. "I guess I could be persuaded. What time?"

"Around six? I can go by your place, or, if you're in the neighborhood, meet me at the police station?"

"I'll call you when I get there."

Okay, that problem solved. I opened my computer and gazed with horror at a mountain of paperwork that needed to be read, approved, signed, or otherwise dealt with. My first thought was to route it all to Louanne, but then I saw that it all came from her. It was everything she couldn't shield me from. Nostalgia for the days of being a sergeant rose up and laughed at me. I reminded myself to be nice to Billie Cargill when she showed up the following day.

৩৩

It was almost six o'clock when Aleks called. I shut down the computer, grabbed my coat, and took the elevator down to the ground floor. Looking around the lobby, I didn't see him, but when I looked outside, he was standing there in the middle of a storm dumping huge fluffy flakes. At least six inches were on the ground already.

"Are you nuts?" I asked as I joined him. "Why didn't you come inside to wait?"

He gave me a beatific smile. "I'm enjoying it. It reminds me of home. Have you ever skied?"

"You mean strap boards on my feet and jump off the side of a mountain?"

Aleks chuckled. "I'll take that as a no. I'll have to take you sometime. The sensation is a lot like riding a motorcycle."

We trudged through the snow. The streets were clear due to the magik spells laid on them, but I knew the sidewalks wouldn't be cleared until the following morning.

"Carmelita showed me a place with great Mexican food," I told him. "The seafood stew is to die for, and the shrimp rellenos will definitely clear your sinuses. Great beer menu."

It was also just down the street from the Harvesting Souls Church.

As we passed the church, I gestured to it and asked, "Who can you feel inside?"

Aleks stopped, and we stood there for a couple of minutes.

"Twelve humans. Why?"

"Is there any magik?"

"One of the humans is a mage." He was silent for another couple of minutes. "There are spells. Several on the front door, and one on all the windows."

"What kind of spells? Can you tell?"

He shook his head. "Mage spells. But what the specific spells do, I have no idea."

"If we walked around it, might you detect any more?"

"Probably, if there are any. What's this all about?"

"I'll tell you over dinner."

I set out around the side of the church. Aleks followed me. He stopped by a side door for a moment, then continued after me. But when we reached the back of the church, where there was a door and a set of stairs leading down to a basement door, he stopped and inhaled sharply.

"What is it?" I asked.

"Demon magik." He pointed to the basement. "There."

The alley behind the church was large enough for a delivery truck or a bus. Aleks walked away from me, going to the end of the alley, then back to the other end before coming back to stand beside me.

"There are veils at both ends of the alley," he said. "I would bet that while they don't impede people from entering or leaving, vehicles won't be able to enter. You'll notice there isn't a trash dumpster in this alley. It's down at the end on the side of the building."

The church took up most of the block, with a few row houses behind it facing the next street over.

"Let's go eat," I said. As we walked through the alley, something else drew my attention. "There's no snow here."

"I was wondering when you'd notice."

We found seats in the restaurant and ordered beers and our meals from the automenu.

"What's going on?" Aleks asked.

I told him about the missing people. "The church's main head-quarters is very near the Rift and demon-controlled territory north of the Waste. And Akiyama-allied forces control much of the accesses to it from the east and north. I don't have anything concrete I can identify, but there's something weird going on."

I spoke with Commissioner Whittaker the following morning, and he assigned two intelligence operatives from his mercenary military force to work with me. Both were mages—an aero-mancer and an electrokinetic—young enough to look like college students, and highly trained in covert operations and weapons.

Carmelita, Mychal, and I met with Sharon and Gordon, briefing them on what we knew, suspected, and hoped to find out, then turned them loose.

I went back to my office and looked at the seemingly endless list of tasks on my computer screen.

"Captain," Luanne called through the intercom, "Lieutenant Cargill is here."

"Send her in."

Billie came into my office, looking a bit unsure of herself.

"Lieutenant Cargill, thank you for coming. Won't you please sit down? Coffee or tea?

She sat, fiddling with her uniform cap in her lap. As usual, she was spit-and-polish, shoes gleaming, uniform pressed and creased. Such a perfect cop that the department had used her photograph on recruiting posters.

"Are you happy in DC?" I asked. "That commute every day must be a drag."

"Oh, you get used to it. Yes, I enjoy my job."

I knew at least half of that was a lie. From her home in north Baltimore, it was a three-hour round-trip commute every day.

"I have a position open," I said. "Senior lieutenant rank, chief administrative officer of the Arcane Major Crimes Unit. Are you interested?"

At first, she just blinked at me. She looked as though she was trying to say something, but no words came out.

"Work for you?" she finally blurted.

"Yes. I need someone to handle all the reports and administrative stuff. I don't have time for it. And it can't be a civilian. I need someone who understands what's in those reports and what to do about it. Someone who understands cops, and can keep them in-line. Someone who understands what should be filed and what needs immediate action."

"Work for you?"

I laughed. "C'mon, Billie. I'm not that bad. And I promise I'll never again mention to anyone that you finished second. The job's a big deal. Right here in headquarters where you'll see the brass every day. Impress them with your performance. One step away from captain. What do you say?"

She stared at me for a full minute, then said, "Oh, hell. You're such a slacker. You want someone to make you look good."

"Yup, but I always give credit to the people who do the work. You make me look good by keeping up with the administrative stuff, and I'll tell Whittaker and Jefferson how wonderful you are."

She shook her head. "I should know better, but yes, I'll take the job." She was silent again, then said, "Do I have to put up with crap from Luanne?"

"Yup. As long as she's not insubordinate. And if she is, you tell me and I'll handle it. But she does report to you, and someone had better have a damned good reason to go over your head to me. I've never done that to my bosses, and I don't like it. She said you're cousins. Do you know each other well?"

"I was her baby sitter when she was little. She had a smart mouth even then."

I chuckled. "She hasn't changed much. Welcome aboard."

With that done, I turned my attention back to the other cases on my desk. I requisitioned a couple of drones and set them to watching Findlay House for any movement by the Mid-Atlantic Produce truck that had been stolen. None of the constant surveillance of the estate showed the truck, but I knew there was a large underground parking garage.

I spent the rest of the day whittling away at the mountain of paperwork—stopping briefly at one point to wonder why we still called it paperwork when it was all done on the computer. When I finished, I wandered around the bullpen, harassing the detectives working for me and getting verbal briefings on the progress of their cases. Eventually, my stomach signaled that it was going to rebel if I drank any more coffee, and I called it a day.

Aleks had flown out to Atlanta that morning, so I walked over to Enchantments to see what Kirsten was doing for dinner. Passing by our favorite candy store, I decided to duck in and pick up some chocolate to share with her.

The incubus standing at the counter didn't really capture my attention, but the face of the shopgirl did. Blank and wonderous, breathing heavily, and her eyes sparkling, she didn't look normal. I stopped and watched as she took all the money out of the cash register and put it on the counter, smiling at the incubus the whole time.

I walked up behind him and stuck the muzzle of my Raider against the base of his skull. "Put your hands up, and give me all your money," I said.

He stiffened, and looking over his shoulder, I saw the girl's expression change.

The incubus slowly raised his hands, and I grabbed one, snapping a handcuff on it, then grabbed the other and finished the job.

"On your knees."

He complied, and I pushed him over so he lay prone on the floor. By that time, the girl's expression had changed to one of horror as she stared at us and the pile of money on the counter.

"You should put that away," I said to her, "and then call the police." Then to the incubus, "You're under arrest for entrancing a human and grand larceny."

It took about five minutes for a couple of uniformed cops to show up. I turned the incubus over to them, bought some chocolate, and continued to Enchantments. For the first time that day, I felt as though I'd accomplished something.

CHAPTER 19

Two weeks after I assigned Gordon and Sharon to go undercover at the Harvesting Souls Church, they contacted me. We set up a meeting at the Kitchen Witch Café that evening.

I didn't have much time to worry about what they wanted since it was Lieutenant Billie Cargill's first day in the office as the new Senior Lieutenant in charge of Administrative Affairs for the Major Crimes Division, and I got busy. It really wasn't a promotion, except in the sense that she was at Police Head-quarters instead of a district sub-station. And the title was completely bogus because I made it up. But I had managed to get her a small raise and wrangled an oversized broom closet for her office. Whittaker had signed off on everything.

I spent the day orienting Billie, getting her computer accesses all set, introducing her to Mychal and the other detectives, and making sure she knew her limits. At five o'clock, I took off and drove up to Hampden to meet with my church spies.

They arrived before me and were sitting in a booth in the back. I sat down, saw they were eating fish and chips with beer, so I ordered the same when the brownie waitress came to take my order.

"So," I said, "what have you found out? Am I crazy?"

"You aren't crazy," Gordon said, and Sharon emphatically shook her head. Gordon continued, "The church preaches an apocalyptic message. The demons were sent to punish humanity for its sins." He raised an eyebrow. "And evidently the greatest of those sins is allowing the evil Magi to subjugate and control them."

"HLA?" I asked.

Sharon said, "I don't think so. The message and the talking points are different. And here's one you probably didn't expect. Salvation can be found in the Rift."

"Huh?"

The brownie came back with my order and set it in front of me. I took a pull on the beer and said, "Run that one by me again?"

"The Rift is actually a stairway to heaven," Gordon said. "That it is dangerous is part of the Big Lie the evil Magi have been telling you. But only the pious, those truly dedicated to God, can cross. You have to give up all your worldly possessions and dedicate your life to holiness, and then you can ascend."

"You're joking."

They both shook their heads.

"I couldn't have dreamed that one up no matter what kind of drugs I was doing," Sharon said. She leaned closer. "The catch is, we haven't seen a single, solitary thing they're doing that's illegal. It's all clothed in the Bible and Christian orthodoxy. The clergy are all human. There's nothing to identify it as a Rifter religion." She shrugged. "I'm not an expert. Maybe you and Whittaker can figure out some loophole to shut them down."

"May not be illegal but definitely subversive," I said.

Gordon chuckled. "Oh, certainly. But they aren't advocating the overthrow of the Council, or sending their followers out to murder Magi in our beds. Just quietly give your wealth to the church and escape to paradise. You don't even have to drink any Kool-Aid. Just step into the Rift."

"And what's your current status with them? I mean, this isn't what they tell someone the first time they walk through the door, is it?"

Gordon grinned. "They're fairly aggressive. They use language that's coded. But it doesn't take a genius to figure out what they're talking about. As to our status, I'm sold. Ready to jump on the horse and ride, whereas—"

"I'm interested, but not quite sure," Sharon said. "My mother is in poor health, and we're very close—"

"And since we're madly in love, I wouldn't do anything without her," Gordon finished.

I gave them my best cop stare. "You rehearsed that."

Both broke out laughing.

"We really didn't," Sharon said, "but we seem to work well together." She cast a glance in Gordon's direction. "We barely knew each other before this assignment. We've each always worked with older partners." She sobered. "May be one of the last times, too. He's getting married this spring, and he'll probably have to go into the Family business."

I wasn't about to touch that one. Perhaps Gordon was in love with his fiancée, but it probably didn't matter. He wasn't going to get out of a business marriage no matter how Sharon felt about him.

"How does the church's process work?" I asked.

Gordon took a sip of his beer. "They continually encourage you to spend more and more time at the church. Once they think you've swallowed their line, then they start talking about what a great life and career you could have with them."

"That happens only with single people or couples of a certain age," Sharon said. "While there are people of all ages at the church, they don't recruit older people with kids, and they don't recruit kids under about seventeen or eighteen to join the clergy."

"We took a trip down to the church in Annapolis," Gordon continued. "Same thing, only the priest there is pushier than Wilding. Anyway, they want us to go down to the Grand Temple in Kensington to see their way of life for ourselves. We'd go down on a bus with other people they've recruited."

"And how many come back?" I asked.

"Dunno. That's why we wanted to meet with you. Personally, a trip across the Rift doesn't sound like a good idea."

I told them to hang on, not make any commitments, and to let me talk to our boss.

"And if you can get a schedule of that bus going to the temple, let me know," I said.

Whittaker asked very few questions when I briefed him on Gordon and Sharon's report. When I finished, he sat in silence for a minute or so, then got up from his chair, went to the side table where he kept his liquor, and poured two glasses of whiskey. He handed me one, and sat back down behind his desk.

"I hate to drink alone, and after that, I need one," he said, holding his glass up in a toast. We both took a sip.

"And what does this church do when the Rift moves again?" he asked. The Rift had a disturbing habit of disappearing from one part of the world and reappearing at random somewhere else.

I shrugged. "Ship their adherents across the globe? Considering the number of people they're talking into doing this, I'm not sure that's their main goal. I think the establishment of an anti-Magi cult is something we should be concerned about."

He seemed to think about it. "Who would that benefit?"

"Besevial and the demons. But the important thing the Council needs to consider is the number of anti-Magi movements we're seeing. The HLA is growing around the world, but they aren't the only ones. I did some online searches, and there's a growing resentment against us. Dozens of grassroot organizations mirror the HLA's complaints. And the only winners in a human civil war would be the demons."

Gordon texted me the bus schedule, and there was one leaving that afternoon. I called Aleks and asked him if he wanted to go for a ride.

Aleks and I sat in my car at the end of the alley behind the church and watched the bus pull in, seemingly without any problems from the veil. A dozen people filed out the backdoor and onto the bus—seven women and five men, all young.

We followed at a discrete distance until we reached the freeway, then I took to the air. The bus got onto the freeway, heading south to the DC beltway, crossed the battle line separating the Council forces from the demons holding Washington, and proceeded to the exit leading to the temple.

As we flew, we could see the Rift in the distance off to our left. A line of sparkling colors cut across the city and out into the Chesapeake Bay, ending just southeast of downtown Silver Spring. The colors rose as high as we could see, so we couldn't see anything on the other side of the Rift. I knew from scientists' repeated measurements all over the world that the breach in reality was exactly sixteen and one-quarter mile wide and seventy-two miles long.

"Absolutely amazing," Aleks breathed. "This is the closest I've ever been to it."

"I've been within about a hundred yards," I said. "I've been told that there isn't any spillover. Once, a robot was sent right to the edge, then it went an inch farther, and disappeared."

"And what's left when the Rift moves on?"

"Devastation. The buildings, streets, all that stuff are still there, but it looks like the aftermath of a battle. No living trees or grass or insects. All that is gone. I have been in such areas, between where the Rift opened and the Waste, which is where the nukes blasted the city. Eventually, the cockroaches, rats, Rifters, and some humans reoccupy the space. Until the Rift comes back again. It's been seven years between the last time and this time."

And in between, it had appeared in a dozen different places between the Mid-Atlantic and China. It never opened in exactly the same place as it had before, but usually nearby. The only exception was White Sands, New Mexico, where my grandfather set off the magikally enhanced nuclear explosion that opened the Rift the first time. It always opened in exactly the same place, signaling a new cycle of movement. Nothing ever came through the Rift at White Sands. We had no idea what was on the other side.

"We have company," Aleks said.

I stopped my woolgathering and looked around. Ahead and to the sides above us were winged demons. The nearest was about three hundred yards away, but there was no mistaking their forms.

"Damn! That really sucks."

"The shield I have around us is pretty good," Aleks said, "but I'm not sure I'm up to taking on a dozen demons."

About that time, there was an explosion ahead and about fifty feet above us. Anti-aircraft fire from the Akiyama troops on the ground. I pulled the car hard left and down, continuing the turn as I leveled it out until we were pointed east, away from the temple and the demons.

Or most of the demons. I immediately spotted two in front of us. One loosed a fireball, and I instinctively pulled the car to the left. The fireball hit our shield on the right side and slid past us.

"How fast will this thing go?" Aleks asked.

"About one-sixty," I said. "Two hundred sixty KPH for you European types."

"The demons behind us are gaining on us."

I took the hint and kicked the Toyota up to its top speed. "Unfortunately, this is just a jury-rigged car, and not an airplane," I said. "Even at this speed, it's not very stable or maneuverable."

An explosion hit us. The shield deflected it, but it knocked the car sideways and rattled our teeth. The gunners on the ground had our range. As soon as I got the car under control again, I cut the power. The car dropped two hundred feet in an instant, and I applied power again, turning more to the north toward friendly territory.

A fireball hit us from behind. The demons were closing in. I began to zig-zag, hoping to throw their aim off.

"There isn't any way to shoot back at them?" Aleks asked.

"It's just a car," I said. "I don't have any high-powered offensive weapons. Besides, even if I did, you'd have to lower your shield to use them."

"Yeah, I don't think we want to do that," he said. "So, Whittaker told you not to come out this way?"

"Yeah. I thought it would be safer in the air." I hadn't given a single thought to flying demons.

Aleks didn't say anything, but he didn't need to.

Something small, maybe a quarter the size of a demon, flew past us going the other way.

"What was that?"

I smiled. "A drone. Someone on our side has decided to help us."

Several more drones whizzed past, one close enough that I could see the three-headed dog painted on the side. A glance in my rear-view mirror showed a drone engaging a flying demon. The demon lost.

Shortly thereafter, a squadron of four fighter planes streaked past overhead, coming from the direction of Baltimore. We weren't being chased any longer, so I took the car lower, found an open stretch of highway, and set us back on the ground.

恓🌹

I woke up to find Aleks crouched down in front of me. I was huddled in a ball in the corner of his bedroom.

"Are you all right?"

"Uh, yeah, sure."

"You were screaming."

Probably not as loud as the guy in my dream, still alive and watching the Demon Queen munch on his liver.

"I guess I had a bad dream."

He reached down and pulled me up, holding me close against him. "Considering some of the things you see on your job, I'm not surprised," he said.

The dreams were coming regularly. Not just of my father with Akashrian, but of her torturing and devouring other humans. Most of the time my father was there, watching. Sometimes Besevial was there as well. I considered asking Kirsten if she could make a charm that would block my dreams, but I was afraid of what that might do to my sanity if I couldn't dream at all.

The worst part was that I recognized some of the people Akashrian was torturing in my dreams. The faces were those I had seen in pictures of missing persons we were investigating.

CHAPTER 20

"Other than discovering that I'm not as stupid as I look, did you learn anything useful?" Whittaker asked me the following morning.

I was standing in front of his desk. I hadn't received an invitation to sit.

"Not really. I didn't have a chance to go in and see the place for myself."

"What a surprise."

It didn't appear as though he was angry enough to start shouting at me or demote me—things that had happened in the past. But his eyes were hard, and the sour twist of his mouth hadn't changed since I walked through the door.

"You know, a couple of million in munitions, aviation fuel, and drones usually have to be authorized in advance. Unfortunately, even if I garnish your wages from now until eternity, I don't think you make enough for us to recover the expenditures. Stay the hell away from that place, Captain James. You're employed as a policeman, not as a soldier, general, or a covert vid-star intelligence agent. Is that clear?"

"Yes, sir."

"You have more important things to take care of. Someone managed to smuggle thallium-laced salt into the jail kitchens. We have a hell of a mess in the basement. Now get out of here."

I tried not to let my relief show as I let myself out of his office. When I got downstairs, I found Carmelita, Mychal, Billie, and Luis Cappellino, leader of the HLA task force, in my office, huddled around Luanne.

"What the hell happened while I was gone?" I asked.

Luanne handed me a piece of paper. The statistics in black and white were almost overwhelming. There had been five hundred forty-three prisoners in the jail. Fifty-seven were on low-sodium diets and weren't affected. One hundred and two received medical attention and the antidote and survived. Three hundred eighty-four prisoners, twenty-three kitchen workers, seven guards, and three policemen died.

"Ten of our own?" I asked. Neither the guards nor the cops were supposed to be eating prisoner food.

"It should make enforcing the rules on stealing food a little easier in the future," Billie said.

"How in the hell, with an all-points bulletin out to every restaurant and Magi family in the Metroplex, did someone manage to smuggle that crap into Police Headquarters?"

Luanne turned her screen so I could see it and started a CCTV vid. I watched a man in a guard's uniform, with an identity badge, walk into the kitchen with a large bag in his arms. He entered a closet or some kind of storage room.

Luanne fast-forwarded about five minutes, then the man came out and left.

"Elesio Gomez," I said.

Carmelita nodded. "Yeah. He finally graduated to the big time. I've already called the police station in College Park and asked them to have a couple of detectives watch his house."

"Tell them to get a warrant. If they see him, pick him up, search the house, and arrest everyone inside. And tell them I want Elesio alive. I'm going to assume that Fast Freddy and Mark Clifford were casualties in last night's poisoning?"

"Yeah," Carmelita said, "they're both dead."

"So Elesio is the only person we know of who can connect Susan Reed to the thallium." A thought struck me. "What about Julia Danner?"

"She's gone," Luanne said. "Her uncle took her to Denver about ten days ago."

I surveyed the group. "I don't think I have to tell you that Commissioner Whittaker considers these poisonings as our top priority. We need to find Susan Reed, find the truck the HLA has been using to transport the thallium, and find their stockpile of the poison. Think about it, and let's meet in the conference room in one hour. I want some solid suggestions as to how we're going to do that."

I wracked my brain about what to do about Susan. If she was ensconced at Findlay House, the place was a fortress. Whittaker's mercenary troops had attempted to take the estate during the last major battle between the Akiyama and Council forces but were repulsed. Even bringing in fighter-bombers to attack it from the air hadn't worked.

In addition to the defenses put in place by Osiris Dillon—using a boatload of magitek devices designed and built by me and my father—my aunt, Courtney Findlay-Moncrief, was a powerful weather mage. Any attacks on Findlay House usually had to deal with both its human and magikal defenders, but also the nastiest weather imaginable.

Sitting alone in the conference room, waiting for my team to assemble, I hoped they might come up with a more feasible plan than I had.

"We didn't come up with any magik beans," Carmelita said when everyone appeared and took a seat. "But we do have an idea that might draw Susan out of the Findlay estate."

Luis spoke up. "Have Whittaker and the Council declare the HLA a terrorist organization. They have yet to do so. That will allow us to arrest every known member of the group and go after their associates. No dancing around the pretty niceties, such as search warrants and finding reasonable cause. Suspicion of terrorist activities. We can apply it to all of her criminal contacts as well. Hit her drug operations, prostitution, weapons dealers, and anything else. Throw the whole police force at her. Totally disrupt all of her activities."

I took a deep breath. "That's almost like declaring martial law. Suspension of civil liberties."

"We are at war, you know," Mychal said. "This is less authoritarian than martial law since it affects only those designated as terrorists. None of the law-abiding citizens would be affected. And if an HLA member buys a drug from a human dealer who got the drug from a Rifter, we can crack down on the whole chain."

"And you think that will draw her out of Findlay House so we have a chance at capturing her?" I asked.

Carmelita shrugged. "It will cause enough chaos that it will disrupt any plans she has. If all the rats are searching for bolt holes, they aren't going to have time to poison anyone."

"We have an empty jail," Luanne said. "What do we have to lose?"

A detective knocked on the door, then came in.

"Captain? Did you put out an APB for an Elesio Gomez?" he asked.

"Yeah. Did you find him?"

"This morning," he replied. "He was found in an alley about five blocks from here with a bullet in his head."

CHAPTER 21

Two days later, Whittaker formally declared the HLA and three affiliated groups as terrorist organizations. The declaration included all areas under the jurisdiction of the Council—North and South America, Europe, and Western Russia.

We drew police officers not only from Major Crimes and the HLA Taskforce but also from the Drug and Vice divisions. In the Metroplex, Whittaker assigned two battalions of soldiers to back us up.

The first raid I personally conducted was on the house Elesio Gomez rented in College Park. Carmelita knocked on the door, and a smiling young woman opened it.

"Hi Dolores. What's up? Come on in. Elesio isn't here right now." She turned and walked back into the house.

Carmelita followed her, I followed Carmelita, and seven SWAT guys followed me. There was a lot of shouting and screaming, people running around, and some futile attempts to escape out the back door. When all the commotion settled down, we hustled twelve young men and women of university age out of the house in handcuffs.

Carmelita and Luanne began searching all the rooms— Carmelita upstairs, and Luanne in the basement. I sat down at the computer in the family room, where a large conference table was set up, along with bulletin boards, a white board, and a projector screen.

The computer screen presented me with a request for a password. Using my magik, I bypassed that and delved directly into the contents of its data storage. It took me about fifteen minutes to wade through all the propaganda, pornography, university coursework, and emails to find what I was looking for —the secure connection to the HLA's dark network. Another five minutes to hack that, and I was in their main server complex.

Forty-five minutes later, I checked to make sure there was a printer with paper attached to my workstation, then plugged a data chip into a slot. I sent the North American member list to the chip and to the printer simultaneously, and sat back.

Carmelita came in, checked the printer, then came over to where I worked. She held out her hand and showed me half a dozen storage chips. "Don't know what's on them yet, but I found these behind a drawer in Elesio's bedroom." She gestured toward the printer. "I also found a lot of paper. Documents, emails, maps. All kinds of stuff."

"Maps? We'll have to go through those. No reason to print out maps unless they're being used for something." Damned near every person in the world had a phone that would display any map they wanted. And why would Elesio keep paper copies of documents?

"Yeah," she said. "A stack of about thirty copies of a map with drawings on it. Another map of the area on the Catonsville campus where that rally was held. I assume the marks on it have some meaning. You having any luck?"

I turned my screen so she could see the email I had been reading. It was from Susan Reed to someone in Austria. It contained the formula and magikal technique for creating the thallium-bound salt that Julia Danner had whipped up.

"I think if we ever manage to apprehend Susan, this might be a crucial piece of evidence," I said. "We'll need to notify our counterparts in Austria."

❧

We arrived back at Police Headquarters and walked in on pandemonium. Hundreds of people had been arrested, and the booking operation was shoving them into cells wholesale, without bothering to identify them. I was informed that the Rifter section of the jail was just as chaotic.

I spent the next few hours attempting to sort through the intelligence everyone had gathered and make some sense of it. About nine o'clock in the evening, Luanne came into my office and put her hand on my shoulder.

"Captain, you've been at it since seven this morning. Have you eaten anything today?"

"Carmelita brought me a sandwich."

"Well, she went home a couple of hours ago. I think you probably need something more than that. And you need some sleep. All this crap will still be here in the morning. Go home."

Since my eyes felt like someone had poured sand in them, I decided she was probably right. I signed out of the computer, stood up, and grabbed my coat. "Thanks, Luanne." As I left, I realized that she had come in at seven like I had. I turned and saw her gathering her coat and turning out the lights.

My stomach growled at me, and I realized I was starving. Instead of taking the elevator down to the parking garage, I decided to grab some dinner before I went home.

Walking through the building and on out into the night, I saw that the chaotic scene I had encountered that morning hadn't changed much. Cops and soldiers were still bringing in prisoners, but the sergeant on the front desk was different. Shift change had occurred hours before.

It was cold out and smelled like snow. As I stepped out from under the building's front portico, I realized there was a fine frozen mist beginning to fall. Few people were out on the street, and traffic was light.

I turned to walk down the hill toward Jack's. Two blocks away from the station, I turned a corner and found Besevial standing in my way. My first thought was that Osiris and Whittaker were correct—I was a slow learner. For the past month, every time I'd gone out alone at night, the demon had confronted me. I drew my Raider but didn't point it at him, waiting for him to speak.

"I don't suppose you've thought about returning Akashrian's avatar," he said, in that deep, rumbling voice.

"No, because I still don't know what you're talking about."

He bared his teeth and snarled. It was very impressive, and in spite of myself, I took a step back.

"Don't play games. You are the one who killed Ashvial. He was weak, and by right, all his possessions pass to you. But the avatar wasn't his. It is Akashrian's, and she has empowered me to recover it."

It might have been foolish, but I decided to take a chance. "Just assuming that I did know where this thing is," I said, "why should I give it to you? What's in it for me? I mean, if it's so valuable, maybe I could sell it."

He made a sound unlike anything I'd ever heard—somewhere between a steam whistle, a rusty hinge, and a cat whose tail has been stepped on. Steam rose from his head, and I took another step back.

"Because I would eat your liver before taking it from whoever you sold it to."

"Oh. I guess I shouldn't do that, then. Well, how much are you prepared to pay for it?"

The steam from his head seemed to dissipate, and he leaned toward me. "I could make you rich beyond your wildest dreams."

I had to chuckle. "My dreams are pretty wild. This is all hypothetical, you know, but suppose I did have it. I would trade it to you for my father."

The demon straightened. He stared at me in silence for what seemed like a long time. Finally, he said, "Hypothetically, what makes you think I could do that?"

"I think Akashrian could do that. Value for value."

He stared some more, then slowly nodded. "You are arresting demons. Why?"

The change of subject caught me off guard. "We're arresting only those who have broken our laws, and those who fight against us at the behest of our enemies."

"I could call them off, abandon Akiyama. Would you trade the avatar for that?"

"You could throw that into the deal, sure. You should do that anyway. Why back a losing hand? My father and demon neutrality. Sounds good to me."

"Akashrian doesn't bargain."

"Aw, c'mon. How stupid do you think I am? She's a demon. You all bargain. It's part of your DNA."

He took a step toward me, and I raised the Raider, pointing it at his chest. There was a movement behind me, and I stepped to the side, risking a quick glance in that direction. Instead of another demon, as I expected, it was Mychal, Raider in hand.

Besevial chuckled. "We shall continue this discussion later."

He disappeared.

"Well, that's a new one," Mychal said. "I didn't know demons could do that."

"Besevial isn't your run-of-the-mill demon."

"Besevial? Oh." He looked down at his Raider, then holstered it. "Will a Raider kill a demon lord?"

I shrugged as I holstered my own weapon. "I hope so, but I'm not sure if he knows, either. I was on my way to get some dinner. Care to join me?"

CHAPTER 22

I walked along in a fog. My head was spinning, and I couldn't see to process what had just happened. Had Besevial confirmed that my father was still alive? That my dreams weren't simply a young girl's wishful thinking? Or was I still caught up in denial about his death?

We arrived at Jack's and found a booth in the back. When I reached out to key the automenu, my hand was shaking. Deciding I needed something more than just a meal, I ordered a beer and a double shot of whiskey to go with my fried oysters.

"Your father?" Mychal asked after we finished ordering.

"Lucky thing you happened along," I said, pretending to ignore his question.

"Actually, I was following you. It seems like you've been having some demon problems lately."

Our drinks arrived, and I retrieved mine from the chute. I took a slug of the whiskey and savored the burn, then washed it down with some of my beer. Mychal continued to stare at me.

When I didn't say anything, he did. "I thought that Lucas James was killed twenty-some years ago."

With a sigh, I said, "Almost twenty-three. He and my Grand-uncle Richard were ambushed about three blocks from here. Richard and seven of their guardians were killed, another six were injured. All of their bodies were left in the street. My father was never found. My Family always suspected Akiyama was behind the attack, and that there were demons involved."

"Why Akiyama? I mean, I know that Findlay and Akiyama have always been rivals, but why assassinate your father?"

"He was the strongest magitek in the world. Findlay and Akiyama compete in many areas, but both were developing magitek products, and both were far ahead of anyone else. Findlay has always assumed Akiyama was making a play to dominate the market."

"If that's the case, it doesn't seem as though it's done them any good. Both Findlay and Dressler continue to compete with them."

I didn't say anything. Both Mary Sue and I had designed magitek devices for our Families since we were teens. We'd become a lot better at it since getting our engineering degrees, but it was magikal strength, imagination, and creativity that made a good designer, not technical skills. Had we caught up to Lucas James? I wasn't sure, but I could duplicate or improve upon anything he'd ever built.

"So, what makes you think demons have your father?" Mychal persisted. "Why do you think he's still alive?"

I shrugged. "I have dreams. Dreams where he speaks to me."

"And you don't think that's just subconscious wishful thinking?"

"How many people can speak and read demon?"

His forehead wrinkled, and the look he gave me showed he thought I was changing the subject. "I don't know. A few hundred, maybe. There were about a dozen people studying it at Johns Hopkins when I was there."

"I have an implant that my father designed. He had one also. According to people who knew him, he didn't speak or read demon. Now, I've never studied the language, but I'm fluent in it. I learned it in my dreams. I know more about demon society and psychology than anyone I've ever met. That includes demon experts at the universities who've been studying them all their lives."

Mychal took a sip of his beer and said, "Tell me about Akashrian and this avatar thing."

So, I did. I didn't tell him where the avatar was, but I did describe it and told him I thought it was the reason for the slaughter at a drug house he and I had investigated. Told him about seeing Akashrian in my dreams, and Besevial's repeated demands that I return it.

"You saw the image over the harbor on New Year's Eve," I said. "That was Akashrian. If I'm hallucinating, then it's contagious."

When I finished, Mychal said, "Have you thought about who's behind the Harvesting Souls Church? Most demons in our dimension are thugs. They don't even think tactically, let alone strategically. Setting up a church as a means of exporting fresh meat across the Rift took some imagination."

It hit me. Mychal was right. The churches showed up at the same time as Besevial took over Ashvial's territory.

I shook my head. "And just when I was ready to write you off as simply another pretty face. Damn! The answer is pretty obvious, isn't it?"

He winked at me. "I think you missed the forest because of all the trees. Now, why does Besevial want that little statuette so badly?"

"I don't know. I wondered if it was a means of communication across the Rift, but when Akashrian's image appeared with Besevial on New Year's Eve, she didn't seem to have any trouble communicating with him. Perhaps it's a means of enhancing his power in this world."

Mychal chuckled. "Or maybe it's just a status symbol, like a fancy sports car."

※

It wasn't a surprise when I fell into dreams about the demon realm that night. Akashrian railed at me for what seemed to be a long time, screaming and threatening. Gradually, I realized she was berating not me but my father.

When she finally left, he turned to me and imparted several key bits of knowledge. He told me that the avatar was actually a portal Akashrian and her minions used to safely travel back and forth between their dimension and ours. Without it, they couldn't be certain of landing back in the demon realm instead of in Alfheim, or the dragon realm, or someplace equally inimical to their kind. The catch was that she needed someone—a demon lord such as Ashvial or Besevial—to open it for her from our side.

I knew there were twelve demon lords on earth, and they had defined territories. But Dad told me there were only three of the avatars, one for each of the demon goddesses in the demon realm. When Kirsten and I threw our wards around the statuette, we severely limited Akashrian's control of the four demon lords who owed her fealty.

Another key piece of information was how to kill her if she did show her scaley head on earth. Father told me that there was no way to destroy the statuette, but if Akashrian died, the avatar would lose its power and strand her worshippers on our side of the Rift with no way to return home except by chancing the Rift.

I had all kinds of questions, but no way to ask them. That was the nature of my dreams. All the communication was one way. Then he gave me a hug and a kiss on the forehead and told me that he loved me. It was one of the few times when I woke up after a dream about the demons and had a smile on my face.

At breakfast, I told Mychal and Kirsten about my dream. When I mentioned the statuette, Kirsten's eyes shifted toward Mychal.

"I told him about the statuette last night," I said. "I also told him some things I've never told anyone before, not even you or Olivia."

I went on to give her an abbreviated account of my dreams and my belief that my father still lived.

"I always suspected something like that," Kirsten said when I finished. "Remember, I've been listening to you have nightmares since we were sixteen."

"You never asked about them."

She scoffed. "Yeah, I have, but gently. I figured if you didn't want to talk about them, then it was none of my business. But I was pretty sure they were about your father. Sometimes you speak of him in present tense, as though he's still alive."

I sat staring at my hands holding a coffee cup. "It's never felt like he was really gone. But I couldn't figure out if that was just denial. But after I got my implant, I started having really vivid dreams. He'd come to me and tell me things. Then one day, I woke up and I was able to read and understand demon." I glanced up at Kirsten.

"Yeah," she said. "That's pretty weird."

Mychal and I drove into work and discovered the previous day's chaos hadn't slacked off. The jails were filled with everyone from idealistic college kids to murderous drug-dealing demons. We had so many drugs piling up that Whittaker had commandeered a vacant office building and turned it into a warehouse. Almost half of the Rifter-run businesses in the Metroplex had been shut down due to illegal activities discovered on the premises.

"Pretty amazing what we can accomplish if we don't have to fiddle with warrants and civil liberties," Whittaker commented. "Of course, the number of complaints from lawyers is up about a thousand percent from last week."

"Authoritarian regimes tend to be very low on real crime," Mychal said. "They have sedition instead. The Families have always tried to avoid that."

I spent the morning browsing through the HLA arrests, trying to make connections between the people we hauled in and Susan Reed. I referred a handful of them to Carmelita for interrogation. I didn't believe that Susan was spending all of her time cooped up in the Findlay mansion. She had to get out occasionally to keep her criminal underlings in-line. She would use those opportunities to touch base with her co-conspirators in the HLA, and if we could figure out when and where she did that, we had a chance of trapping her.

In the afternoon, I went over to the office Mary Sue had set up so I could meet the Dressler Robotics magitek engineers and start work on redesigning the battlebots. The young man was technically very good. The young woman was creative. Both had several years of experience and immediately understood what we needed to do. By the time we knocked off that evening, I felt a lot better about the project.

That gave me the freedom to go home for dinner and begin designing the device my father imagined for use against Akashrian.

CHAPTER 23

L uanne burst into my office. "A stretch limo just left the Findlay estate going north."

"Have a drone follow it."

"Already happening."

"What color?"

"The limo? Gray. Maybe silver. Why?"

My grandmother's car. All but two of Findlay's limos were black. But Olivia preferred to be different.

"Tell the surveillance team to keep to their stations. It could be a decoy, or it could be nothing at all," I said, getting up from my chair. I grabbed my coat. "Are either Carmelita or Mychal here in the office?"

"Carmelita is. She's interviewing one of those HLA members you tagged."

"Call her and tell her to meet me in the parking garage."

The limo might possibly be a decoy, but I would bet it held either Susan or Courtney. My grandmother's cars were softer, plusher, and more girlie than the other Findlay limos.

The week had dragged since my encounter with Besevial. I had met twice with the Dressler engineers, and they agreed with my assessment that it would be easier to design new battlebots from the ground up. There had been too many scientific advances over the past eighty years. Some of the older designs could be imported into the design software and used as a starting point, but those were the basic physical parts, such as the tank treads.

The roundup of HLA suspects and criminal Rifters had slowed down as well. The police force had grabbed all the low-hanging fruit, but any of the drug dealers and flesh peddlers with any sense that we missed in the first sweep had gone to ground. Junkies who couldn't find a fix were flooding the area hospitals. We had put a severe crimp in both Besevial's and Susan's operations.

I reached my car at the same time Carmelita did. We jumped in, I started the engine, and we drove out onto the street. I took the first freeway onramp, not caring that it went in the wrong direction. I just needed clear space so I could take the car airborne.

"Coffee?" Carmelita asked as I completed my turn and leveled out heading north about five hundred feet over the freeway. She handed me one of the to-go cups she was holding.

"Thanks. How did you have time to pick this up?"

"Your timing's good. I just had them delivered from the fancy coffee place down the street. What's going on?"

I filled her in, and she fiddled with the radio until she connected with the drone operator.

"The limo turned off from the main road that Akiyama holds between Wilmington and the Findlay estate," the operator said. "It's heading west now."

We told him to keep us informed, and I adjusted our course a little to the west.

"Call Luanne and ask her to search for any construction permits issued in the past three months for Tina Stewart's address north of Columbia," I said.

Carmelita did so, then asked, "You think Susan is using the place?"

"No idea, but what happens to drug dens and other criminal hangouts when the owners die?"

"The government takes them?"

"Yeah, theoretically. For the most part, they sit until they rot waiting for the bureaucracy to get off its ass. Susan probably didn't have any construction work done, but she might have sent in a cleaning crew after we hauled all the bodies away. She can't use her place anymore, and she had to sleep somewhere between the time she killed Crozier and when she shacked up out at Findlay."

"No-tell motel, probably," Carmelita said.

I didn't comment but privately agreed. The drone would prove me either right or wrong fairly soon.

We flew on for a few more minutes, then the radio said, "Another gray limo has left Findlay House in convoy with six SUVs."

Carmelita glanced at me.

"Probably Courtney going up to Wilmington," I said. "Track them."

It soon became apparent from the roads it took that the first limo was headed to the old mansion Tina Stewart had stolen from Brian Crozier. I adjusted course.

"Call Whittaker and get a SWAT team out to Stewart's mansion," I told Carmelita. "And see if there are any drones in that area."

Sure now as to where we were going, I increased our speed. We reached the mansion before the limo, and I climbed high enough we wouldn't be identifiable from the ground. A drone had arrived before us, and Carmelita asked its operator to share its camera to the screen on our dashboard.

Half an hour later, the limo showed up and parked to the right of four other cars in front of the gates to the estate. Someone in a gray coat with a hood got out of the limo. Even with a telescopic lens, it was impossible to tell from above who it was. He or she went to the door of the gatehouse and entered. Shortly thereafter, the figure emerged inside the compound.

Instead of approaching the main house, the person went around it and entered a door to the servants' quarters behind the mansion.

"I'll bet that's Susan," I said.

But in barely a minute, the person came out again. This time the camera showed me enough of her face that I could verify that it was Susan Reed.

She hurried across the compound, went through the gatehouse, then back to the limousine. As she passed the other four cars, she put out her hand and patted the hood of each of them. As soon as she crawled back into the limo, it backed out and sped away.

The servants' quarters and all four remaining cars simultaneously erupted into flame.

"What the hell?" Carmelita squeaked.

We sat there, stunned, looking at the scene below us. It took me a moment to recover my composure, then I snapped, "Don't let the drone lose sight of that limo."

"I'm on it," both drone operators said through the radio.

The SWAT team arrived a couple of minutes later, and their helicopter set down on the road outside the compound. I gave a quick briefing to their commander and asked him to hang around until the fires were out. While I broke out of my circling pattern to follow the limo, Carmelita called the fire department and our office to send a couple of detectives and a forensics team to the mansion.

"What do you suppose all that was about?" she asked when she got off the radio.

"I'm not entirely sure," I replied, "but the first thing that comes to mind is Susan eliminating witnesses. With her entire criminal empire crashing down, maybe she's trying to distance herself. If you stop and think about it, the only thing we have on her is that she attended some HLA meetings and broke out of the prison in Gettysburg. She could find a good lawyer to make the case that she was innocently in the wrong place at the wrong time."

"And the prison escape?"

"Wasn't her idea. Crozier kidnapped her as a hostage. With him dead, who could prove she's lying?"

Carmelita nodded. "I hate to think she's that slick, but she's been ahead of almost everyone ever since we met her."

We followed the limo as it retraced its route to the Findlay estate. It was admitted to the compound, a lone figure in a gray coat exited the vehicle a few yards inside the walls, and then the limo blew up, taking the driver with it.

"Holy—" Carmelita exclaimed.

"Yup. Eliminating witnesses," I said. "That woman has no conscience whatsoever. No wonder she and my Aunt Courtney get along."

CHAPTER 24

I was getting a little bit tired of Susan Reed. I had pegged her as a sociopath from the first time I spoke with her, but I hadn't seen her as a psychopathic serial mass murderer.

Reading the email for the fifth time—sent to my personal email from a free email account established the previous day—I decided I needed to do something about her.

Dani,

I'm tired of this cat-and-mouse game. My life is a shambles, and I admit you're winning. All I want is a new identity so I can move somewhere else and start over. In exchange, I'll hand you Courtney on a platter. Think about it.

SR

Whether her offer was a trap or not, the idea of giving Susan a free ticket to resume her activities somewhere else was a nonstarter. The last thing I wanted was to hear about Magi being poisoned in Denver or blown up in Vancouver. And I had little faith that we had rounded up all her contacts for cross-rift drugs. No police force in history had managed to completely stamp out a drug trade.

I wasn't naïve enough to believe I could set up a sting by offering her a new identity. Susan was too smart to fall into that kind of trap. Besides, with the computer systems used all over the world, a new identity wasn't an easy thing to manufacture. It required erasing Susan Reed from the international computer network and inserting a completely new person. I could do it officially, or as a hacker, but it was too much work either way.

Whittaker would never go for it officially. Courtney Findlay-Moncrieff wasn't nearly as important to the Council as the assassin of dozens of high-status Magi.

The question was how to lure Susan Reed out and capture her.

I sat back in my chair and thought about my options. Normally, I tried to stay true to my oath as a police officer. I didn't even fix speeding tickets for Kirsten, or diddle our utility bills, though either of those things would be child's play for a magitek hacker with my skills and my implant.

But if I got the chance again, I would settle with Susan permanently. The woman was too dangerous. Considering her track record, I wouldn't trust the high-security arcane prison in Antarctica to hold her.

That evening after dinner, I went out to my workshop behind my and Kirsten's house. The ward Kirsten had set on the little building behind the kitchen would admit only me and her. Inside, there were some storage spaces that even she couldn't access.

I went through my inventory of devices I had either made or picked up over the years. Some, such as the magikally enhanced laser rifle, were legal for me to have as a cop but not as a private citizen. A few were illegal unless specifically sanctioned by the Council.

Setting aside those devices and weapons I thought would be useful, I locked everything else up and went to bed.

The following day, I told Whittaker I needed the next day off. I spent an hour or two checking all the drone video taken of the Findlay estate for the previous thirty days. Susan didn't go outside much—not that there was a reason to in the middle of winter. Considering the number of tunnels on the property and the size of the mansion itself, a person could probably live inside all the time. But I was able to identify her a few times on the vids and note which doors she used going in and out. That helped me to figure out where in the mansion her room was most likely located.

After work, I rode my bike out to Worthington Ridge. It was cold, but the motorcycle was my personal property. The car I drove belonged to the Police Department and had a tracker on it.

I had never lived in the mansion full time, but I had my own suite of rooms and had spent considerable time there when I was in high school and university. In other words, when I was old enough that I wanted to sneak out and back in occasionally.

The walled enclave covered about forty acres, and although the normal and magitek security systems made the place almost impregnable, a smart teenaged girl could figure out a way around such things.

I parked the bike in some trees about two hundred yards from the wall, past a bend in the road that ran by the estate. I knew that none of the sensors or cameras could see me. A short hike through the woods brought me to a large oak tree near the wall. Using the oak to shield me from the estate's watchers, I was able to approach close enough to use my magik.

There was a magitek warning sensor on the wall opposite the tree that was different from all the others. If it was turned off, it didn't transmit that fact back to the central monitoring system. When I was seventeen, it had taken me three tries to get it right, and I hadn't used it in fifteen years. But since I was the one who did the maintenance checks on the estate's magitek system, I also knew it hadn't been replaced and still worked the way it was designed.

I deactivated the sensor, then activated two of the devices I carried. One was a device I had built with Mychal's help that generated an airshield around me. The second was a cloaking device I pocketed when I arrested HLA member Carl Beaver for conspiracy to murder. Between the two, I hoped I would be invisible and protected from any weapons.

With butterflies in my stomach as large as bats, I stood in front of the wall. When I was a teen, sneaking in and out of the estate was a game. Losing then would mean a scolding. Now, it would probably get me killed.

Pulling on a pair of special gloves and taking a deep breath, I edged around the tree and walked directly toward the inactive sensor on the wall.

Almost invisible, unless someone looked very closely, were indentations in the wall. I had ground them out using a power tool to create places for fingers and toes so I could climb the wall, and I'd done the same thing on the other side of the wall.

I climbed up until I reached the top, then carefully unclipped the razor wire where I had cut it long ago. Small brackets on either side held it to the wall and kept it from springing away from the cut.

Chuckling to myself that I couldn't remember either the name or the face of the boy who inspired such elaborate measures, I pulled myself onto the wall, turned around, and climbed back down inside the compound.

The path to my old room was one I had navigated many times so high on weed and alcohol that it was a wonder I hadn't broken my neck climbing over the wall.

Twenty feet in front of me was a gardener's shed full of tools and equipment. I walked along behind it until I reached the end, peeked around the corner to make sure no guardians were present, then crouched low, and sprinted across an open space to a hedgerow that formed a border around a gazebo used for lawn parties.

I skirted through a copse of flowering cherry trees, past the east rose garden, to the main gardener's garage with all the lawnmowers and heavy power tools, and finally came to the main barracks for the bachelor guardians who lived on the estate.

From there, through a small peach orchard, I arrived at the wall bordering the inner garden that surrounded the house. I hopped over the wall and found a stone pathway that led me around the back and directly under the window of my old room. The windows were dark.

Until recently, that room had been occupied by young Mr. William Moncrieff, Courtney's grandson. I had been part of the operation that liberated him and returned him to his mother. Unless Courtney gave that suite to Susan Reed, I couldn't imagine who else might be living there. And if it was Susan, then my task would be considerably simpler.

A concrete drain from the roof ran right next to the balcony. By standing on it, I was able to jump high enough to grab two of the spindles of the balustrade. Since no one else in the family was a six-foot-tall part-elf, no one had ever considered that as a means of entry.

I pulled myself up and over. My magik unlocked the French doors, and I slipped inside. Pulling on a pair of magitek night goggles, I looked around. As far as I could tell, the room didn't look any different than the night I rescued William Moncrief. A football still sat on a table in the sitting room, and I doubted Susan would have left it there.

So, not in my old room, but I still suspected Susan was housed in the same wing. I couldn't imagine that Courtney would put a stranger in the family wing. That would be both a breach of security as well as protocol. For one thing, Denise Butler-Findlay, Courtney's mother, still lived there. Even moving one of Courtney's paramours into the family wing would probably cause questions my aunt wouldn't want to answer.

There were a lot of times I wished I had witchy magik. Kirsten would have been able to cast a spell and locate Susan's exact location. The only thing on my side was that I didn't expect many people in my grandmother's wing of the house.

A pair of magically enhanced earplugs served as auditory enhancements. Even on the plush carpet, I should be able to hear anyone long before they might see me.

There were a dozen suites in that wing of the house, most with either two or three bedrooms and two or three bathrooms, and a sitting room. My grandmother's apartment was even larger. Olivia had her own kitchen, although she never cooked, a second sitting room, or parlor, a study-slash-library, and an office.

I started at the far end of the hall, quietly unlocking the door and peeking inside, then going to the next suite. The first six suites, including mine, were dark. But the next one showed light when I cracked the door. I waited, listening, but didn't hear anything, so I ventured inside.

No one was home, but someone definitely was living there. Reminding myself that the cloaking device made me invisible, I searched through the rooms. I had to smile to myself. In spite of all the empty rooms in the mansion, Courtney couldn't help spreading a little spite. I had no idea what her relationship was with Susan, but it was the smallest bedroom suite, with larger empty accommodations on either side of it.

I found the confirmation I needed in the bedroom closet. I had seen Susan wearing one of the dresses at least twice.

There was an electric kettle, a drip coffee pot, and a pound of expensive Caribbean coffee on a buffet in the sitting room. I made a pot, poured myself a cup, found a comfy chair, and sat back to wait on Susan to return. I laid the Raider on the arm of the chair, but it was intended to be a distraction. Far too noisy to use inside. The magitek lightning box I set next to the coffee cup was much more practical.

I switched off the cloaking device. It required me to use magik continuously to keep the effect. The box for the airshield also required a steady use of magik, but I kept it on.

I waited for two hours before someone unlocked the door. Susan must have been at dinner with Courtney, because she was wearing a much fancier dress than I'd ever seen her in. She came in, set her clutch on the table by the door, and walked into the sitting room. It took her a moment to realize I was there. The startled expression along with a sudden jerk as though she'd been slapped were quite satisfying.

"Hello, Susan. I got your message."

CHAPTER 25

S usan's eyes darted to the Raider, then around the room.

"It's all over," I said. "Of course, I didn't have to come in person. I could have just forwarded your note to Aunt Courtney."

"There's no way you could prove that email came from me."

I chuckled. "You assume that Courtney is less of a psychopathic murderer than you are. I would consider that a dangerous assumption. And as far as power is concerned, you're playing in the big leagues now. I doubt you can even conceive of what she's capable of doing."

She tried to project a casual nonchalance, but her posture was still fairly rigid.

"Courtney's clever, but not too bright," Susan said. "She thinks she's a lot smarter than she is. But we're friends. She'd never believe you. Besides, that note did what it was intended to. It brought you here."

I smiled. "Right into your trap?"

She smiled back, and raised a small pistol.

Without warning, I activated the lightning box, loosing an electrical charge that was enough to knock out a man or stun a demon. Susan's gun went off, the bullet hitting a cabinet ten feet to my left. She did a little shaking dance and dropped to the floor in a heap.

Rising from my chair, I walked over to her, placed the box against her temple, and activated it again. She jerked, and then lay still. I checked her pulse and felt it slow and then stop.

I knelt beside her for a moment, curious about whether I might feel anything, but I didn't. I had come to kill her, not talk to her, not to arrest her. It wasn't any different from killing a demon, or a vampire, or any other monster. I didn't feel guilt or sorrow.

Taking a quick look around, I grabbed a laptop computer and shoved it in my knapsack. There was a knock on the door, and I froze.

Whoever was outside in the hall waited for a few moments, then knocked again. I triggered the cloaking device and retreated, as quietly as I could, to the chair where I had been sitting. Holstering the Raider, I crossed the room to the window overlooking the back garden. Susan's room didn't have a balcony.

"Susan?" my Aunt Courtney called out, knocking louder on the door. "Susan? What was that noise? Are you all right?"

Unlatching the window, I pulled on it gently, hoping I could raise it without making too much noise. No such luck—it was stuck. Taking a deep breath, I put some muscle into it and pushed it. The window slid up with a screech and a thump.

I drew my knife and slashed the screen. Courtney started pounding on the door, shouting Susan's name. A quick glance down showed a twenty-foot drop to the garden, but at least there weren't any rose bushes below.

Plunging through the window, I grabbed the sill and hung for a moment before I let go, and landed hard just as an explosion sounded from the room. Light flashed from the window. Courtney was a storm mage, and it sounded as though she had blasted the door with a lightning bolt.

I took off running, vaulting the low garden wall, and fell to the ground on the other side. Sure, I had the cloaking device and the airshield device, but I had little faith in their ability to withstand Courtney's magik. Anyone who could call a tornado from a clear sky had power to burn.

For a few moments, I debated with myself as to whether I should simply hide and hope things would blow over, or make a break for it. But as I reviewed what might go wrong, I realized that all of Osiris's security procedures were probably still in place. Staying close to the wall, I started crawling in the direction of the peach orchard.

I had made about fifty feet of progress when the alarms went off, followed quickly by high-intensity lights turning the night into a nightmare scene brighter than daylight. Even cloaked, I was still solid and would still cast a shadow. Continuing to hug the wall, I crawled faster. Eventually, I made it to the orchard and slipped in among the trees. The shadows there helped to hide me and break up my silhouette, so I rose to my feet and ran in a crouch toward the guardians' barracks.

It was a calculated risk that the guardians would all be running in the opposite direction, but I had to get to a place where I could get over the wall and out of the compound.

My luck held, and I was able to reach the barracks, then slip around to the back of the building. There was an open space between the barracks and the gardener's garage that I had to chance. No one was in sight, but of course that had nothing to do with what the monitors could see from all the CCTV cameras set up all over the area.

I could use my magik to disable the cameras, but that would be like setting off fireworks, not only telling the guardians where I was but also who I was. I took the chance and crossed the opening, gritting my teeth as I saw my shadow. For anyone watching on TV, they would see a shadow but not the person casting it. I realized I should have killed the cloaking device, trusting to hope that I wouldn't be identified, but it was too late.

A door to the garage was ajar, and I slid inside to darkness partially illuminated by flashes of light through the windows. Donning my night goggles, I looked around and assured myself that I was alone.

The place was filled with strange shapes—lawn mowers, electric carts, a ditch digger. At the far end, parked in front of a large garage door, was a bulldozer. I needed to get past a two-foot thick brick wall. Would a bulldozer break through the wall? I honestly didn't know. My only other options were to go over the wall the way I came in, punch a hole in it using the concentrator weapon I had in my pocket, or hide out until I could slip out through one of the gates.

The problem with the concentrator was that I wasn't sure if it would penetrate the wards set on the walls. Whittaker's mercenaries had repeatedly assaulted the compound and failed to penetrate its defenses. Modern warfare in the age of magik had moved past most of the explosive weapons of previous centuries. Artillery and aerial bombardment were considered anachronisms.

I trotted over to the bulldozer and looked it over. When people tell a girl she should study engineering, they shouldn't be surprised when she makes it her business to play with every engine she comes across. That bulldozer was newer than the one I had learned to drive twenty years before, but not that much different. I checked the hydrogen tanks and discovered that they were full.

Another thing about being an engineer was that I could easily envision what would happen when the bulldozer hit the wall. The garage door was about twelve feet high, and the wall was twenty feet high. The driver's seat was open to the air, and while the airshield might keep me from getting my skull crushed, it wouldn't keep me from being buried under an avalanche of bricks.

The earplugs brought the sound of voices outside the garage, not close, but coming nearer. It wouldn't be long before someone decided to check the garage.

Wanting to increase my chances of success, I attached a magitek converter and an enhancer to the engine. Then I locked the steering controls so the machine would go only in a straight line. I switched off the cloaking device and the airshield, then used my magik to start the bulldozer's engine. Once it was humming, I triggered the mechanism to open the garage door, and put the big machine in gear. It lurched forward.

When it cleared the door, I kicked in the converter, then the enhancer. The machine accelerated and leaped toward the wall a hundred feet away. Satisfied that I'd done as much as I could,

I triggered my airshield and cloaking devices and followed the bulldozer.

As soon as I was outside, I hugged the wall of the garage and watched. Shouts from the other side of the garage were followed by gunfire. Explosive bullets hit the bulldozer, but it lumbered on.

The gunfire, voices, and everything else were drowned out by the crash of the bulldozer hitting the wall. My earbuds, designed for use in combat, cut out, so I watched the show in silence. The wall bulged, the blade on the front of the bulldozer bent, and the wall above the machine shook. Then the machine pushed through the hole. As if in slow motion, the bricks above the hole collapsed, raining down on the driver's seat and controls in a cloud of dust.

The caterpillar treads kept moving. The engine's power transferred from speed to torque, and the bulldozer climbed over the rubble, down the other side, and sped up toward the woods.

Men ran by me, and my hearing returned. They shouted, cursed, and fired at the machine as it crawled away. And then a bolt of lightning, far larger than the machine, lanced from the sky. The bulldozer froze, sparked, and burned. The hydrogen fuel tanks exploded. The sound and the concussion from the blast leveled every man in sight, and more of the wall collapsed.

From my vantage point, with my back against the garage wall, I felt the pressure push on me, but the airshield held. Figuring I would never have a better chance, I raced toward the wall, through the gaping hole, and into the woods.

CHAPTER 26

By my reckoning, I was about half a mile, maybe a little more, from where I'd left my motorcycle. The people nearest me weren't a concern, as it would take them some time to recover from their proximity to the lightning bolt and subsequent explosions.

But they weren't the only people who would be hunting me, and the bulldozer gave them a location to focus on. I made my way through the woods as quietly as I could while still moving quickly. Although the people hunting me lived on the estate, I doubted any of them knew the grounds as well as I did. Exploring the woods had always been my preferred choice compared to spending time with my family.

Two or three times, I heard someone crashing around in the undergrowth and changed course to avoid them. Once I almost ran headlong into a deer escaping my hunters. One of my fears was that if I took too long, they might discover the motorcycle.

I could hear vehicles on the roads, and about fifteen minutes after I escaped through the wall, a helicopter passed overhead, training a searchlight on the ground. That was something that would become more worrisome after I retrieved my bike. I had flown over the area many times and wasn't concerned that while on foot I could be seen through the trees from above, even in winter.

It took me about half an hour to reach where I stashed the bike. I had never checked to see if the cloaking device would render both me and the motorcycle invisible. If it didn't, then it would be pretty silly to continue using it.

I circled around, making sure there wasn't anyone lying in wait. No one was close, and I could tell the bike hadn't been tampered with because there weren't any electrocuted bodies lying near it. I jumped on, started it, and turned onto the road going south, away from the compound. I switched off the cloaking device but kept the airshield on. Thankfully, the motorcycle's electric motor was almost silent.

It was half a mile to the main road, and another fifteen miles to Mom's house. I had to slow down for a hard curve just before reaching the main road and heard a gunshot. Something ricocheted off my airshield, and I gunned the throttle, putting my foot down as the bike slid around the corner.

More gunshots sounded as I took the next corner, then I goosed the bike while lying down on the battery casing to reduce both air resistance and my silhouette as a target. I was concerned about a bullet disabling the bike. If that happened, they'd have me.

The road had two long curves, then ran essentially straight for several miles. I kicked the bike up to one hundred twenty miles an hour and concentrated on not hitting any cars.

I triggered my phone and called Mom. When she answered, I told her, "I'm on my way to your place with a bunch of Courtney's goons following me. Can you help me out with an ambush?"

"Come in from the south," she said. "Are you in a car?"

"On my bike."

"How long until you get here?"

"Ten minutes maybe?"

"We'll cover you. Drive carefully."

Of course, she'd say that.

I passed a car that was doing less than half my speed, then wove between a car in front of me and one coming toward me. It was getting late, and there wasn't much traffic, but there was still a lot more of it than I was comfortable with. Thankfully, the bike was more maneuverable than the armored personnel carriers that Courtney's people were probably driving. That was one of the reasons I'd taken the bike.

I hadn't counted on Courtney's people using lights and sirens, in addition to blithely running cars off the road. They couldn't match my speed, but I didn't lose them, either. I knew their APCs—or at least the ones Courtney inherited from Findlay— were equipped with magikally enhanced telescopes, because I had designed them.

When I reached the freeway, I really cut loose, pushing the bike as fast as it was capable of going. That didn't last long as I soon reached a traffic jam. Checking on my police band, I discovered there was a wreck ahead. Slowing down and driving on the shoulder, I managed to make it to the next exit. The cars following me had a much more difficult time. They could also drive on the shoulder, but only until they reached the first idiot who was blocking it, while I was able to take the bike between cars.

The helicopter caught up with me, however, and followed me along the off-ramp. I wouldn't have minded that so much, but they started shooting at me, seemingly indifferent whether they hit innocent bystanders or not.

Weaving and zig-zagging, I managed to avoid a catastrophe through the copter's first two passes. When I reached a park on my right side, the copter pilot decided to use the open space to come in low and bring a machinegun into play. I hit the brakes, fish-tailing and fighting to stay upright, and he passed in front of me. As he flew over the road, I keyed the third setting on my lightning box, launching a lethal hundred-thousand-volt lightning bolt at the copter.

Helicopters don't glide, and when their electrical system burns out, the engine stops and they drop like a rock. Which was what that helicopter did. The hard landing, incorporating an unfortunate collision with a tree, solved my aerial problem.

But it had radioed my position before it went down and slowed me enough that the ground pursuit gained on me. I took off again but could see the lights of an APC behind me.

The next few miles were harrowing, and I left the main road to try and ditch pursuit by going through a couple of residential neighborhoods. It didn't work, but the people behind me didn't gain on me, either.

My phone rang. My mother. "Where are you? Are you all right?"

I gave her my location and hung up. I didn't need the distraction.

When I finally reached Loch Raven drive and turned onto it, I had at least three APCs behind me, and they were almost in shooting range. I hit the first bend in the road about the time the APCs turned onto Loch Raven behind me. I breathed a sigh of relief. Almost home.

I knew when I passed through the veil the elves had cast around the reservoir, and backed off on the throttle. I pulled into Mom's place, drove the bike into her garage, and plugged it in.

But when I tried to walk, I discovered my legs were barely strong enough to hold me up. I leaned against the wall, and as the adrenaline bled out of me, I found myself shaking. At least some of that was from the cold. My hands had been wrapped around the handlebars, and I couldn't straighten my fingers. I wondered how bad it would have been without the airshield.

Mom came out, gave me a shoulder to lean on, and helped me into the house.

"Would you like something warm to drink?" she asked.

"Hot chocolate with spearmint schnapps?"

"I think I can do that. You sit over there by the heater."

She brought me the hot chocolate, and it warmed me all the way down. I felt my body start to relax.

"So, what inspired you to visit your Aunt Courtney?" she asked.

"I'm going to have to tell this all over again when Joren comes in, aren't I? Let's just say that Courtney wasn't the reason I went over there."

"But she was the reason you left in such a hurry?"

"That's pretty accurate."

Joren came in about forty minutes later, poured himself a drink, and sat down with us. "You need to find a better class of boyfriend," he said. "A nice elf boy who takes no for an answer."

"You dissuaded them?" I asked.

"Hell of a mess out there. You need to call your government or Council, or whoever, to come clear the road."

Cautiously, I asked, "What happened?"

"The lead APC ran into a rock, and the two behind it were going too fast and following too close."

Something didn't make sense. The road and the area around it were perfectly flat. "What rock?"

"The one we dropped in the middle of the road right after you passed. Just past that first curve. One hell of a crash."

"Uh, how big a rock?" I asked.

"Oh, about the size of one of those APCs." Joren chuckled. "If the driver had been quick enough, he could have chosen one of the trees on the side of the road instead. Why were they driving so fast?"

I told them about Susan, giving them a brief history of the woman, the HLA, and how she managed to become the drug boss of the Mid-Atlantic.

"So she was the one responsible for all those poisonings you've been investigating?" Mom asked.

"Yeah. Her idea, and she was a master at manipulating people to commit murder. We found out she wormed her way into Findlay House. Heaven knows how she met Courtney, or managed to make friends, but as I said, she was a manipulator."

I went on to tell them about our crackdown on the HLA and the drug trade, and Susan's reaction to it.

"I just decided that enough was enough," I said. "I went out there, snuck into the house, and killed her. Sometimes justice and the law have issues coming together."

"And you got caught," Mom said.

"Yeah. No sooner did I kill the witch than Courtney came knocking on her door. Just bad luck."

Joren shook his head. "I'm not sure I'd call it that. Some people think luck is a magikal talent. If that's true, then you've got more of it than anyone I've ever met."

CHAPTER 27

I stayed the night at Mom's and drove back into the city around noon. I dropped by Enchantments and agreed to go out to dinner with Kirsten. Aleks was in Atlanta again, and Mychal had a Family function to attend.

Then I went to the office and told Whittaker and Carmelita that I'd heard a rumor that Susan Reed had been assassinated. Whittaker gave me a raised eyebrow but didn't challenge my story.

The sun was just setting as I stepped out of Police Headquarters and started off toward Kristen's shop. And ran head-on into Besevial.

"This is getting tiresome," I said, laying my hand on my Raider. "Can't you call and make a date like all the other boys?"

The demon grinned, a sight I wished I had missed.

"Akashrian has agreed to your terms," he said.

"My father is alive?" I blurted out.

"Of course. I assumed you knew that. Where is the avatar?"

"Oh, no. She gets the statuette when she returns my father, and you pull your minions out of the battle lines with the Council's troops."

His grin turned into an ugly scowl. "How can we trust you to keep your end of the bargain?"

I barked out a laugh. "That's rich. I'm supposed to trust a demon? The concept, let alone the word, doesn't exist in your language. What surety do I have that you won't just kill me and grab the statuette? No, first you pull back your troops. When you do that, we'll arrange a place of my choosing to exchange your avatar for my father."

He seemed to mull that over, then said, "In four days' time. Where?"

I thought furiously, then the perfect place hit me. "Gunpowder Falls. It's north of the city, and there's a turnout from the road. At sunset." It was just outside the veil the elves had drawn around Loch Raven. Any chances of demon treachery could be covered by surrounding the exchange location with elven warriors.

"Done. You do realize that I have to use the avatar to bring him over," he said.

"I figured as much."

He nodded and disappeared.

I walked on until I reached Enchantments. The shop was still open for business, and I had to wait for Kirsten to finish helping several customers. When she was done, we walked back to get my car and then drove to the Kitchen Witch. On the way, I told her about my meeting with Besevial.

"And your mother knows nothing about any of this?" she asked when I finished.

"About my father? No. She knows about the avatar."

"Duh. It's at her house. But does she know what it is?"

I shook my head.

"And you just assume the elves will help you with this crazy scheme?"

I grinned. "A chance to hunt demons? They'll jump at it."

❧

After dinner, we drove up to Loch Raven to see my mom and grandfather. The elves Joren had brought with him from Iceland, and those who came later, had built quite an extended village along the eastern side of the reservoir. But Joren lived with my mom in her house at the southwest end of the lake, below the dam.

When we arrived, we found Joren and Mom in the sitting room with a magikal fire in the fireplace, playing the elven equivalent of chess. They poured us each a glass of wine, then finished their game while we watched.

"Do you remember how to play *sjakk*?" Joren asked me after Mom beat him.

"I don't get to practice much," I said with a laugh. "We played a couple of times when I stayed up here last fall, but if *you* can't beat her, then you can imagine what she did to *me*."

"She cheats," he said, and we all laughed.

"What brings you up here?" Mom asked.

"That little statuette we stashed in my workshop," I said. It was uncomfortable, but I went on to tell her about the demons wanting their avatar back. Then I got to the really uncomfortable part.

"You know the implant I got when I graduated university? The one designed and built by Dad? It turns out he has one, too. So, for the past fifteen years, he's been visiting me in my dreams."

As I continued, all three of us kept glancing at Mom to see how she was taking the news that my father was still alive. She sat, completely poker faced, occasionally sipping her wine.

When I finished, Mom asked, "And what makes you think this demon queen will trade fair? You say that Besevial needs the avatar to bring Lucas across the Rift, but he also needs it to bring Akashrian across. What's stopping them from killing you, taking the avatar, and going on their merry way?"

"Well, I was hoping I could talk a few elves into coming along with me." I raised an eyebrow in Joren's direction, and my grandfather returned a feral grin. "And I also made *this* according to Dad's specifications."

I held out the device I had been working on. Instead of a box, it was a square U-shape with a place for my hand and spiked ends that protruded from my fist on both sides.

"It's an energy projector. It converts energy I pull with my magik from the world around me, concentrates it, and projects it as pure energy. He says it will kill Akashrian, or any other demon."

Both my grandfather and mother had seen the statuette and felt its magik. Their lifted brows showed their surprise at my statement.

"Have you tried this device?" Joren asked.

"Not yet. I was afraid to try it in the city. But perhaps we could go over to the lake. I thought I could use Goose Island as a target."

Mom shrugged. "There shouldn't be much wildlife on the island this time of year."

We all got up and trooped out to Mom's truck. Joren and I got in the back, and Kirsten rode up in the front with Mom. She drove north to the end of the little peninsula jutting out into the lake, just before the road crossed a bridge to the east side. She parked, and we made our way through thick forest to the lake.

There was a half-moon, so we could see the island about two hundred yards away. I held up the energy projector, pointing my hand at the island, then used my magik to trigger it. Beams of light shot out from both ends, merging about three feet in front of me into a white, cohesive band about a foot wide that was too brilliant to look at.

I held it only for a moment, then cut it off.

"Danu's tits!" Joren exclaimed.

I was blinded, my night vision destroyed. I looked to my grandfather, whose elven eyes were far keener than even an eagle's.

"What is it? What did it do?"

He shook his head. Taking an arrow out of his quiver, he spelled it and fired it into the air in the direction of the island. It lit up the scene like a flare. At first, I couldn't comprehend what I was seeing. Then the enormity of it struck me. The end of the island pointing at us was gone. Instead, there was a perfectly semi-circular bay at the island's eastern end. A circle of at least twenty yards had been vaporized.

"Well, if Akashrian's corporeal," Mom said, "that should do the trick. Do me a favor and put that thing somewhere safe, though. Okay? I'd hate to have an accident that took out the dam or something."

CHAPTER 28

On our way into town the following morning, I didn't bother to turn on the radio. So, when I reached my office, I wasn't prepared for the level of excitement. Police Headquarters was a madhouse.

"You've heard, right?" Luanne greeted me.

"Yeah, they made me queen. I've known about it for weeks."

She snorted. "Right. I mean about the demons."

Considering my meeting with Besevial the night before, I wasn't sure I wanted to know. "What about the demons?"

"They seem to have abandoned the anti-Council forces. Just disappeared overnight. The Council has attacked Akiyama forces along several fronts."

I wheeled around and trotted to the elevator. On the way up to Whittaker's office, I thought about what Luanne had said with a feeling of unreality. Besevial had really abandoned Akiyama? Pulled all the demons out of the fighting?

"The Commissioner is busy this morning, Captain," Whittaker's secretary stopped me cold.

"I just have some information to give him."

She shook her head. "He's not here. He took a helicopter up to Novak at five o'clock this morning. If you need something urgently, you should see Deputy Commissioner Jefferson."

"Uh, oh, okay." Jefferson was officially my boss, a man I avoided like the plague. He and Whittaker had an agreement about me. I stayed out of Jefferson's way, and he stayed out of mine.

I went back to my office, turned on the screen, and checked what the media had to say. They didn't seem to know much but reported renewed fighting near the airport, south of Baltimore Harbor, and south of Wilmington. All of those areas had strong demon presences the day before, but it appeared the demons were gone. The Council forces were fighting human soldiers, witches, and mages.

I checked internal reports, and cops all over the Metroplex were reporting zero demon activity. Zero. Not even any unusual murders or stray body parts. I had talked to Besevial about six o'clock the previous evening, and I couldn't find a single report of demon misbehavior filed after seven.

That was scary. It was an article of faith among human magik users that the demon lords controlled the demons in their territories, but I never guessed their communication was that good or their control so complete.

I was pretty sure Akiyama Hiroku was surprised as well. Our intelligence suggested that two-thirds of the Akiyama-alliance fighters in the Mid-Atlantic were demons. Another ten percent were vampires, usually working for the demon lord.

The really surprising thing was that Whittaker had pounced so quickly. No hesitation. Hit the Akiyama forces before they had time to regroup. For the first time, I realized just how good Whittaker's intelligence services were. And how strong a general Tom Whittaker was.

I called Carmelita into my office. "Is there any fighting going on around the temple in Kensington?" I asked.

"I can check. Are you thinking about going over there?"

"If the demons aren't guarding the place any more, then yeah."

She came back a few minutes later.

"There's a major battle going on southeast of there, with the Council forces making a major push to reclaim the beltway. But we should be able to get in there from the north, through Clarksville and Colesville."

"Let's go. Gather up everything we've got on those missing persons."

When I went to get my coat from the peg where it hung by the outer door, Billie Cargill approached me.

"Are you going out to the temple in Kensington to check on missing persons?" she asked.

"Yeah. We think it might be tied to something bigger. Hold down the fort."

"Dani, I had about half a dozen missing persons reported to the Northwest Station. Young people who had connections to the temple, but I never had the manpower to really follow up on them," Billie said.

That stopped me. We had tied missing persons to the peripheral churches but not to the main temple.

"Can you get me pictures? Any interviews done with those who reported them missing?"

"Sure. Give me about fifteen minutes."

I waited for Billie and Carmelita to get their stuff together, then my partner and I got my car from the garage.

"Do you think we could grab something to eat on the way?" Carmelita asked. I realized I was hungry, so we swung by a place with crab-cake sandwiches-to-go before getting on the freeway and taking to the air.

We flew west until we passed beyond the city, then I swung south, passing over suburbs and occasional areas with grand estates and horse farms. When we got within ten miles of the temple, I found a straight road without any traffic and set the car back on the ground.

Carmelita had been monitoring what little information was available about the battle in the north DC area, and it appeared we were well away from the fighting. I wasn't taking any chances, though, and had her maintain an airshield around the car. If Akiyama forces tried to retreat from the battle, I assumed they would head north, toward their main base in Wilmington.

I also didn't completely trust that all the demons had completely disappeared from the area. When Ashvial had been demon lord of the Atlantic region of North America, there had been demons that disputed his authority. One had even been so bold as to steal Akashrian's avatar.

We were stopped at the gate leading from the public road. I showed my ID, and that seemed to cause considerable confusion among the guards. One of them got on the phone, and then he waited for a while, talked some more, waited some more, and finally someone on the other end made a decision.

"If you'll follow that car, ma'am," the guard in charge said, pointing to a white electric car one of his men was climbing into.

I thanked him and followed the car around the parking lot to the front near the main entrance to the temple. He drove slowly, and by the time we parked, there were several more guards there to meet us, along with a couple of men in priestly cassocks.

"I'm Captain Danica James, Metropolitan Police," I said, showing my ID to the guy who was evidently in charge.

"Welcome to the Harvesting Souls Church, Captain," the ramrod-straight, gray-haired priest said in a melodious baritone that I was sure could melt the heart and resolve of any woman still breathing. "I'm Reverend Blake. How may I help you?"

To say that he had a charismatic aura would be an understatement. In spite of his age, he was incredibly handsome and held himself with an easy confidence. I had to drag my eyes away from his face in order to find my voice.

"Uh, we've had a number of reports of missing persons who are members of your church," I said. "We spoke with Reverend Wilding in Baltimore, who said that a couple of his parishioners on our list had come down here to—how did he say it?—to 'seek a more contemplative relationship with God.' Their families have filed formal reports, so we have to investigate. I'm sure you understand."

"Of course. Please come in."

He led us inside, where we got a glimpse of the magnificent sanctuary before he took us through a door and along a corridor to a cozy little office the size of the major crime's detective bullpen that contained forty desks. It was only a little fancier than my Uncle George's study. Of course, Uncle George had only been a trillionaire, and not the head of a religion no one had heard of six months before.

"You've done a marvelous job restoring the place," I said. "I saw it a few years ago, and it was close to being a ruin."

"The Lord doth provide, and we have worked very hard," Blake said. He bade us sit at a table, offered us tea or coffee, and sat down with us.

Carmelita handed him a list, along with a folder containing pictures of the missing people. He thumbed through the pictures, then called three more priests into the room. They conscientiously went through our list and the pictures for almost three hours.

I sat with them while Carmelita interviewed the missing people in a room close by. The church authorities provided sixty of those who were on our list. About twenty more were identified as, 'They were here, but they have left us, and we are no longer in touch with them.' That could mean they were on a commune somewhere off in the woods, crossed the Rift, or were served up at a demon banquet. I had no grounds for suspicion and couldn't ask. The priests denied that the church had any records of seventeen more. That one I believed more readily.

Still, the number of people on our list that the church acknowledged rather shocked me. I had been going on the idea that where there's smoke, there's fire. It was rather disconcerting to discover I had a raging inferno on my hands.

The priests showed us back to our car and watched us drive away. As soon as we were out of sight, I took the car airborne.

Call me paranoid, but I didn't discount the idea of some kind of ambush.

"What do you think?" I asked Carmelita as soon as we leveled out and were on our way back to Baltimore.

"True believers, every one of them. Ready to give their souls to the church," she said. "But there's something about them that sets my teeth on edge."

I nodded. "There's something off about the priests. I swear, if any of them had asked to get in my pants, I would have been tempted to strip right there."

"I know what you mean about the priests," Carmelita said. "Maybe some kind of pheromone? I probed the girls, but I didn't get a hint that any of them have been exploited. Actually, they didn't seem to be attracted to the priests like I was." She shifted in her seat so she was facing me. "Dani, all of the people I interviewed were wearing a small pendant—a cross inside of a symbol I've never seen before."

"Can you draw it?" I asked.

She pulled out her notebook and sketched the pendant. I went cold when she turned it to me. The cross was surrounded by the two glyphs that spelled Akashrian in the demon script.

CHAPTER 29

I t had been a long time since I visited the international scholarly database on demons. Amongst the data stored there were academic papers on demon social systems and mythology, in addition to research detailing demon anatomy and physiology, sexual habits, eating habits, and anything else someone managed to be curious about.

Akashrian: Variously translated as a goddess or a queen, Akashrian appears to be one of the top-level personages in demon mythology and social hierarchy. When associated with mythology, she is considered the goddess of lust and pain. This is the goddess that sex demons, such as succubae, incubi, and lilliths, worship. When associated with social hierarchy, she is considered a queen, holding fealty from the demon lords of fire and water. As far as Earth is concerned, the majority of demons in North America owe their allegiance to Akashrian. She is an antagonist to Lakasvian and Delevidat, demon goddesses thought to control the demons in Europe and Asia, respectively. As far as can be determined, the top level of the demon pantheon consists wholly of the female and pan genders. No evidence of gods in the male, common, or neuter genders has been documented.

Interesting, to say the least. I dug a little further and found that Lakasvian was the goddess of fertility, knowledge, and intelligence, while Delevidat was the goddess of cunning and business. Lucky us in North America. I wondered about the relationship between Akiyama and Delevidat's followers.

"It must be interesting," Kirsten said, coming up behind me. "It's almost midnight, and you've had your head in that screen since dinner."

I leaned back and had problems focusing on my roommate. Gradually, my eyes adjusted.

"Just reading up on our favorite demon," I said, pointing to the screen.

Kirsten leaned over and read the section on Akashrian.

"Oh, goody. Pain? One of my favorite subjects. And you're saying I can jump into the Rift and get the full treatment from her?"

"That's only a theory," I said.

"I'm happy to leave it at the theoretical level."

I showed her the sketch Carmelita had given me. "These small pendants seem to be in vogue amongst the adherents of the Harvesting Souls Church. A Christian cross mixed with the demon glyphs signifying Akashrian. Any ideas?"

She studied the drawing, then said, "I could guess, but if you can get your hands on one of those, it would be better."

"Thoughts off the top of your head."

Kirsten shrugged. "They're probably charms. Coercion? Suggestion? A spell that just makes you feel good? Almost certainly something that provides the giver of the charm with some kind of control."

"So, I need to get you one of the charms."

"Yeah, otherwise, I'm just speculating." She looked at the screen and then the sketch again. "You know, the charms could be demon magik, not witch magik. A lot of the jewelry the sex demons wear incorporates that symbol. Sex and pain. Carmelita probably focused on trying to determine if those kids had been abused sexually. Keep in mind that masochists revel in pain. Unless you see scars, you probably wouldn't know if their rapture came from suffering. From what you've told me about your dreams, Akashrian likes to mix her pleasures."

❦

Gordon, my undercover operative inside Harvesting Souls Church, called me two days later and asked me to meet him in a semi-dive bar in Highlandtown. I knew the place had good food, so we agreed to meet for lunch.

The Raven had been a Baltimore fixture for centuries and was still run by the original owner's descendants. It had been a hangout for me and my friends when I was a university student. Just enough off the beaten track to be less rowdy than the bars nearer to the harbor—gentrified enough that you didn't have to go armed.

Gordon had taken a seat at the end of the bar, and I slipped onto the stool beside him. The barman brought me a beer and a menu, I made a quick choice, and he left us alone.

"What's up?" I asked.

"The Harvesting Souls Church is planning a special festival the weekend after this one," Gordon said. "They've contracted thirty buses to haul their worshippers down to Kensington, starting Friday night. The big event is scheduled for Sunday, and they're calling it a 'mass ascension.' A guy we befriended in Annapolis told me. He's all excited about it."

"How many people are expected to attend this religious extravaganza?"

"I was told about a thousand."

"And this is going to happen at the temple?"

Gordon shook his head. "Rock Creek Park."

The northern end of the Rift extended right to the edge of the park. Before the wars, the area surrounding it had included some of the wealthiest neighborhoods in the DC area. After DC was nuked the first time, the rich had moved out in the country, so they weren't around to witness the original appearance of the Rift in DC. Currently, the park was wild and overgrown, its major inhabitants being feral shifters.

"I don't want you and Sharon anywhere near there," I said.

He chuckled. "Don't worry. We're planning on disappearing a couple of days before all this goes down. Pass the word on to the Commissioner. I'm taking a trip up to Montreal with my fiancée to go skiing, and I think Sharon and her roommate are planning a trip to a beach in Mexico. We don't want to get inadvertently caught up in anything. I've seen the Rift, and it scares the crap out of me."

I nodded. "Good plan."

"I have a present for you." He held out his hand and dropped one of the charms Carmelita had seen into my palm. "Don't put it on, it's loaded."

"I was hoping you could get hold of one of these," I said.

We ate our lunches, then I paid, thanked him, and we went our separate ways.

Back at the office, I checked with Whittaker's secretary and made an appointment for late in the afternoon. Then I called Mychal and Carmelita into my office and briefed them on what Gordon had told me.

They agreed with me that the easiest way to prevent a slaughter would be to prevent the buses from picking up the church's congregations in the first place. As a magitek, it would be easy for me to prevent the entire bus fleet from even starting their engines.

We could also close the roads leading to DC. Or we could just bust the churches before their plans progressed that far. That option was most appealing to me, but I doubted Whittaker would go for it.

I was right. Whittaker didn't like any of the options I presented.

"We need to catch them in the act of doing something illegal," he said.

"Such as?"

"If you can prove those pendants have a coercion spell, or that people are being forced into the Rift, that's illegal."

"Gordon supplied me with one of the pendants. I'll have Kirsten look at it tonight."

CHAPTER 30

Kirsten and Aleks rode with me out to Mom's place. Kirsten had to be there to remove her ward, and Aleks said he went just to get some of my mom's cooking. I could tell he was lying and was feeling masculinely protective. I found I didn't care. The venture I was embarking on was as scary as anything I'd ever done.

We arrived at Mom's a little after noon. She fed us lunch, and then we went out to my workshop. I dissolved the ward set in place through a magitek device and opened the door. A closet in one corner had the same kind of magitek protection, along with a heavy lock and a ward that Kirsten had set. We opened that, then removed two more sets of wards to unveil the wooden box, about a foot square and a little over two feet tall.

I carried the box out to Mom's truck, and we drove down to Gunpowder Falls. We pulled off at the turnout, and I carried the box to a small clearing in the woods near the river. We cast wards around it and sat back to wait.

We had about an hour until sunset, but I wanted to be set up when Besevial arrived. Hidden in the trees were two hundred elven warriors armed with bows and swords. I carried the new magitek projector I had built, Aleks had his spirit magik, and Kirsten simply sat on a large rock, cast a ward around herself, and complained she should have brought popcorn.

I paced, nervous as a girl at her first dance. My mind raced with all the things that could go wrong. What would happen when Besevial actually took possession of the avatar? And what were the odds he would really fulfill his side of the bargain? Would I actually get my father, alive and whole, or would I get a corpse, or a demon wearing my father's shape? That was the one that scared me the most. I'd get Dad back, but he'd be possessed, not really Dad at all.

The sky lit up as the sun sank in the west, and I stood fidgeting over the box. Without any fanfare or warning, I realized I wasn't alone in the clearing. Besevial stood ten paces in front of me, a leering grin on his face.

"Is that what I seek?" he asked.

"Yes. Where's my father?"

"In my world. I must have the avatar to bring him across."

I backed away from the box and cast my magik at its lock. I drew my Raider while holding the energy projector with my other hand behind my leg.

"It's yours," I said.

His grin widened. "You don't trust me."

"Not as far as I can throw you."

He made a tsking sound as he approached the box, then he bent over, and lifted the box, revealing the avatar sitting on its base.

"Ahhhh."

He set the box aside, then lifted the avatar. He held the statuette against his chest and turned around so his back was to me. I didn't hear anything, but red light—I assumed from the avatar's eyes—shot out like a flashlight across the clearing. The air shimmered and seemed to part.

A hole formed in reality. The light on the other side was red, the same red as I had seen in demon dens. Akashrian stood there, and in her hands, she held a human. The man had snow-white hair, and he was very thin.

She reached through the portal and sat him down on his feet. He had my father's face, though it was much older and more worn than I remembered.

"Daddy?"

"It's me, Dani," he said. I heard it both with my ears and through my implant.

"Oh, God!" I rushed past Besevial. Dad took only two steps before I reached him and threw my arms around him. I tried to say something, but all that came out were sobs.

And then my mother was there, taking his face in her hands, staring into his eyes, and then kissing him.

I caught movement out of the corner of my eye, and turned my head to see Besevial carrying the avatar through the portal into his world.

"Hey, wait!" I shouted.

Besevial didn't turn, but my shout caused half a dozen archers to loose their arrows. His back looked like a pin cushion, but he didn't seem to notice. A white ball of spirit energy staggered him, however. And then the portal closed, the last rays of the sun disappeared, and we were left in darkness.

My mom was crying. I had never seen her cry before. Dad held her and stroked her hair.

The elves melted back into the forest, and after a while, the five of us who were left got into Mom's truck, and I drove us home. When we got there, Mom and Dad sat on the couch, holding each other and speaking in low tones while I helped Kirsten fix something for us to eat. She was a great cook, but I knew how to operate a kitchen powered completely with elven magik.

After our meal, we sat around, and Dad told us of his twenty-two years among the demons.

"Everyone thought you were dead," I said. I winked at him. "All except for three irrational females who refused to accept it. Mom and Grandmother still tend to speak of you in present tense rather than past. What happened?"

He took a sip of his wine. "You have no idea how good that tastes. Well, your Uncle Richard and I were on our way to a meeting with representatives of the Akiyama Family at the Palace of Commerce when we were ambushed. Our lead car hit a mine in the road, and the car we were riding in crashed into it. At that point we were attacked by demons along with some human mages. I took a knock to the head, and when I woke up, I discovered I had crossed the Rift and was in the possession of the demon goddess Akashrian."

"So, you didn't see anything about the attack?" I asked.

"Oh, I saw enough. I assume Richard didn't survive. He was shot. And I did recognize the men who captured me."

"Akiyama," I said.

He shook his head. "No, two of Moncrieff's assassins. Tell me, is Cousin Courtney still as big a bitch as she was back then?"

"Worse. But why take you across the Rift?"

He drained his glass. "You wouldn't happen to have any more of this, would you?" We were drinking Mom's peach wine.

Mom started to get up, but Kirsten hopped to her feet. "I'll get it."

He waited until she came back from the kitchen and poured wine for all of us. He took a sip, then said, "Well, I assumed I would be tortured and killed. I was half right. You know that demons feed on emotions. Fear and anger are two of the strongest emotions, and Akashrian is a very needy goddess. Anyway, one of her underlings, a demon lord named Ashvial, got the idea that a magitek could help them to understand technology. Help them to build magitek devices that used demon magik. He convinced her to keep me as a pet."

Dad shook his head. "It didn't work. At first, she suspected that I was purposely sabotaging my efforts. Giving them bad information. Eventually, she figured out that demons are just not able to comprehend how technology works. Like a human with no talent can't understand magik. But by then, she had become —I guess the word would be comfortable with me—and she enjoyed playing with me. So she kept me around."

I remembered my dreams and didn't ask what he meant by 'playing with him.' I really didn't want to know more.

So, I switched the topic. "Do you know anything about what they call an avatar? A little statuette of Akashrian about this tall?" I held out my hands two feet apart.

"It's how she controls her minions in this world," he said. "It also conveys some of her powers to them. You saw how they used it to create the portal so I could cross."

"But why would they take it back across?" Mom asked.

Dad shrugged. "Maybe they didn't trust you and were afraid you'd take it away from them? Or they plan to use it somewhere else? Or for something else?" Taking another sip of wine, he asked, "How did you convince them to let me go?"

"I had the avatar," I said. "I traded it for you."

"What?" He sat bolt upright.

Mom turned to him. "Ashvial ruled demons in the Atlantic Seaboard. I killed him, and Dani stole the statuette and hid it."

I chuckled. "The demons actually think I killed him, but it was really Mom bailing me out of a tight spot. When Besevial came looking for the statuette, I told him I'd trade it for you. That was the first time that I really knew you were still alive, because they agreed. Before that, I always wondered if my dreams were real."

I had to explain why Dad couldn't just waltz over to Findlay House to see Olivia, but before we all went to bed, I called my grandmother in Ireland.

"Grandmother? Are you sitting down?"

"Why? What have you done now?"

I handed Dad the phone.

"Mama? How are you?"

I heard only his side of the conversation, but it was very emotional. As they talked, I realized that with my father back, I was no longer her heir. That made me feel almost as good as having him home.

CHAPTER 31

The following morning, I called Luanne and told her I was taking the day off. Kirsten called her assistant and told her the same thing, and Aleks cancelled a meeting. Mom fixed breakfast for everyone, then we hiked up to the dam.

It was only half a mile, and not much of a climb, but Dad had to take several stops to rest.

"I didn't get much exercise," he told us, "and the food...well, let's just say the food wasn't very good. They fed me enough to keep me alive, but that's about it."

"Don't worry," Kirsten said, "Amelie won't let you go hungry."

I didn't ask what they had fed him. I didn't want to know. He looked as though he'd aged a hundred years.

But his mind was sharp, and he wanted to see the turbines and the enhancements I'd made while he was gone. We also talked about the Cerberus factory, and he sounded very interested in what Mary Sue and I were doing.

"Maybe I could help," he said.

"I'm sure you could. I could really use some help with the design work on those battlebots."

On our way back to Baltimore that afternoon, Kirsten said, "I hope he's all right. He doesn't look too good."

"It's been an incredible ordeal, but he's with one of the foremost healers in the area, and there are a couple of other healers in the elven village," I said. "I think we'll have to give it some time and see how he does."

"And what about the demons and that statuette?" Aleks asked.

"You don't suppose having the avatar is necessary for their grand ascension, do you?" Kirsten asked.

Ah, back to reality. "What did you learn from that pendant I brought you?" I responded.

"It appears to be a suggestion charm rather than a charm carrying a coercion spell," she replied. "It's more subtle, but more difficult to break because it doesn't force a person to do something. Some people might call it a persuasion spell. You know, the person who gave you the charm says, 'It would be so joyous to ascend to heaven with all your friends.' Which is a lot more subtle than, 'Jump in the Rift so a demon can eat you.'"

I sighed. "Any chance of a spell that neutralizes a thousand of those charms at once?"

"Nope. And even if someone takes it off, depending on how long they've worn it and how much suggestion has been used, they may have internalized those suggestions. So, even if the charm is removed, the person probably still has those thoughts."

When I spoke with Whittaker the following morning, I told him about Kirsten's analysis of the charm pendant.

"The difference between a coercion spell and a suggestion spell sounds like splitting hairs to me," I told him. "I think we should bust the churches and toss all the leaders in the clink."

He sighed. "Let me think about it. In the meantime, we've had another poisoning. This time it got into the food shipped to my troops assigned to contain your aunt's imperialistic ambitions. Almost three hundred soldiers of the regiment dug in west of Findlay House."

"Any idea how it got into their food?"

"Mychal and Carmelita have arrested three people, all soldiers working for me. They think the suspects were bribed." He leaned forward. "Dani, we have to do something about this. I thought you said Susan Reed was dead. Who else is distributing this stuff?"

I thought about it. ""You notice the target is a little different this time. Courtney probably has Susan's supply of thallium. Drop a nuke on Findlay House. Order your troops to take the place."

Whittaker shook his head. "I wish it was that easy. You and Osiris made that estate one of the most secure and well-armed fortifications in the world. Nothing we've tried can breach the magitek shields, and the lightning generators are huge. Where did you get that much power to feed them?"

I didn't want to explain that I had built cut-outs at the reservoir so that Findlay could override the entire Baltimore electric grid if necessary. I didn't think my grandmother would appreciate me revealing one of Findlay's deepest secrets.

On the other hand, I could disable that cut-out at the dam. Findlay House also generated its own power where the Gunpowder River flowed into the reservoir. Two run-of-the-river turbines were installed there, and the output from them didn't feed into the main power grid. One generated electricity for the Findlay estate, and the other sent electricity to the Findlay shipyard in Wilmington.

I wanted to slap myself. I had the ability to cut off all of Akiyama's power in Wilmington as well as Findlay House. But before I suggested that to anyone, I wanted to talk to my dad about it. He had installed those generators, as well as the electrical lines to their destinations. And while I had maintained the generators in his absence, I had never dealt with the power lines. I wasn't even sure exactly where they went, or how much branching they did. Could we cut off power to Findlay House or the Wilmington shipyards selectively?

Realizing that Whittaker was waiting on me to stop woolgathering, I said, "So, what do you want me to do? I don't have a magik wand that will stop people from eating thallium. Aren't there some kind of metal detectors or chemical tests people can use on their food shipments? Kirsten gave me a charm that tells me if my food is safe or not. That's what I would do if I were you."

He pursed his lips, and I could tell he was unhappy with me.

"We did distribute the antidote widely to our troops," he said. "We had only a handful of deaths."

"Wouldn't it have been easier to test the salt in the kitchen?"

His glower deepened. "Yes, it would have been. Someone would have to think about doing it though."

I wanted to say that should have been pretty elementary. Kirsten had started testing all of the food she bought after the Danner family poisoning. I did realize that checking a bag of groceries was easier than doing the same thing for truckloads. But, discretion being the better part of valor, I just shrugged and excused myself. I glanced back as I slipped out the door. Whittaker was already on the phone and I heard him say, "Why in the hell aren't we scanning food shipments to our troops?"

In my mind, the Harvesting Souls Church had crossed the line from a legitimate religion into a cult. A death cult. And I had only a week to come up with a plan to prevent that weird cult from marching a thousand people into the Rift.

Something I had no doubt about was that Whittaker and the Council might not be taking it seriously ahead of the event, but they would be completely up in arms afterward. From the missing persons reports and the interviews Carmelita had conducted in Kensington, it was obvious that at least a dozen members of Hundreds Families were involved with the church. Maybe twenty more were from Thousands Families. And the mothers of those people who disappeared forever were not going to be happy.

For some reason, I didn't expect Whittaker and the Council to accept the blame. They were a lot more likely to look for an underling to sacrifice.

Time to pull out the big guns.

"Carmelita, come into my office."

"What's up?"

"I know you said that you and your uncle, the one who's a Catholic bishop, don't get along that great," I started.

She snorted. "What do you want?"

"Well, I was hoping that if someone dropped some information about the Harvesting Souls Church in the right ears, perhaps someone might get indignant and bitch to the Council..." I let my sentence tail off. Her uncle was the Archbishop of Baltimore, and her grandfather sat on the Council as head of the Domingo Family.

She pursed her mouth and dropped into a chair, a thoughtful expression on her face.

"Maybe," she said after a minute or two.

I waited while she thought about it some more.

"I'd have to present it the right way," she said. Then her face brightened. "I know! I'll invite Danny to go watch with me!"

She lost me. "Danny?" I asked.

"Yeah. Uncle Danny. He's Archbishop Rodrigo's younger brother, and just a little bit older than I am. He's a Comparative Religion professor at Loyola. There's a birthday party for one of my nieces tomorrow night and both of them will be there." She gave a little shrug. "I hadn't planned to go, but this should be fun."

CHAPTER 32

I took a drive up to Loch Raven, had dinner with my parents, and then Dad and I dusted off the plans for the Metroplex electrical grid. The plans and schematics were stored in the main computer system, but he also had paper copies in a locked closet off the computer room.

Personally, I thought it was amazing that the scheme he created had lasted twenty-three years without any breakdowns or maintenance. Sure, I had maintained the turbines, generators, and magitek enhancers, but the switches, control computers, and cables hadn't been touched since his kidnapping.

"You're joking," Dad said, staring at me. "You've never touched the computers? They're still running? The programs have never glitched?"

I shrugged. "I've rebooted everything a couple of times. I have to use the computer to take a generator off-line so I can work on it. But the computers themselves? No, they've been rock solid."

"And you never considered that..." he sputtered, looking for a word, "...unnatural?"

"Not really. My daddy built them."

He continued to stare at me for a moment, then he pulled me into a hug. There were tears in his eyes.

When we really got into the plans, I discovered that not only was there a dedicated line going to Findlay House from one of the run-of-the-river turbines but also the turbine that fed Wilmington had a switch so its electricity could be diverted to another line that ran to Findlay. There was also a third line to the estate from the main power array at the dam. If the primary line went down, the computers would automatically cut over to the next line, and then the next.

"Were you paranoid that Olivia might lose power for her hair dryer?" I asked.

Dad chuckled. "My mother and Uncle George's generation were very fond of triple redundancy on anything that might protect them from demons. And although I doubt they would ever admit it, the idea of using their control over the power system as a weapon surely figured into their thinking."

"You mean, they could cut power to anyone in the Metroplex— or the whole Metroplex—and still have all the electricity they needed."

"Something like that."

"They looked only outward for threats," I said. "Too bad they never considered that dear, sweet Aunt Courtney might murder them in their beds."

He shook his head. "George always had a blind spot as far as she was concerned. So, now that you know how to kill the power to the estate, what do you plan to do?"

"Good question." I stood and started rolling up the plans to put them away. "It does provide me with a weapon, but we have to figure out how to use it. Even without power, she still has a thousand guardians armed to the teeth at the estate, and Akiyama has a lot more than that to back her up."

As we locked up and got ready to go back to Mom's house, Dad said, "Don't let all this talk about war and battles constrain your thinking. Courtney didn't get where she is through a massive frontal assault. Firepower may be the way to defeat a demon horde, but subterfuge and smart thinking might work better when your target is a single person."

I grinned. "In other words, I might be better off hiring a pretty-boy assassin."

❦

Carmelita came in the morning after her family birthday party whistling a popular tune that she knew I hated. Leaning against the jamb of my office door, she gave me a lopsided grin.

"Let me guess," I said, "your Family elected you queen."

"Almost. Uncle Rodrigo plans to hit Whittaker first thing this morning, or at least that's what he said. But Uncle Danny said he'd come and watch the show with me. He was very enthusiastic."

"Great. Just what we need. More civilians putting themselves at risk."

"Don't be a party pooper. I'll bet we can find someone willing to advertise it and sell tickets. We could get rich."

I immediately thought of Aleks, my business-obsessed boyfriend, then pushed the thought away.

My phone rang.

"Captain James," I answered.

"If you can spare me a moment, I'd like to see you in my office. Now," Whittaker growled.

"Right away." I hung up and grinned at Carmelita. "Our boss sounds as though he's had a chat with your uncle. He also sounds like he wants to shoot the messenger. Wish me luck."

When I reached the commissioner's office, I found a dark-haired man in a black suit with a clerical collar chatting with my boss.

"Reporting as ordered, sir," I said as I entered.

"Captain Danica James, this is Archbishop Rodrigo Domingo," Whittaker said. "The archbishop has learned of the event the Harvesting Souls Church plans for this weekend, and wants to know what we plan to do about it."

I had done some research, and come up with what I thought was a masterful plan, and perfectly legal.

"As soon as you approve the necessary resources, I plan to arrest everyone who shows up," I said. "Except for the first twenty-five people, of course. We'll need a lot of buses to haul them away, as well as officers to keep the crowd in-line, and probably extra booking officers on duty."

Domingo gave me a satisfied, tight-lipped smile and settled back in his chair. Whittaker's mouth dropped open and his eyes bulged a little.

"And what charge do you plan to use for the arrests?" he asked.

"Unlawful assembly. Holding an event with more than twenty-five people without a permit," I replied. "Rock Creek Park is part of the National Park System, and you need a permit to hold large gatherings in a national park."

Whittaker blinked at me. "National park? There's no National Park System. At least, there hasn't been since the first time DC was nuked."

"Ah, but there is," I said. "When the Magi Council established itself as the world's formal governing body, they decided it was too messy and cumbersome to adopt a whole new set of governing laws. So, they accepted all the established laws and said if any of them needed changing or repealing, they would deal with them on an individual basis."

I took the liberty of sitting down. "Among those laws from long ago that we still enforce are speed limits, parking laws, laws against dumping trash on downtown sidewalks, murder, and armed robbery. There are still national parks, and there are even people who administer the various national parks. What doesn't exist is an administrative office that issues special-event permits for Rock Creek Park. But the law requiring them is still on the books."

The archbishop barked out a laugh.

Whittaker's stony-faced glower slowly cracked, and a grin appeared. "How many men and how many buses?"

"I figure about three hundred officers and as many buses as we can wrangle. The Harvesting Souls Church will have the buses they use to haul their worshipers to the park, and we can commandeer those."

"Oh, only three hundred officers," Whittaker leaned back in his chair and chuckled. "I'm sure I can find a little loose change in my budget for that."

I leaned forward. "Good. But I'm not sure things will be that simple. I suspect that the church is actually run by demons. And if they decide to object to our operation, then I'm going to need troops to protect both the cops and the church's followers."

Archbishop Rodrigo nodded. "When my niece first told me about this church, and what they're trying to do, I also suspected demon involvement. Who else benefits from this blasphemous charade? I think your captain's right, Tom. Demons have little sense of humor, and very short tempers. When they're thwarted, the whole thing is liable to blow up."

Whittaker didn't look happy. "I don't suppose the Catholic Church is willing to contribute some resources to the cause?"

Rodrigo gave him a beatific smile. "Our thoughts and prayers will be with you."

CHAPTER 33

Carmelita and I took a drive down to Rock Creek Park that afternoon. A battered old sign, barely readable, told us when we reached Picnic Area 21. The map we were following on my car's computer showed the Rift extending to the edge of the open area there.

There were a couple of cars parked there, just off the road. I parked a few yards away, and we got out. The forest was as thick as hair on a cat, and we couldn't see more than thirty or forty feet in any direction.

Drawing my pistol, I let it hang next to my leg. I raised an eyebrow at Carmelita, and she drew her pistol as well.

We walked over a small bridge into an open area with picnic tables, firepits and grills, a sandy area for volleyball, and a covered gazebo. At the end of the open space, a picnic table was cut in half by the Rift. A wall of sparkling colors rose into the sky as far as I could see. We were looking at the very northern end of the Rift, and it was only a few feet wide in the part closest to us but widened into the distance. The forest stood on either side of it, but we couldn't see into the Rift at all.

"Absolutely amazing," Carmelita breathed.

We walked closer, stopping about fifty feet away from it. I had never ventured closer, though I had talked to a couple of scientists who had poked instruments into it. They didn't get any readings, and never retrieved what had gone in.

"I don't see how they're going to get a thousand people into this space," my partner said.

"Yeah, me neither. I guess they're just going to march the sacrifices in as they arrive."

"How do we know they go to demon land? I mean, if the Rift was in Norway, would they go to the land of the elves?"

"Not according to the elves," I said. "My grandfather said that they never saw anything come out of the Rift. As far as we know, only upper-level demons can go back and forth, and they use some kind of magik to do it."

"Your grandfather has been here a long time. Maybe at the time he was in Alfheim, there weren't any elves here who tried to go back."

I shook my head. "We just don't know, and the dangers of experimenting are too great." I didn't tell her that my dad might have more knowledge on the subject. I hadn't even told Whittaker that Dad was back.

"So, you think the priests are going to use some kind of demon magik?" Carmelita asked.

"I'm not sure what to think. Let's map out where we plan to station our forces, and then go back to Baltimore and start putting this operation together."

We drove back to Police Headquarters and held a planning session in one of the conference rooms.

"I envisioned it as a large production, with speeches, or at least a sermon," Mychal said when he looked at the photos we had taken of the area. "Lots of pomp and ceremony. There isn't room for any of that."

"Yeah, well, it's more like a funnel," Carmelita said. "Get off the bus, walk through a relatively small clearing, and pass out of this reality. A really low-budget operation. I assume there will be a priest there to bless them as they cross over to the other side."

"This may be easier than I thought," Commissioner Whittaker said. "There isn't space for a large force of guards. We take out the guards, substitute them with our own people, and direct the would-be sacrificial lambs out the other side of the clearing." He pointed on the map. "Here. Then we load them onto our own buses and take them to a holding area."

He was right. Doing it his way would be super simple. But I was inherently suspicious of anything that looked too easy. I couldn't escape the feeling that we had to be missing something.

৩৩৩

On Friday afternoon, we had our people in place, stationed at all the road entrances to Rock Creek Park, with communication and food stations set up at the other picnic areas, and a hundred SWAT officers in the woods surrounding Picnic Area 21.

Drones monitored the various Harvesting Souls Church's locations and alerted us when the buses filled up and hit the roads.

But none of the buses went to Rock Creek Park. They all went to the main temple in Kensington, their occupants got off, and the buses turned around to pick up another load of passengers.

It continued that way all evening until midnight and started up again at eight o'clock on Saturday morning.

Whittaker and I spent some time on the phone, then we sent most of our force home, telling them to report back at six o'clock Sunday morning. I also went home and caught some sleep.

On Sunday morning, I was back at the park, expecting that we'd soon see some of the church people show up to start staging their event. By mid-morning, nothing had happened.

Around noon, Luanne called me from Police Headquarters in Baltimore. "Captain, I think you should take a look at what the drones over the temple in Kensington are showing."

I hiked up the road to Picnic Area 22, where our main command post was set up. Entering the large van packed with electronic equipment, I glanced around at the screens covering the walls. Two of the screens showed the temple.

As I watched, two buses pulled into the parking lot and drove up to the entrance. The passengers got off and filed inside the building. Then the buses pulled away and drove back to the highway.

"Any idea how many people those buses have hauled in there this weekend?" I asked the room.

"Nine hundred and fifty-six so far," someone answered.

I stood and turned in the direction of the voice. "Any idea how many people total are in the building?"

A uniformed cop with sergeant's stripes on his sleeves shrugged. "Hard to be precise, as we don't know how many people were in there before we started keeping track. One thousand one hundred and eighty-three people have gone in since Friday, and seventy-six have come out. If someone went in and out twenty times, we'd have them counted as twenty people."

I studied the screens some more. Three buses were parked in the lot. That meant twenty-seven buses were out on the road. As I watched, another bus came in, discharged its passengers, then parked next to the other three. The driver got out, went to a car parked nearby, and drove away.

Pulling out my phone, I called Luanne. "Hey. I'm watching the drone feed. What am I missing?"

"Seventeen rented buses have already been returned to the company that owns them," she said.

I waited for her to say something more. When she didn't, I thought about what she'd said. "How are they going to get all those people to Rock Creek Park?" I asked.

"Teleportation? Divine intervention? Walk?" she replied.

Duh. Forest and trees. "They aren't going to the park at all."

"So it appears. They aren't setting up anything outside, so they must plan to hold their mass ascension ceremony inside."

But the rift was six miles away. Unless the mass ascension was only a metaphor. Or they had a way of opening a portal...

I contacted Dad through my implant.

When you were kidnapped, did the demons take you through the Rift, or did they open a portal? I asked him.

Ashvial opened a portal. Why? He answered.

I'll tell you later.

"Crap! Is Whittaker at headquarters?" I asked Luanne.

"I don't know."

"Get hold of him or someone who can get hold of him. We need to change our target site. They're going to open a portal inside the building."

"How are they going to do that?"

"Long story. Tell Whittaker."

I hung up and found the commander of the SWAT team. He wasn't overly-enthusiastic when I told him we had set up our ambush in the wrong place. He was even less enthusiastic when I told him the real event was going to take place inside a building. Especially when I said that I had little knowledge of how the inside of the building was laid out. The only plans I had been able to find were two hundred years old, and we had no idea what kind of renovations the Harvesting Souls Church had done.

"We need to move all of our personnel six miles north of here?" he asked.

"Looks like. And can you do it without drawing too much attention?" His face made me wonder if a person's head could really pop like a cartoon thermometer. "Okay. I'll take fast and efficient over quiet," I said.

CHAPTER 34

I commandeered the SWAT team's second-in-command, as well as a communications technician and his equipment. Along with Carmelita, we all got in my car and took off. I wanted to take to the air but waited until I was out of the park and could reach a major street. Going airborne in the middle of a forest was too chancy. It was winter, and the trees didn't have any leaves, but that made any branches hanging over the road more difficult to see.

The SWAT guys proved to be deficient in the sense-of-adventure department. I was too busy dodging traffic to pay much attention to them, but Carmelita did warn them before I took the car off the ground. I assumed her laughter had something to do with their reactions.

I bypassed the gate and set the car down on the road leading to the main parking lot. We didn't see any people. I drove around a bit, and finally parked where I'd seen the bus driver's personal car parked. The captain and the technician melted into the forest next to the parking lot while Carmelita and I loaded up on weaponry and crept around the side of the enormous building.

I led her past a loading dock. It would have been an easy way in, but I was afraid it might also be too public. The door I wanted was all the way around the building in the back by the trash dumpsters. The door had no handle or knob on the outside, just a lock that required a key. Child's play for a magitek.

I unlocked it, then used a knife to pry it open enough to slip my fingers through, and pull it open.

"Isn't this breaking and entering?" Carmelita asked.

With a shrug, I said, "The door was open. I dare anyone to prove that it wasn't."

She grinned and followed me inside. I blocked the door open in case someone else might want to use it, such as the SWAT team.

We were in a room with a lot of trash cans and bags of trash no one had bothered to take out yet. I went to the other door in the room, opened it a crack, and peered out. The hallway was bare concrete, unadorned and undecorated. Not something a lot of people other than the maintenance staff used. The building was an elongated hexagon with large, square towers at each point, and we were on one of the short sides on the east end.

I assumed the ceremony would take place in the main sanctuary, the only space large enough to hold more than a thousand people, but I had no idea how that room was laid out. My only guide was the two-hundred-year-old pictures.

"Let's try to the right," I said as I slipped through the door. The light in the hallway was dim, but we could see all the way to the end. No chance someone wouldn't see us.

There were two doors off that hall, and when we turned the corner, we looked down an identical stretch of hallway.

"It's going to be a maze in here," Carmelita said. "But from what I could tell from some old pictures, the main room is on the ground floor. We need to be up from there. Find a place overlooking it all."

I opened the nearest door and peeked in. It was a stairwell, leading both up and down. Glancing down the stairs, I saw the glow of red light below. I decided to climb instead.

We went up two flights of stairs before we reached the next door. I pushed the door open slightly and saw carpet on the floor beyond. The light was also much brighter than what we had seen in the first hallway or on the stairs. I ventured in a little farther.

It was another hallway, but brighter, painted white, with a beige carpet. What caught my attention was the first sound that we'd heard. The distant sound of a voice over a loud-speaker system.

I stepped out into the hall and followed the sound. We soon came to an opening that turned out to be a balcony overlooking the temple's main room below. Looking up, I saw the floor of another balcony directly above me, and across the room, there were two balconies on the other side, one on our level and one above.

No one was on either of the balconies across the way, or on the one where we had emerged. The other end of the huge room also had four balconies on the same levels, but they were empty as well.

Below us, the room was almost filled with seated people. At the far end was a raised dais with what looked like an altar and a lectern. A man stood at the lectern, talking about the joys and rewards of ascending into heaven while we were still alive rather than waiting until we died. To the sides of the room at that end was raised seating behind railings. The people sitting there all wore clerical garb. Men on one side, and women on the other.

On the wall behind the altar was a huge cross with the glyphs spelling Akashrian.

"How much do you want to bet that the priests are possessed?" Carmelita whispered.

It hadn't occurred to me before, but what she said made some sense. Due to the red light I'd seen emanating from the basement, I was fairly sure there were demons in the building. If she was right, we had more than a hundred major demons sitting in the room below. That was a lot of fire power, more than she and I could hope to fight.

I was loath to abandon our position, though. We were in a great place to watch the proceedings below, and if it came to a fight, we held the high ground. But I needed to communicate with our forces outside. Reluctantly, I backed off the balcony and tried another door down the hall.

We found ourselves in what looked like a formal sitting room. A quick search revealed a closet, but no other doorways. It also had a window, which allowed me to get my bearings and see the grounds below.

"Can you cast a sound shield on that door?" I asked Carmelita.

She nodded, and I pulled out my phone to call Luanne.

"What's going on in the world?" I asked when she answered. "We're inside the temple, and there are a lot of people in here with us."

"Commissioner Whittaker wants to talk to you. I'll switch you over," she replied. And before I could say anything, she did.

"Where are you?" Whittaker asked.

"Sitting inside the Harvesting Souls temple. All the people they bussed down here are sitting listening to a spiel about how going to heaven when you're still alive is better than waiting until you're dead."

Silence on the other end.

"Boss?"

"You're kidding." Before I could answer, he asked, "How did you get in there?"

"Through an unlocked door by the trash dumpsters. Boss, there are steps down to the basement, and the light down there is red."

I held the phone away from my ear. I appreciate fine creative cussing as much as the next cop, but I could hear him just fine with the phone a foot away. I saw Carmelita's eyebrows go up, and she was across the room from me.

"Dani, you're miles away from the Rift. How does this fit in with your theory that they're sending people across?"

"I think they plan to open a portal. Boss, Carmelita thinks the clergy might all be possessed, and I think that makes sense."

"I never heard of any magik that can open a portal."

"My father came through one last week. The demons know how to do it."

More silence. I waited.

"I'm sending people onto the property. When you want them inside, let me know. Lucas is back?"

"Yes, he's back. He's out at my mother's place. Send me some mages now. Especially aeromancers, and if you have any witches who can cast wards. Back door by the dumpsters. We'll guide them in."

"As soon as I can," he said and hung up.

CHAPTER 35

Half an hour after I spoke with Whittaker, I received a call from Mychal.

"I'm outside the building by the dumpsters, and there's a half-open door in front of me. Where do I go?"

I sent Carmelita down to get him while I snuck back onto the balcony across the hall to watch the show. The guy who had been talking was now leading everyone in a song. I pulled out a set of magik-enhanced binoculars and studied the clergy, trying to discern any signs that Carmelita was correct. I didn't see anything, of course. Normally, I wasn't able to tell if a person was possessed until they tried to kill me.

I lay there on my belly for about twenty minutes, then I heard a faint sound in the passage behind me. Using the periscope setting on the binoculars, I peeked around the corner and saw Carmelita leading a bunch of people down the hall. I crawled out into the hallway and crossed to the room she and I had used before.

Mychal had brought eighteen mages and two witches with him. That was when I realized how seriously Whittaker regarded the situation.

"So, what's the plan?" Mychal asked once everyone was inside the room, Carmelita had sealed the door, and he had introduced everyone.

"I think there are demons in the basement," I said. "I was hoping that we could cast wards on the stairwells to block anything from coming up to join the party."

"Yeah, we can do that," one of the witches, a young blonde woman, said. "How many stairwells are there?"

I shrugged. "I don't know. I've seen only one. I was thinking we could send two or three mages with each witch, have them go in opposite directions, and try to plug up the basement."

"Sure, we can try it," the other witch, a middle-aged man, said.

Carmelita spoke up. "The more people we have out running around, the better the chance we get discovered."

"I really don't care. I think things are going to hit the fan pretty quickly, and if there's a demon den in the basement, I'd rather even our odds."

"I agree," Mychal said. "A Magi SWAT team and a thousand of Whittaker's mercenaries have taken control of the grounds. As soon as anything happens, that SWAT team will be coming through the front door, the loading dock, and that trash-room door."

I kept one of the mages with me and Carmelita, and sent the rest of them to occupy the other three balconies that I could see above the main room. The three of us snuck back onto the balcony nearest us and settled down to listen and wait. I glanced at my watch. An hour before sundown. Not that demons couldn't operate during the day, they just preferred nighttime.

Half an hour later, Mychal called. "One of the witch teams ran into a security guard, and it got a little noisy. They had to retreat from the last stairwell, so it's unblocked."

"Acknowledged," I said. "When the action starts, make sure no one has their backs to those stairs."

I passed Mychal's information on to my companions. Shortly thereafter, one of the witch teams joined me. The other climbed up another level and joined Mychal on the top balcony at the other end of the room.

Everyone had reported that the building was almost deserted except for the main sanctuary. A total of twenty-three people had been rounded up outside the building. I really couldn't see directly below me without exposing myself, but it seemed there had to be more people somewhere. Of course, we had seen only the central part of the main building. Whittaker's people hadn't attempted to enter any of the peripheral buildings as yet.

A burst of organ music brought my attention back to the proceedings below. As I watched, all the people rose to their feet and began singing. The presiding priest turned and faced the demon cross, and began chanting. A wave of cold washed over me as I realized he was chanting in the demon language.

"All teams, on the alert!" I said into my phone. "Something's about to happen."

The air around the cross began to shimmer, just as it had that night at Gunpowder Falls when Besevial opened the portal. And sure enough, when the portal stabilized, Besevial stepped through it into our world. He was holding Akashrian's avatar in front of him.

A human, dressed in priestly robes, climbed the steps of the dais and stopped in front of the demon lord. I watched in horror as Besevial handed the avatar to the priest, then stepped forward, and merged with him. The priest screamed, the demon disappeared, and only the priest remained.

"Did he just possess that guy?" Carmelita asked.

"Yeah. That's how it's done."

None of the people I could see below acted as though anything strange had happened. Personally, that creeped me out more than anything else that had gone on.

Akashrian emerged from the portal. She stood there for a moment, then walked to the center of the dais and in a loud, sibilant, and faintly musical voice said in English, "Come to me, my children. Come to me and take your place in heaven."

The people standing on the floor started forward, forming two lines, and began streaming past her toward the portal.

"Now!" I shouted into my phone on the general wavelength. "All troops, assault the building."

Standing up, I aimed with my new projector weapon, and triggered it with my magik. Two beams of white light merged and shot toward the dais. The light hit the man Besevial had possessed, and he disappeared. The avatar fell to the floor.

Akashrian looked up and pointed her hand in my direction.

"Duck!" I yelled, diving into the hallway. Carmelita, the blonde witch, and two other of my companions landed beside me. The others disappeared in a yellow flash along with the balcony.

I used the periscope to look beyond the gaping hole in the wall and saw the sanctuary devolving into pandemonium. The mages on the balconies were involved in a full-scale battle with the priests and nuns below. Akashrian, holding the avatar in the crook of her arm like a baby, destroyed another balcony.

The worshipers on the floor continued to form two lines and march through the portal, as though nothing was going on around them.

My phone rang. "Captain," a voice I didn't recognize said, "there are tons of demons coming up those stairs we couldn't block. We're retreating."

"Go! Be safe!" I responded, but he had already hung up.

I waited for Akashrian to direct her attention to something at her end of the hall, then aimed and fired my weapon at her. She waved her hand in my direction, and the white beam of light hit something that absorbed it.

"Dani, someone's coming up the stairs!" Carmelita called.

Crap. I ran down the hall to the door leading to the stairs. Pausing a moment with my ear against the door, I listened and could hear footsteps on the metal stairs but didn't hear anything directly on the other side of the door. I pulled it open and stuck my head through.

Below me, on the intermediate landing, I caught a glimpse of a demon.

"Any humans in here?" I yelled.

My only response was a demon growl. I sent my magik into my weapon and destroyed the stairs. There was an awful sound of crashing mixed with demons' screams, a lot of dust, and then quiet.

"I hope the elevators are working," Carmelita said from behind me. "The SWAT team is in the building."

I raced back to the hole where the balcony had been. The battle below was still chaotic, and the idiot worshippers were still marching through the portal.

In desperation, I fired at the portal. The results were far more satisfactory than trying to kill Akashrian. The air in and around the portal shimmered.

Akashrian sent another energy beam at me, and I ducked back into the hallway just in time. The hole where the balcony had been got a lot larger.

I waited until Akashrian was distracted by someone shooting at her, then I fired again at the portal, and it convulsed. Two people who were in the process of walking into it seemed to convulse along with it, and then it collapsed in on itself.

Akashrian let out a scream of rage. She lashed out indiscriminately, shooting yellow sizzling balls of energy all over the place. Worshippers died, clerics died, cops and SWAT soldiers died. Everyone who was able, including me, fought back.

I fired bolt after bolt of energy at her, but it seemed as though the weapon took longer and longer to recharge. Bullets and missiles exploded all around her. Balls of fire bathed her. Bolts of lightning struck her. It didn't seem as though anything could harm her.

Suddenly, she whirled around, blasted a hole through the wall of the church, leaped through it, and was gone into the night. No sooner did the tip of her tail disappear than the side doors into the sanctuary burst open and waves of demons poured through.

I thumbed my phone to the general wavelength. "Red alert! The demon goddess has escaped the temple. Repeat, she has escaped. The temple is full of demons. Pull back, pull back!"

I turned to Carmelita. "Come on, let's get out of here."

"How?"

I led her and the others with me into the room where we had originally made our plans. Drawing my Raider, I blew the window out.

"We just need our friendly local aeromancer to ferry us to the ground," I said.

"All of you?" She took a deep breath. "You're buying the drinks."

CHAPTER 36

Sitting around the table with me at Whodunit were Carmelita, Mychal, the blonde witch, and five others who had come out of the debacle at the Harvesting Souls temple unscathed. I had been introduced to everyone but hadn't bothered to memorize their names. I had the presence of mind early —after I had bought the third round—to realize I wasn't driving home. I had called Aleks and had an invitation to spend the night, if I could walk or crawl that far.

The bar suddenly quieted, and I instinctively looked toward the door. Police Commissioner Thomas Whittaker, wearing his uniform but with the coat unbuttoned and the tie loosened, came in and walked over to the bar. The instant that he put his hand on the bar, Ed Donatello, the owner-bartender, set a shot glass in front of him. Whittaker picked it up, drained it, and slapped it down.

Whittaker and Ed exchanged a few words, Ed poured him a pint of ale and a double shot, and Whittaker turned away, focusing on our table.

Most people assumed that Ed—a retired detective sergeant—never charged Whittaker out of respect. While I knew Ed respected the Commissioner, I also knew that Whittaker owned a third interest in the bar and had put up the initial capital to buy it when Ed lost his leg and took early retirement. No one but Ed and I—and possibly Whittaker—knew that I owned five percent. Ed had been my partner, and if I had been a little quicker the night he and I ran into a snake monster from the Bay, he still might have had two legs. But I always paid my bar tab.

Whittaker made his way across the room, carefully balancing his drinks while acknowledging people who called out to him and occasionally stopping to chat with someone.

"Clear a space and get him a chair," I ordered.

Mychal jumped up, found an empty chair, and brought it to our table. People scooted around to create a space. A couple of people got up as though to leave.

"Sit down," I growled. "Nobody's going anywhere until he says you can leave."

A couple of startled looks, then everyone settled in their chairs.

Eventually, Whittaker came to our table, set his drinks on it, and collapsed in the chair we had provided. He looked around the table, his gaze pausing on every face. Then he picked up his shot glass and held it out.

"To law and order and survival," he said. "One hell of a cluster-fuck, and I commend you all for getting out of it in one piece."

We all clinked our glasses together and drank.

Whittaker set his half-empty shot glass on the table and said, "Okay. I'll get your *official* reports tomorrow. Tonight, tell me what happened. What *really* happened."

I started, but everyone had a tale to tell him from their perspective and experience. It took a lot longer to tell than it had to live through.

When no one had anything else to say, I asked the question we all had. "What happened to the demon woman?"

Whittaker chuckled and downed the last of his whiskey. "She plowed a fifty-yard path of destruction between the temple and Rock Creek Park, then disappeared. We're not sure if she crossed into the Rift, or into the Waste. She incinerated any drones we sent after her. Slaughtered any troops that got in her way."

He pulled out his phone and projected a hologram into the middle of the table. The carnage was even worse than I feared. In addition to the people killed and injured during the battle at the temple, Akashrian was obviously in a hurry, and her trail could easily be followed—a straight line of devastation that included bridges, roads, forests, buildings, and housing developments. It looked like a killer tornado had torn through the area.

He fixed me with his eyes. "You called her a 'demon goddess' at one point."

"My father variously called her a demon queen or a demon goddess. He said he didn't know which, or if it mattered."

He sat back in his chair and took a pull on his pint, only to find it empty. He raised his hand and a robowaiter was there immediately.

"Another round, and tell Ed to put it on my tab," Whittaker said.

I noticed that the robot trundled over to the bar, and Ed loaded its tray with drinks already waiting. The robot was back within a couple of minutes of its leaving.

Whittaker cast his gaze around the table again. "I assume no one here is driving. There will be cop cars waiting outside to take you home." He raised his glass again. "Sláinte."

⊗⊗

The cop Whittaker detailed to babysit me and Carmelita dropped me off at Aleks's building, then drove her out to the Domingo estate. I was still able to walk, but barely. Aleks steered me into the bathroom and helped me undress. I popped the top on a vial of Kirsten's hangover cure and drank it before I fell into bed.

The following morning, Aleks and I hit the Kitchen Witch for breakfast, and then he dropped me off at my house. The day was sunny and clear, not too cold, so I hauled out my motorcycle and drove up to Mom's house.

I sat in her kitchen with a cup of an herbal tisane and a fruit pastry, and told her and Dad about the disaster at the Harvesting Souls temple.

"I haven't seen the official reports yet," I said, "but I'm sure there are hundreds dead, hundreds injured, and I doubt anyone will ever know how many missing."

Dad was most concerned that the weapon I built seemed ineffective against Akashrian.

"You know," he said, "that Akashrian knows only two humans, you and me. This setback will enrage her. You're going to need to be extra careful."

"If she was unprotected, then maybe I could have killed her," I told him. "It certainly vaporized a demon lord, but he was holding that avatar-statuette, and it was unharmed. She shielded herself, and nothing anyone threw at her penetrated."

Mom had different worries. "No one has any idea where this Akashrian went?"

I shook my head. "Whittaker said either the Rift or the Waste. I'd bet the Waste. I don't think she's very happy with her situation. She probably didn't plan to stay in this dimension."

Dad snorted. "The problem is, there has never been a demon as powerful as she is on earth. She's an apex predator, and if she's stuck here, she'll seek complete world domination. She can command every demon in this world."

"But she has the avatar," I said. "She can open a portal anytime she wants to."

Dad shrugged. "Let's hope she wants to. It may take a demon lord to do it, and she doesn't have one handy."

He wanted to take a look at the projector weapon I had made from his instructions, so we went out to the workshop. I had questions about the device, and wanted to take the opportunity to explore the theory behind it. It was canon that there were three kinds of magitek devices—enhancers, converters, and disrupters. Enhancers and converters were used to channel magik into operating electrical and mechanical devices. Disrupters did the opposite, and except for specific uses, were illegal.

"This thing violates the laws of magik, at least as I learned them," I said, laying the device on a workbench.

"Yes, it does, but that's because those laws encompass insufficient knowledge," Dad said. "It incorporates a concentrator, which is something I learned about in the demon realm. It's the principle behind Akashrian's avatar."

"The avatar is a magitek device?"

He shook his head. "No, because they don't have technology in the way we know it. All their efforts to make me build a magitek device for them failed. The laws of physics are different there. An internal combustion engine doesn't work. Gunpowder doesn't explode. But they are much farther advanced in magik than we are, and I learned how to concentrate magik. In their world they use it to create things like the avatar, but I figured it would work on mechanical or electrical devices in this world."

I watched as he took my device apart, both physically and magikally, studied it, and put it back together.

"What would happen if you coupled it with an enhancer?" I asked.

I received an astounded look in return. I told him of my experience adding an enhancer to the magitek lightning box he had made for me decades before.

Dad shook his head. "Interesting question. If it will vaporize part of an island and a demon lord in its present configuration, I'm not sure I want to enhance it that much. Enhancement of some technologies can have disastrous results."

"Like a magitek nuke?"

"Yeah, like your grandfather found out the hard way."

"Yeah, like that."

He got a far-off look in his eyes and stared off into space for several minutes. Eventually, in a dreamy tone, he said, "But if we could regulate how much enhancement..."

"Like the step switch on the lightning box?" I asked.

"Maybe something like that. Do you have the lightning box with you?"

"Always." I handed it to him.

He placed it on the workbench next to the concentrator. Then he started pulling parts out of various bins, and I could feel his magik as he began work.

CHAPTER 37

Two days afterward, I led a SWAT team from the Arcane Division into the Harvesting Souls Church in downtown Baltimore. Simultaneous raids were conducted at the other facilities owned by the church.

"Captain James," Reverend Wilding greeted me. "How good to see you again. May I be of service?"

I handed him a search warrant and said to the cops following me, "Please show the Reverend outside and make sure he doesn't go anywhere."

About that time, there was a sound like an explosion from the alley in the back of the church. Reverend Wilding's cheerful expression froze, and he reached for me. I expected that reaction after we proved Carmelita's theory at the temple. All of the church's clergy had been possessed.

I drew and fired in one motion, the Raider's magikally enhanced incendiary-explosive round catching him in the chest. That slowed him down temporarily as the human body died and the major demon inside re-manifested itself.

The real Reverend Wilding was blue, seven feet tall, with scales, gills, and horns, and his muscles were clearly delineated like a weightlifter's. His teeth and claws appeared capable of ripping through an armored car, and he no longer wore that happy-to-see-you smile.

Back-peddling, I fired again. Twice. Both shots hit him, and I managed to create a little space between us. I shifted my aim to his head, but by the time I pulled the trigger, he had jumped out of the way.

I hesitated, as the demon moved past a cop a few feet to my left and I didn't have a clean shot. The cop didn't react quickly enough, and the demon tore off his head in passing. I fired at the demon's back, and then half a dozen guns discharged all around me. The demon's head exploded, and his body stumbled forward and fell.

"Heads up, ladies and gentlemen," the SWAT captain called out. "This isn't a garden party."

The head of the dead cop sat on the floor, staring at me accusingly.

A fireball whooshed past me, and I triggered my airshield box. A bolt of lightning flashed from my right toward the hallway where the fireball originated. A fusillade of bullets followed the lightning.

Half of the SWAT team was assigned to enter the basement through the door to the alley behind the church. I heard an explosion from the basement, and demons boiled out of the stairwell to the left of the nave.

I fired the Raider until the magazine ran empty, then pulled out the concentrator, switched it down to its lowest power setting, and discharged it. The three demons closest to me disappeared, but it didn't blow a hole in the wall of the church. Encouraged, I slipped behind a pew for cover, and started picking off demons as they came out of the basement.

The fight lasted about half an hour. When it was over, we had lost a dozen cops and had killed at least nine major demons, seven standard demons, and taken sixteen demons into custody. Mentally, I could add to the tally seven more demons who had been vaporized. The SWAT team captain led me downstairs into the basement.

"There's also a subbasement," he said, "But it's full of water."

Understandable, considering how close to the harbor we were.

"The demon in charge of this place was a water demon," I said. "Check that subbasement out thoroughly, but carefully."

The only light available in the basement was the dark-red light. I paused and put on a pair of night goggles. The basement was similar to other demon dens I had seen. A large, open space with low divans and tables. There were a lot more sleeping places than the number of demons we had encountered.

I looked toward the stairs leading to the alley.

"Yeah," the captain said. "I think we should post some people here to see who else comes home. Looks like a center of activity."

"I agree. With Lucifer's Lair closed, I knew they had to be hanging out somewhere."

Carmelita wandered over to where we were talking.

"The number of demons we saw here was nothing compared to the number who used to hang around Lucifer's," she said. "This church can't be the only den."

Unfortunately, I had to agree with her. I wondered if anyone in the Police Department had informants among the sex demons. They were the only ones who still populated the city in large numbers, and they weren't involved in the war—at least not overtly. But they had answered to Ashvial just like the other demons, and I assumed to Besevial. That meant they answered to Akashrian.

No one knew if a demon lord was born to that status or elevated to it, but the suspicion was they rose in the hierarchy. With Besevial gone, that left a void. Would Akashrian bring one over from her realm or promote a major demon already in our world? After I got back to my office, I called Dad through my implant and asked him about it.

"Well," he said, *"that doesn't have a simple answer. The closest analogy I can make is that a demon lord is prepared rather like a queen bee in our world. They're born as normal major demons, but at some point, when they're very young, they're selected and from then on, they receive special food along with training and education."*

"Is it the same for the top of the hierarchy, like Akashrian?" I asked.

"Not exactly. She was bred to be what she is, then fed specially. At some age—I'm not sure when because I wasn't there when it happened—she and her eleven twin sisters engaged in a battle royale, and Akashrian was the survivor."

Reports from the raids at the other churches contained similar information to what I had seen in Baltimore—clergy revealed as being possessed by major demons, demon dens in the churches' basements, and evidence of human worshippers being abused, eaten, or conned into crossing the Rift.

Unfortunately, the demons hadn't felt the need to keep records of the humans they ensnared, so we had no way of knowing how many unsolved missing-persons cases were due to the Harvesting Souls Church's activities.

Archbishop Rodrigo and his counterparts in other religious denominations lost no time condemning the Harvesting Souls Church and banning any contact or interaction with them. They also set up a couple of counseling centers to help deal with those people rescued from the temple and its outlying churches.

The major question I had was what Akashrian's next gambit would be. I had no illusions that she would give up trying to build an empire in our world. As long as the Rift existed, humans would have to deal with the Rifters. And as long as demons viewed other species as prey, there would be conflicts.

CHAPTER 38

Akashrian's response came quickly. A wave of demons poured out of the Waste, overrunning Akiyama's positions between the Waste and the airport. Obviously, the demon goddess didn't care much about Ashvial's carefully nurtured alliances. That didn't mean she was targeting the Council's enemies. The Akiyama forces just happened to be the first humans to get in her way.

At least the Akiyama forces provided a buffer that gave the Council time to prepare. Caught between the demons and Whittaker's mercenaries, Akiyama's soldiers were unable to retreat. The anti-Council threat to the airport and the seaport was decimated.

The demons from the Waste were one threat, but not the only one. Carmelita's comment that there had to be more dens in Baltimore than the one housed at the Harvesting Souls church was prescient. We had demons everywhere, especially downtown and in the harbor area.

"If the police don't control these damned demons," Kirsten said as she served Mychal and me dinner, "I'm going to stop paying bribes, and you two can feed yourselves. Business has completely dried up."

Mychal snorted. "We'd have to nuke the city to get rid of them all, and that wouldn't be very good for business, either."

"Or you could modify your business model," I said. "Try stocking the kind of goods that appeal to demons."

Kirsten glowered at us. "You're treading on very dangerous ground."

Mychal and I set out for downtown the following morning, but I had gone no more than a mile or two when I was presented with a wall of brake lights in front of me. I hastily sketched a rune in the air in front of the dash. A matching sigil lit up in red, and I sent my magik into the converter. The sigil turned silver, and the car lifted off the ground.

Traffic accidents on the freeway were uncommon, given modern collision-avoidance systems, but not unheard of. And I always kept in mind something my father told me when he was first showing me how to use my magik.

"Dani," my father had said, "it's almost impossible to make anything foolproof because fools are so damned creative and persistent."

As we rose into the air, I could see the traffic jam extended in front of us for miles. And in front of all the cars there was indeed a wreck. A massive one.

"There's something going on with the train, too," Mychal said, looking out the window on his side of the car. "It's stopped, and people are abandoning it."

"Call it in," I said as I angled the car so I could better see the freeway. As Mychal talked to the dispatcher, I realized what was going on below us. At least a dozen demons were wreaking havoc on cars and their drivers and passengers—smashing windshields, ripping off doors, and hauling the terrified occupants out to be maimed or killed.

"Tell them we need a Rapid Response Team out here ASAP," I said. "And probably another one for that train."

If the demons were launching an all-out assault on the transportation systems, I shuddered to think what might be going on in the underground metro. That would be the perfect hunting ground for demons. There would be no way for their prey to escape.

"Dispatch says the same thing is happening all over the Metroplex," Mychal reported. "The freeway from the south is also under attack, as well as the east side of the DC beltway. Do you mind if I call Kirsten so she doesn't get caught up in this mess?"

"Yeah, call her." Kirsten usually drove in later than Mychal and I did.

I didn't see anything that Mychal and I could do by ourselves, except get killed, so we just waited until the RR teams showed up on the scene, then we got out of the way.

Luanne grabbed me as soon as we arrived at the station and sent me to the main situation room where Whittaker and all the major department heads were monitoring the morning's disasters.

I gave them an update from my personal perspective of the mayhem on the midtown freeway, grabbed a cup of coffee, and sat down to listen. The police, Whittaker's mercenaries, and the private guardians of the Magi Families were battling demons all over the eastern seaboard. Demons had attacked the main police station in Atlanta, and there were reports of heavy fighting in Pittsburg, Buffalo, Toronto, and Detroit.

A number of people in the room were concerned that Akiyama might try to take advantage of the situation, but Akiyama was still trying to extract their troops caught in a squeeze between the demons and the Council forces around the DC area.

Others suggested that the Council send forces into the Waste to exterminate the demons and take out Akashrian. Such ideas were often accompanied with grumbling that the demons never should have been allowed to stay in our world in the first place.

Whittaker looked straight at me and raised an eyebrow. With a sigh, I realized that he wanted me to explain to people above me on the food chain some simple facts of life.

"During the Rift War," I said, "we fought the demons to a standstill because our most powerful mages were directly engaged in the conflict. The police, the guardians, and the armed forces we field today are usually staffed by the Magi's younger sons and daughters, and those who really don't have a place in running the Family businesses. If you want to try and convince the Council members and their heirs to get off their duffs and march into the Waste along with our standard forces, then your plans might have a chance of succeeding. But otherwise, we just don't have the strength to go up against Akashrian. I've seen her, and she's far more powerful than any human mage who ever lived."

"Then we need to lure her out and take her," Deputy Commissioner Howard Jefferson said. "I understand that there are two humans she has a particular grievance against."

I batted my eyes at him. "If you think I'm going to volunteer as bait, you're living in a dream world. As far as the Findlay heir doing that, I'll let you suggest it to Olivia Findlay."

"You wouldn't have to be bait," another man said. "We just have to make her think you're someplace she can get at you."

I sat back and acted like I was considering their mad plan. "So, we have a creature who can translocate back and forth between dimensions, whose power is beyond our understanding, and you propose to trick her. Have I got that right? Sure, I mean, what could go wrong? And after she eats a couple of battalions of low-powered mages for breakfast, what's your fallback idea?"

"Look here," Jefferson said. "That's not a very cooperative attitude."

"Nope. I've used up all my cooperation for this month. I resign." I stood up and started to leave.

Whittaker's voice cut across the room. "Like hell. Sit back down. And the rest of you, come up with some ideas that make sense. James is right. We have to be able to throw power at Akashrian. Luring her out makes sense, but if we can do it, we have to be able to finish the job."

By the end of the day, no one had come up with a plan that seemed workable, and Whittaker mercifully allowed me to go get some dinner.

On my way out, he drew me aside. "Talk with Lucas and see if he has any ideas."

"Okay," I said. "I'll talk to Olivia and Osiris as well. Perhaps you can speak with Frank Novak and Jorge Domingo. They've fought demon lords and know what kind of power it takes. Believe me, a demon lord is a child compared to Akashrian. We're going to need serious magik for her."

He nodded, a grim expression on his face.

CHAPTER 39

While I was drinking coffee until I thought my bladder would burst and listening to a bunch of windbags try to come up with a plan that didn't put their own asses on the line, Mychal and Carmelita had been fighting demons.

I checked in with Luanne in my office, and she said Billie was out helping to keep the peace as well. Billie was a more-than-competent pyromancer and an excellent shot, so I assumed any demon she ran into would regret it.

Against my normal better judgement, I cruised through the police cafeteria and picked up a sandwich that didn't smell spoiled and wolfed it down. That soaked up some of the coffee and settled my stomach a little. Then I ventured out onto the street.

I walked up the block to the ruins of the Palace of Commerce, where a battle between some standard demons and some of Whittaker's soldiers was providing the entertainment. From there, I swung by Aleks's apartment building, where private guardians had two machinegun nests set up in front of the building. Out of curiosity, I wandered around the back, was challenged twice by guardians who were a little too jumpy for my taste, and found another machinegun nest guarding the backdoor of the property.

The machineguns were fifty-caliber, firing explosive incendiaries similar to those in my Raider. Satisfied that they had the situation under control, I continued toward Enchantments.

Other than true demons, destroying property and fighting with the police and soldiers, there weren't any Rifters on the streets. No sex demons or minor demons, such as devils and imps. No vampires. And all the 'legitimate' demons, who owned businesses or had jobs, were staying out of sight.

Whittaker had told me the situation was a scaled-down version of the Rift War. The police were operating on wartime rules. Any demon we ran into was assumed to be hostile. As a result, when a demon emerged from an alley and faced me, I shot him without calling a warning. Then I turned around and shot his buddy who was rushing toward me from behind.

Kirsten had chosen a different means of dealing with the situation. A sign on the door instructed customers to call, and she would lower her wards to admit them. I also noticed that she was running specials on demonbane, anti-demon charms, and a number of other defensive spells. I didn't bother to call. She had my DNA and always exempted me from her spells.

When I entered the shop, she was sitting behind the counter with her feet up reading a book.

"Land office business today?"

Her response wasn't very ladylike.

"Why stay open? Go home and lay around there," I said.

"After all the trouble I had getting here? I'm putting off the drive home as long as I can. Maybe I can talk someone with an aircar into giving me a lift."

"I have to go up to Loch Raven. Want to go?"

She tossed the book onto the counter, dropped her feet to the floor, and pulled her coat off its hanger. "I thought you'd never ask."

We walked back to Police Headquarters to get my car and had to shoot only one demon on the way. But when we drove out onto the street, I almost crashed avoiding a demon who either thought she was invincible, or was trying to commit suicide by jumping in front of us. I took the car into the air as soon as I could.

The cops had closed the north-south freeway, and the mess Mychal and I had seen that morning still wasn't sorted out. The wreckage had mostly been towed away, but the roadway was completely blocked with abandoned cars. Ambulances were parked at both ends of the blockage, and we could see emergency personnel searching for injured people and bodies.

"That's just incredible," Kirsten said. "Thanks for giving me a heads up. Even taking surface streets, it took me three times as long as usual to get downtown."

I brought the car down on Loch Raven Road, and the elves waved us through a new checkpoint they had set up at the edge of their veil. We drove up to Mom's house and parked. When we walked inside, my nostrils were immediately alerted to fresh-baked bread.

"Banana bread?" Kirsten asked, her nose up in the air like a hound stretching for a scent.

"Yup. From an old elven recipe handed down from my ancestors," Mom said.

Joren, sitting with Dad at the kitchen table, snorted. "I didn't even know what a banana was until I crossed into this realm."

Mom dropped a couple of fresh loaves on the table, poured tea for everyone, and sat down.

"To what do we owe this visit?" she asked.

"Demons," I replied.

"Oh, lovely. I'm afraid I don't have any good recipes for them. Are you sure they're edible?"

I chuckled. "Doubtful. I'm not sure how you'd purge the sulfuric acid in their blood." I went on to outline the issues presented at the meeting that morning.

When I finished, Dad said, "You're definitely right about the kind of power it would take to defeat Akashrian. And you're probably right about what it would take to lure her into an ambush. The problem is, she would know it was an ambush, and she's so strong that she wouldn't care. Her mindset is that she would walk into a trap to punish anything that dared to challenge her."

Kirsten spoke up. "What I don't understand is, demons are intelligent, and they feel pain. From what I've seen, they're being slaughtered without really making any progress. I mean, it's shutting down the economy, and people are terrorized, but what's the purpose?"

"That is the purpose," Dad said. "Demons do eat people, other beings, and animals, but the main thing that sustains them is strong emotions. Fear, anger, and pain are far more satisfying for them than anything they can put in their bellies. And

Akashrian is soaking up those emotions through all of her minions. But demons don't fear death. I'm not even sure if they have a concept of death like we do. They do fear her. I saw Akashrian torture a demon lord for years. He was begging to die, but evidently the emotions were so enjoyable that Akashrian kept him alive."

I nodded. "The demon lord who used to rule here was addicted to the emotions projected by human empaths. In the end, that's what got him killed."

We batted ideas around for a couple of hours, then Dad and I went out to our workshop while Kirsten helped Mom fix dinner.

CHAPTER 40

Over breakfast the following morning, my grandfather had some disturbing news.

"You were followed yesterday. Humans wearing Moncrieff-Findlay guardian uniforms have taken up posts on all the roads leading out of here."

"I doubt we were followed," I said. "We flew in most of the way."

"But you were followed the night you killed that witch woman over at the estate," Dad said. "They've probably put surveillance on the roads in, waiting for you to show up again."

That made sense. I had fled to the closest place I knew I'd be safe, but in doing so, I had given my greatest enemy a location to target. And I preferred to take off from a straight road without any trees around. That didn't describe the narrow, twisty roads around the reservoir.

Joren shrugged. "We can take them out, but it could get messy if they have drones watching and we don't have the element of surprise."

"Or we could try that idea we talked about last night," Dad said.

Deciding it was worth a try, Dad, Joren, and I hiked over to the dam. From the top of the dam, Joren pointed out where Court-ney's guardians were stationed. It was a good place for an ambush. Minebank Run, a tributary to the Gunpowder River below the dam, ran under the road.

"Anything we do needs to leave the bridge unharmed," I said. "That's the only way a large truck can bring equipment to the dam."

My father nodded, then took the drone we brought with us, and sent it toward the bridge. He turned to me and asked for my lightning box. I gave it to him, and he gave me the drone's controller.

We trooped down inside the dam to the generators. As Joren and I watched, he coupled the lightning box to one of the huge enhancers that multiplied the electricity the generators produced.

The drone didn't show the two groups of men Joren said were hiding on both sides of the bridge.

"They cast shielding illusions," he said, "but there are about a dozen men there altogether."

My dad nodded. "Well, shall we see what happens?"

He triggered the lightning box, and an enormous bolt of light-ning lanced out across the three-quarters of a mile to the hollow on the west side of the bridge. The thunder was deafen-ing. Before the echoes faded away, he triggered the box again, and another lightning bolt struck the hollow on the east side of the bridge.

My ears ringing, I zeroed the drone's cameras on the hollow. The illusion was gone, and I could see sprawled and twisted bodies lying around. Shifting the camera to the other side of the bridge, I saw more bodies.

"I don't know if they're alive or dead," I said turning the screen so Joren and my dad could see it, "but they're clearly incapacitated."

Dad grinned. "I love it when an experiment is successful."

"I'll send some warriors in to check it out," Joren said. "You should be able to safely head into town."

Unfortunately, the dam was too low, and we didn't have a direct line of sight to the areas where Courtney's guardians had set up on the other roads leaving the reservoir. On the way back to Mom's house, Dad and I discussed possible designs for a magitek device that could jam Courtney's drones. He said that he'd do some experimenting and let me know his results.

༺✦༻

I met with Whittaker that afternoon after I got back to the office.

"Dad says that the odds of luring Akashrian out using him or me as bait are about as good as you or him getting pregnant," I said.

My boss laughed.

"Basically," I continued, "do you care if one of the worms from your private bait shop escapes?" Whittaker was an avid fisherman, part of why his Family estate sat next to a river.

"So, that line of thinking leads to a dead end," he said with a sigh.

I grinned. "Not completely. Bait is in the eye of the beholder. He suggested that the one thing she does care about is competition. Akashrian is one of three demon queens with interests in this realm. Lakasvian controls the demons in Europe, and Delevidat controls the demons in Asia. If one of them were to encroach on her territory here in North America, she would react."

"And how would we invite one of these other demon queens to grace us with their presence?" Whittaker asked. "Strikes me as a stupid thing to do."

"Indisputably," I answered. "But Joren thinks we can create a doppelganger for one of them. The only problem is to make the illusion feel like a demon queen to another demon queen. How to give it evil magik, if you will."

He leaned back in his chair and looked thoughtful. "And if it worked, how would we deal with her? I heard you yesterday, even if everyone else was more concerned with talking than listening. I fought through the Rift War. The idea of facing a creature who scares demon lords is not something I relish."

I winked at him. "My dad and I think we have an answer."

That evening, Kristen, Mychal, and I brainstormed ideas over a couple of bottles of wine.

"Aren't there traditions where witches create straw men, or mud men, or some kinds of dolls and give them some kind of pseudo life?" I asked.

Kirsten rolled her eyes. "I think you need something a little more complicated than a voodoo doll."

She jumped up and got her phone off the table in our foyer.

"Hello, Mom? Are you and Dad going to be home tomorrow night? Oh, good. Do you mind if Dani and I drop by? We have some questions about some rather esoteric forms of witchcraft."

Their conversation went on for about half an hour before Kirsten said, "Sure, we can make it for dinner. See you then."

Kirsten hung up, dropped the phone back on the table, and came back to the living room. "I'm pretty sure some traditions of witchcraft involve simulacrums, I just don't remember which ones. But if anyone knows who the experts are, Mom and Dad are the ones to ask."

CHAPTER 41

I reported to Whittaker that I was working on a solution. He looked disappointed but didn't press me. It shocked me that he actually expected I might come up with something overnight. Hell, humanity had been dealing with the demon problem for almost a century.

And the demons were a problem. The assaults continued. Citizens were upset. The media was ecstatic, sticking a microphone in front of anyone who had a story or a rant.

Kirsten had switched over to delivery, taking orders online, and paying a courier service. She told me that Julie, her assistant, was boxing up orders while Kirsten spent her time in her laboratory creating the charms, potions, and protections.

"Hell, Dani, I'm making almost as much as I was before all this happened, and I don't even have to put up with my customers in person."

But almost two-thirds of her orders had to do with protection from demons.

She closed up her shop early, Mychal escorted her from the shop to Police Headquarters, and we took my car down to her parents' place in Annapolis Junction.

Kirsten's parents were two of my favorite people. Aileen was an older version of her daughter—blonde, beautiful, a bit curvier, and brilliantly intelligent. Blair looked typecast as a dark warlock—dark hair, dark eyes, swarthy skin, over six-feet tall and husky. He always dressed in black and rode a motorcycle.

Blair swept me up in a hug. "Dani, more radiantly beautiful than ever. When are you going to make my dreams come true and join my harem?"

Aileen laughed as hard as I did. "You're too old for me! Hell, you're as old as my *father!*"

"Like fine wine. You don't know what you're missing," he said as he set me down on my feet.

"I think I'll survive."

We made small talk for about fifteen minutes, until the doorbell rang. Aileen answered it and admitted one of the oldest-looking people I'd ever seen. He was dressed all in black, with a black wide-brimmed hat, and his white hair and beard were very long, as were his sidelocks. He was hunched over with age, but I could tell he'd never been a tall man.

Aileen introduced him as Rabbi Mordechai Feitler. His voice, deep and strong, belied his apparent age, and the sparkle in his blue eyes revealed someone who was still quite aware and lively.

Kirsten had learned to cook from her mom, and the dinner Aileen prepared was spectacular. Rabbi Feitler raved about it, and so did the rest of us. After the table was cleared, we were served small cups of thick, black coffee and shots of slivovitz.

"And so, what is the reason for this bribery?" the rabbi asked. "I'm not complaining, obviously, but I assume there is something you need."

I explained our problem.

"A golem to imitate a demon?" Feitler asked. "Yes, I can create a golem, but I'm not an artist. I doubt very seriously that it will fool this Akashrian. Even with all the illusions you wish to clothe it in, it will still be a mud doll. Demons are very good with illusions, and I would not trust any that I—or you—might cast."

I nodded. "My father suggested that our best chance might involve using multiple people's talents. I don't know anything about creating a golem, but could you work with an elven sculptor?"

The old man's eyes lit up, and he regarded me for a long minute. "It would be interesting to try. Do all the demon goddesses look alike?"

"No, but my father has seen all three of the ones who exercise power in this realm. He can describe Lakasvian and Delevidat. We can create a physical likeness, but it wouldn't be alive."

"And how are you going to clothe it in magik?" Feitler asked. "The demon won't be fooled by a magikless golem."

"My grandfather says that, working with a witch and a magitek, he thinks he can simulate demon magik," I said.

"Very interesting. I'm intrigued. When do you wish to begin?"

"As soon as possible. The devastation the demons are wreaking is too much to withstand very long."

He nodded. "Today is Thursday, tomorrow the Sabbath begins. Let us start on Sunday."

We worked out logistics. I would pick him up at his temple Sunday morning and transport him out to Loch Raven. In the meantime, he said he would email me a list of materials, tools, and working conditions he would need.

As we flew back to Baltimore, I prayed the wild idea would work.

CHAPTER 42

"For the creation of a faithful servant, mute and of great power, resistant to the demons of fire and air," was written at the top of the email the rabbi sent me. I scanned the list and saw that the process of creating a golem would take the whole week. Luckily, finding the clay he specified wouldn't be a problem in Maryland, and the rest of the items didn't look difficult to obtain, either. I passed the list on to my father.

Kirsten and I picked up the rabbi at his temple in Kemp Mill early Sunday morning.

"There have been many demon incursions in this area," he informed us as he climbed into the car. "I would advise taking the roads going north instead of east."

I grinned at him. "I hadn't planned on taking the roads at all. Fasten your seatbelt."

When I took the car airborne, I glanced in the rearview mirror and saw his eyes widen, then he glared at me. But soon he was too busy watching the ground below and seemed to have relaxed.

Although I saw a few flying demons in the distance, none of them came closer or tried to challenge us. We also saw several Council aircraft, and a couple of them flew close enough to check us out and decide we weren't a threat. On the whole, the flight was smooth and uneventful.

I landed and drove up to Mom's house. She fussed over the rabbi, showed him to his room, and fed us all. Then he sat with Dad, Joren, and Lenokin—the elven sculptor who would be working with him. I saw that they had several full-color drawings labeled "Delevidat," as viewed from different angles. She was very different-looking than Akashrian. Her form was suggestive of a human woman but far more snake-like and less voluptuous than Akashrian. Long horns grew out of her forehead and swept backwards, ending in sharp points at mid-back. Her face was one of the most human of any demon I had seen, but sharper and crueler than any human face, with tusks similar to a saber-toothed tiger of ancient times.

"She's about eight feet tall," Dad said. "Her body is mostly pink in color, fading to green on her back and tail. The horns are a darker green, and so are her eyes."

"Usually, we don't prettify our golems," Rabbi Feitler said. "The body must be formed in a single night, and the hands, feet, and mouth are of the first importance. The fingers must be fashioned for grasping and the toes for balance. The legs must be of equal length, or else he limps. I don't know how I can do all this."

Lenokin picked up a cloth-covered bucket he had brought with him. Setting it on the table, he stripped the cloth away and took out a large lump of clay. Placing his hands on either side of it, he stared at it. The lump started to vibrate, twist, and change shape. It took twenty minutes, but when he leaned back in his chair, a rough miniature sculpture of the creature in the drawing sat on the table.

"If you can cast your spells while I mold the clay," Lenokin said, "then this will work."

The rabbi rose out of his chair and studied the sculpture. "Can I touch it while you work?" he asked.

The elf shrugged. "I don't see why not. As long as you don't change the shape."

Feitler looked up from the little statuette. "We won't know until we try, will we?" he said with a grin and that twinkle in his eye.

When the old rabbi discovered that my grandfather was actually older than he was, he latched onto Joren and tended to direct his instructions and conversation to his new friend. As a result, Joren was the one who took Feitler to the river to dig the clay to mold the watch-eye.

The rabbi brought a bucket full of clay back with him and formed the mass into a watch-eye using Kabbalistic spells. He was a little taken aback when he discovered that the kiln the elves provided to bake it was fueled by magik rather than wood, but he adapted. The eye had to bake for three days and three nights until the clay was hard.

While that was going on, Feitler returned to the river, and with the help of the elves, gathered a large amount of clay. Working at night by candlelight, he and Lenokin fashioned the clay into the semblance of Delevidat. The old man insisted the work must be done in a single night, so they started at sunset on the third day the watch-eye was baking. As dawn broke, the rabbi scooped a hole in the creature's forehead and embedded the watch-eye. They covered it with the cloth, ate a meal, and went to bed.

That night, Joren and I flew Feitler to a Jewish graveyard north of DC, and waited while he dug up a small square of dirt. We then flew him back to Loch Raven, where he combined the dirt with silver and his own blood to form an ink.

He inscribed a spell on a small piece of calfskin parchment. When he finished, he was visibly shaking, pale, and sweating. He explained that with each stroke of his pen, he had infused the spell with his own life essence.

Next, he chanted a spell over a crystal the size of my fist and inserted the parchment into the creature's mouth. The body immediately rose and silently stood in front of the rabbi. Absolutely creeped me out.

"I now control the golem," Feitler said, sitting heavily on a chair. "I control it by directing my thoughts through the crystal into the eye. The creature will obey as if it is my own flesh."

Abruptly, the golem turned, walked across the room, stopped when it reached the wall, turned around, and walked back toward us. It stopped and saluted.

The rabbi explained that it could not be stopped against his will. Unless Feitler was killed, or the parchment was taken from the golem's mouth, it would continue to be animated. If the parchment was removed, the creature's energy would diminish, but it would use its remaining strength to return to its master's side.

Mom and Joren helped the old man to bed, and he slept the next twenty-four hours.

"Okay, we have it," I said. "Any ideas how to let Akashrian know it's here?"

"All we need is a major demon," Dad said. "We show the golem to the demon, and turn the demon loose. Akashrian will know within the day."

I was appalled. "I have to go capture a major demon? What should I use for bait? Candy? Human sacrifice?"

"Relax," Joren said. "We can supply all the demons you need. A master demon, you say?"

"Yes," Dad answered. "Anything lower won't have any credibility."

"Have we figured out how we're going to imbue this thing with the feeling of demon magik?" I asked.

Dad smirked. "What exactly does demon magik feel like? Demons are chaotic creatures. We just simply layer on some of every kind of magik we can, and create chaos."

"Simple, huh?"

His grin faded a bit. "Well, that's the theory, at least."

CHAPTER 43

We invited so many people to work on the golem that we had to hold the work in the elves' meeting hall. My father had gotten very creative as to what kinds of magik he thought would contribute to chaos.

My boss, Tom Whittaker, was an earth mage. Blair, Kirsten's father, was a master of light and dark witchcraft. Joren was a storm mage, and several other elves had rare and unique talents. It did surprise me when Olivia, an electrokinetic, and Osiris, a pyromancer, flew in from Ireland, completely unannounced. Rabbi Feitler, my boyfriend Aleks, an aeromancer, a hydromancer, and a witch doctor from Africa also showed up. Even several of the Council members showed up to donate their magik to the golem.

The reunion of my grandmother and father brought tears to my eyes, and the way Mary Sue hugged him as though she was never going to let him go confirmed my suspicions about her parentage.

The golem stood in the middle of the room, looking quite fearsome.

"So, how is everyone going to infuse it with all of these different magiks?" I asked my father.

He chuckled. "They aren't. You, and I, and Mary Sue are going to do it."

My expression caused him to laugh.

"The golem is really just a kind of machine," Dad explained, and I saw the rabbi nod. "We'll take the magik all these people direct at us, and redirect it into the golem, the same way you'd build a magitek storage device using magik from someone else."

"But I've never tried to combine different kinds of magik in a single device," I said.

"Why?" he asked.

After a moment, I realized he wanted an answer. "Well, because it would get all confused, it would be chaos." The corner of his mouth quirked up. "Oh," I said.

Dad instructed all the magikers to use their darkest, most potent spell for loading the golem. Then he turned his attention to Mary Sue and me.

"I know you've done this a thousand times, but with the kinds of spells we're going to be dealing with, you have to stay alert and focused. Treat it the same way you would if the spell was cast at you and you needed to deflect it or shield from it. If you get tired, or feel overwhelmed, take a break. Okay?"

"What do you mean, 'deflect it or shield from it'?" I asked. A glance at Mary Sue's expression told me that she was as confused as I was.

Dad's brow furrowed. "You know. Say, if a pyromancer tosses a fireball at you. You choose a place for it to go, grab it with your magik, and send it on. You do know how to do that, right?"

I thought back to a time I had used Aleks's spirit magik to destroy the water pipes in the tunnels under the Moncrieff estate.

"I always use a converter to catch the magik, then redirect it to enhancers," I said.

Mary Sue nodded. "Yeah, you need something to catch it."

Dad hesitated a moment, then said, "Okay. I can show you another way, but for today, we'll use what you know how to do."

He went over to a satchel he had brought with him and came back with two converter boxes. "You won't need enhancers. Just redirect the spells into the golem."

It took several hours, but by the time we finished, we had stored magik from twenty-three different magik users in the golem. I felt like I'd been through the ringer. I was starving, but all I wanted to do was go to bed for a week. I reached out to touch the golem and drew my hand back immediately. It felt like my fingers had been burned, shocked, and frozen all at the same time.

Mom, Aileen, Kirsten, and several of the elves laid out a feast for everyone, and then we went back to mom's house. I dragged myself upstairs and fell into bed. I didn't even notice when Aleks joined me.

⬡

"Now all we need is a major demon," Dad said to Joren the following morning.

"We have five," Joren responded. "We weren't sure what kind you might need, so we gathered an assortment."

He took us to an elven building. Inside were five cages grown from some kind of wood. They didn't look substantial enough to contain a demon, but I noticed that all of the demons kept well away from the bars.

They did have a variety of demons. I could readily identify fire, water, and flying demons. Joren told us the other two were an earth demon and a frost demon.

"Where did you catch them?" Dad asked.

"All within a hundred miles of here," Joren said. "From what you told us, that means they are Akashrian's creatures, right?"

Dad nodded. "That's correct. Now we need to have the rabbi animate the golem, and turn the demons loose."

Joren raised an eyebrow. "They aren't going to be very happy when we let them out, Lucas."

"Don't worry about it. They'll be far too worried about the golem to pay you any attention."

The rabbi took the golem to the dam and had it stand on top. He had told us that distance wasn't a problem. As long as he had the crystal, he could see and hear what the golem saw and heard, and direct the golem's actions. We gave the old man an enhanced magitek communicator, then I flew him home in time to adhere to the Sabbath. While I was in Kemp Mill, I confirmed that our setup worked. Using the communicator, Dad could tell the rabbi what he wanted the golem to do.

Lucas James might have been the only human on earth who was truly fluent in demon. I spoke it, too, but like a little kid. I understood a lot more, and my reading was quite fluent. Using an auditory illusion spell that one of the aeromancers set up, Dad could say something in demon, and it sounded like the golem was talking.

Before I arrived back at Loch Raven, Joren had freed the captive demons, and our Delevidat golem had given them a challenge to be conveyed to Akashrian. All we had to do was wait—and pray our gambit worked.

CHAPTER 44

After four days, we were truly beginning to wonder if our ploy was going to work. We heard nothing from or about Akashrian, and the demon assaults showed no sign of slacking off.

Whittaker reported that the Council members were getting antsy.

"The good news is," Whittaker said, "they are taking Dani's suggestion that they get more actively involved seriously. The economic damage is hitting them where it hurts most."

In other words, they didn't give a damn how many people the demons slaughtered, but when their profits shrank to millions instead of billions, it got their attention.

Olivia helped with that. Having her back where she could visit with Frank Novak and Jorge Domingo forced them to pay attention. She also wanted to come home. The climate in Ireland wasn't to her taste, and she pressed the other Council members to think about resuming the conflict with Moncrieff and Akiyama to push them out of North America.

On the fifth day after we introduced the golem to the major demons, the elves standing watch reported that the air over the river—about four hundred yards downstream from the dam—began to shimmer like a heat wave.

Dad and I rushed to the dam. We watched as the disruption widened, and then a portal opened.

What I could see through the hole in reality looked like the Waste, rather than the demon world. The light was white instead of red, and the ruins of buildings could be seen. Dad and I took up our posts and waited. My heart hammered in my chest, but I couldn't imagine what *he* might be feeling as he contemplated facing the monster who had held him captive for more than twenty years.

There was movement on the other side, and then Akashrian came through the portal. She was directly over the river but floated in the air. The statuette—her avatar—was cradled in her left arm, just as she had carried it at the temple. The portal closed behind her, and she let out a roar that shook the world.

The golem responded with a roar of its own, followed by a stream of Demonish so harsh and nasty that I knew only half of the words.

Akashrian strode toward us, and when she reached the river's bank, she unleashed a glowing yellow ball of energy. It hit the golem but didn't seem to faze it.

Now, Dani! my father said through my implant.

I pulled energy from the massive generator inside the dam, directed it through its converter, and triggered my energy projector. A white beam shot out and converged with the beam from my father's weapon at the other end of the dam.

At first, Akashrian stood, facing the dam and the golem, bathed in the ravening energy the enhanced weapons discharged. Using the power of the hydroelectric turbines behind me, I poured my magik into the concentrator.

One of Akashrian's globes of energy hit the dam directly beneath the place where the golem was standing. A chunk of the dam—five feet deep and five feet wide— disappeared. The golem stumbled and fell to its knees in the rubble, but otherwise, it didn't seem to be harmed.

Akashrian tossed another ball of death at the golem, and more of the dam crumbled. A few more strikes like that, and she might reach the level of the water the dam held back.

The golem fought to its feet and let loose a quivering, almost amoeba-like black ball. It floated toward the demon goddess, and when it reached her, it exploded, coating her with an oily gelatinous substance.

Dad and I fired again. The demon goddess screamed, a sound that hurt my ears. And then Akashrian was gone. The energy beams Dad and I held on her hit the water where she was standing, and with an explosive burst of steam, vaporized the river. I cut off the concentrator, and a moment later, Dad did the same.

A large crater—half on the bank and half in the river—filled with water. But I thought I saw something in the bottom of the crater before the river covered it. The avatar.

One of the hydromancers working with us cleared out the crater, revealing the avatar sitting in the bottom. It was unscathed but powerless. The malevolent magik everyone had felt from it before was gone. The red, glowing eyes were black and lifeless.

The elves used their magik to help fix the dam, but it took them three days. Joren told me that rock wasn't as amenable to manipulation as wood, and none of them had worked with concrete before. It wasn't as simple as just patching the hole Akashrian had blasted in it. They had to reconstruct part of the west generator room. Mom had to order a new generator, converter, and enhancer. It would be weeks before all the equipment came in, but I didn't think anyone in Baltimore would complain about reduced electricity if it came with a reduction in demon attacks.

Aleks and I brought the rabbi back to Loch Raven, and he decommissioned the golem. He told us that the black blob that had hit Akashrian was the sum of the chaotic magik we had filled it with. He had taken a chance, cast a spell through his crystal, and that was the result. He speculated that it had disrupted Akashrian's protection, allowing the energy beams my father and I employed to destroy her.

We showed him the avatar, and he said, "This is very similar to a golem. I'm not surprised that you were unable to destroy it. But I think this is the proof that she has been destroyed. You said it was active when she was still in the demon's realm? And now it is harmless."

I asked him if he wanted it, and he acted as though I'd tried to hand him a venomous snake. So I tried to give it to Dad.

He shuddered. "No. I'll never get her out of my nightmares, I don't need a likeness of her sitting around."

"Maybe you should keep it," Kirsten said. "It is a beautiful piece of work."

I took a long look at it. She was right, viewed in isolation, it was beautiful, if disturbing.

"I think I'll donate it to a museum," I said. Everyone seemed to think that was a good idea, so I gave it to Olivia to decide on a fitting place for it.

Demons' coordinated attacks ceased. Without either Akashrian or Besevial to direct them, major demons seemed to wander around aimlessly. Lesser demons looked to the major demons for direction, and not finding any, wandered off themselves. Minor demons listlessly went about their business, but without the enthusiasm for disruption and mayhem they had always displayed. Since the demons lost their focus, I expected their activity to revert to the random attacks we had always endured.

When Aleks, Kirsten, and I arrived back in Baltimore, we were struck by how peaceful it seemed. There had been a lot of destruction over the previous few months, but walking the streets was downright peaceful.

CHAPTER 45

Frank Novak had invited Olivia to stay at his estate north of Baltimore and east of Loch Raven. The Novak Family was large, the main house expansive, but she was given one of the guest houses on the property. She described it as 'cozy' and 'quaint but comfortable.' I thought it was huge and was glad I wasn't the one who had to keep it clean.

A week after the confrontation with Akashrian, Olivia invited Kirsten and me for a 'family dinner' and told us to bring our boyfriends. Remembering what family dinners had been like at the Findlay estate, I feared the worst, but it turned out the guest list comprised only about twenty people.

Mary Sue caused a bit of a stir when her escort turned out to be an elf. Mom surveyed all the whispering and winked at me. Olivia didn't betray any surprise at all. He wasn't the only elf present, as Joren evidently was included in the definition of family.

Olivia had brought several servants with her from Ireland, including her cook. Dinner was semi-formal, the food excellent, and the company very comfortable.

"So, what's been going on, besides demons and occasional battles with people who prefer larceny to proper work?" Olivia asked as dinner was served. "I thought I had a deal with my granddaughter to keep me updated on this part of the world, but as you all know, she's never grasped the concept of answering her phone."

Everyone took turns telling their recent history, most of it having to do with demons and the 'Akiyama bandits,' as Olivia dubbed them. But when Kirsten's turn came, she held out her left hand. The diamond was proper trophy-wife size, and the smile on her face was as big as the one she wore after spending her first night with Mychal.

"He finally worked up the courage to ask you? Took him long enough," I said.

"He finally worked up the courage to tell his father," she replied.

"And?"

Mychal laughed. "He asked me what took me so long, and told me I was lucky she hadn't given up."

After the dessert, over drinks and coffee, Olivia revealed the real reason for inviting us.

"It appears that the demon menace has diminished, at least for a while," she said. "The Port of Baltimore and the airport are firmly in Findlay hands. Since Akiyama no longer has its demon allies, and Moncrieff has cut off all support for Courtney and Akiyama, they are significantly weakened. Most of their allies show no appetite for continuing the conflict."

She smiled—a rather predatory look, it seemed to me. "Osiris has hired several regiments from Whittaker, and we plan a three-pronged offensive against Akiyama's interests in Vancouver, Montreal, and Wilmington. The objective is to drive them out of North America completely."

"Are the rest of the remaining members of the Council involved in this?" my father asked.

"Oh, yes," Olivia said. "Novak, Domingo, and their allies are completely on board, as are the Europeans. We plan to knock Akiyama down a peg and shut them out of Europe and the Americas, except on our terms. Akiyama Benjiro made his play and failed. It's time for consequences."

She let that sink in, then said, "Dani, Lucas, we need your help at the Cerberus factory. Mary Sue can't do it all by herself. We need as much output there as possible before we launch our attack. And we have only a month. Dani, I've already spoken to Tom Whittaker, and he's granted you an indefinite leave of absence until this is all over."

And to think I had been happy to see her.

"I want to go home," Olivia said with a catch in her voice, "and I want to bring my family home. I've been away from it for too long."

Dad and I met with Mary Sue outside as the other guests were making their way to their transportation.

"Where are you living?" I asked. "You're not commuting up there from Baltimore every day."

"Not a chance. Too dangerous, for one thing. I rented a town-house in New Castle." She shrugged. "It's cheap. I'm working fifteen hours a day, so it's mainly a place to sleep. I can't even remember the last time I cooked a meal."

I couldn't either, but I had Kirsten. Dad and I shared a look.

"It's really that bad?" he asked.

Mary Sue nodded. "Akiyama runs military patrols up and down the main highway and supply convoys to the Findlay estate. They've never bothered me, but I don't drive my own car. I'm pretty sure they have Dani's picture, though. You'd probably be okay unless they find out you're back."

"Yeah," I said to Dad. "Courtney's tried to knock me off multiple times to solidify her claim to Findlay. She'd go crazy if she knew you were still alive."

He thought for a while. "Tell me why we have a magitek munitions factory right under Akiyama's nose instead of somewhere safer."

"Because the Port of Wilmington belonged to Findlay when we started. Too difficult and too much time and money invested to move it," Mary Sue said.

Kirsten was waiting for me by Mychal's car. We hugged. "I'm happy for you," I said. "Where are you going to live?"

She bowed her head, not meeting my eyes. "At Novak. Mychal's going to build a place for us on the estate. But the wedding isn't until June. I'll still be at our place until then. And I'll still pay my half of the mortgage. I won't leave you in the lurch."

I leaned forward, and she raised her eyes.

"I'll be fine," I said. "Mary Sue says I'm making money, so I'll buy you out, but I'll keep your room for you in case Mychal is ever mean to you."

Her smile flashed. "I don't think he knows how to be mean. Besides, I'm tougher than he is."

The following day, Aleks drove me up to New Castle so I could look for a place to rent. Mary Sue had rented her place before Akiyama took the port, and housing Akiyama's people had soaked up the market. We didn't find anything, so we expanded our search area. I did find a townhouse in Newark that wasn't too rundown. They asked an outrageous price for it, but it was large enough for both Dad and me so I took it.

Tired but happy, we went back to Baltimore, where Frank Novak loaned me a car that no one could connect to me. Dad and I spent the next few days adding magitek options to it so it would fly, as well as some shielding and stealth abilities.

After all that, we drove over to the factory Mary Sue had set up in old warehouses near the port in Wilmington.

I hadn't seen the place since Olivia first showed us the empty warehouses. Since then, Mary Sue had erected wide, paved, covered pathways between the buildings. Inside, there were work cubes, assembly lines, parts rooms, and all the things one would expect in a manufacturing facility.

Dad commented on the covered pathways. "That's a great idea. I'm sure it makes it much nicer walking between the buildings in bad weather."

Mary Sue chuckled. "That's kind of a nice side benefit. We actually did it to confound aerial surveillance. I think the wards we have in place will protect from most assaults, but I'm not sure they will withstand a concentrated aerial bombardment. I'd rather not find out."

She gave us a tour, and I discovered the two Dressler engineers I had been working with had already moved their work to Wilmington. Dad was impressed and acted like a kid with a new toy when Mary Sue showed him his office and the workshop she had set up for him.

Afterward, she took us out to eat at a funky little crab shack and brew pub south of New Castle. I figured it would be one of the last chances we would have to relax before work and the upcoming resumption of war took all of our time.

CHAPTER 46

D ad considered evaluating the Cerberus factory and its work processes his first priority. Mary Sue and I trailed along after him like a couple of ducklings.

After a morning spent doing that, the three of us sat down at lunch.

"What is your failure rate in quality control?" he asked.

"A little less than half of one percent," Mary Sue answered.

Dad nodded. "After a magitek finishes with a drone, he or she tests it, right? And what is your failure rate at that stage?"

"About three percent."

I saw the faint trace of a sly smile. "How long does it take for the magitek to load the magik in the drone, and how long to test it?"

Mary Sue shifted uncomfortably in her chair. "About an hour and a half for each step."

"And how long for quality control?"

"Two hours."

He pounced. "So, to increase your quality numbers by two point five percent, you're slowing your production at the critical stage by fifty percent. Does that really make any sense?"

Mutely, she shook her head.

I had done an internship at one of Dressler's factories when I was at university. Mary Sue, in spite of being a Dressler, had landed an internship in Italy with a fashion designer. I realized for the first time that I should have paid more attention to how the factory processes were designed. I had handed it all to her, and failed her. She had done well, but together, we could have done better.

By the end of the week, we had overhauled the production flows and increased total output by thirty percent. Then we set to work on the design process. The result of our analysis there was to cut the design staff by a fifth and put them to work in production.

At that point, Dad turned us loose and devoted his attention to the battlebots.

I was used to working twelve- to fifteen-hour days but found myself far more exhausted coming home from the factory than when I was chasing bad guys. Both Mary Sue and my father told me I was an adrenaline junkie, and I found it hard to argue with them. Especially since Kirsten and my mom had been telling me the same thing for years.

There was a downside to the absence of demons. With time on their hands, the Akiyama troops had more time to snoop around. Mary Sue told us that patrols in the area of our factory had increased, but the patrols didn't appear to be very enthusiastic or alert.

"They're going through the motions," Dad said. "They were told to patrol, so that's what they're doing. But they don't act like they expect any trouble."

"Maybe," I replied, "but if they're anything like cops, boredom can be dangerous. You never know what kind of stupid ideas they might come up with to stick their noses into somewhere they don't belong."

He looked at me a little oddly. "I never thought of it that way."

"Believe me. Half of the shootings at traffic stops could be avoided if the cops had better things to do than worry about broken taillights."

What I said must have worried him, because over the next few days, about fifty Findlay guardians with magikal ability filtered into the factory. They didn't wear uniforms, and were introduced as new employees, but I recognized a number of them.

In his spare time, Dad took the six old-fashioned battlebots Whittaker had given us and refurbished them. He gave each of them a thorough maintenance, upgraded their control systems, installed modern weapons, and added magitek. They weren't even close to what we were designing, but they were a lot better than what humans had during the Rift War.

I was detailed to taking care of the electricity. The line that ran from Loch Raven to the port followed the main freeway. An automated electrical substation south of the port split the main line and fed smaller lines into the city and the port. I had never touched that substation in my life, but Dad said that he had overseen its construction. He gave me the plans for it, and told me to modify it to our advantage.

There was a fence around the substation, and its gate and the building were locked, but that was no obstacle. I took two of the guardians with me in a service van and drove right up to it one morning. We got out, pulled tool boxes from the van, I unlocked the door, and we walked in.

The tool boxes contained our weapons, in case we needed them. While my companions played cards, I found the lines for our factory and installed a new computer and new switches on them. Then I installed a shutdown switch on the main computer.

When I finished, and we were loading our stuff back in the van, an APC with Akiyama soldiers pulled up.

"What's going on?" the sergeant in charge asked.

"Routine maintenance," I answered. "You don't want to wait for things to wear out. Better to take care of it and not have any disruptions."

He watched me lock the building up and didn't even bother to ask for identification. My pals drove the van out of the enclosure, and I locked the gate behind us. We said so long to the soldiers and took off in the opposite direction of the Cerberus factory.

CHAPTER 47

The week before the offensive was scheduled to start, Mary Sue gave all the employees three weeks' pay as a bonus, and told them to take a three-week vacation. Only fifty core people and the guardians showed up the next day. We loaded all of the completed drones into trucks and vans, along with three more trucks filled with spare parts, and sent them on their way to Whittaker.

After everyone was gone, Mary Sue gave Dad a ride back to Loch Raven, leaving only me and the guardians in Wilmington. The following morning, two hundred of Whittaker's commandos and one hundred of Osiris's special operations people showed up and converted the factory into a command center.

The operation was scheduled to start at seven o'clock on a Wednesday evening. At six o'clock, I got in my car, drove past the electrical substation, and used my magik to flip the switch that cut power to most of the Wilmington area and the port. The metropolitan area went dark, with the exception of the Akiyama barracks and ships in the harbor. I knew that Dad would have pulled the plug on the Findlay estate's power at the same time.

As I drove south out of town, fighter-bombers from Whittaker and Novak began bombing the Akiyama installations. The parts of the Akiyama operation that were still lit up made incredibly easy targets to identify, and I chuckled as I heard the sound of explosions behind me.

I avoided the freeway, instead taking the old highway, the one Akiyama was using to provide supplies to Courtney at the Findlay estate. I still ran into a checkpoint manned by Whittaker troops about ten miles out of town. I showed them my ID, and they let me pass.

I had to pull over twice to let Whittaker troops go by—once for a troop convoy and the second time for a convoy of rocket launchers and artillery.

My route took me past a road that led directly to Loch Raven, but that wasn't my destination. Instead, I continued to Hunt Valley and Oregon Ridge. At a trailhead there, I pulled off and parked next to the only car in the lot. Aleks got out, locked his car, got in beside me, and gave me a kiss.

"Thanks for backing me up," I said.

"No problem. I can wait to wash my hair until tomorrow."

As I pulled back out of the parking lot, he said, "Dani, your dad disappeared. Right after he did what he had to do at the dam. He took an APC and drove off."

I processed that, then said, "I shouldn't be surprised. I think he's headed to the same place we are, with the same goal in mind."

"I wondered about that."

As we drew close to Worthington Ridge—the wooded hill on which the Findlay estate was built—we saw flashes of light and a lot of aircraft flying over. It started to rain. Pretty soon we began to hear the sounds of fighting—explosions, lightning flashes, rolling thunder. The rain came down harder.

"Crappy weather," Aleks said.

"Probably courtesy of my Aunt Courtney. Keep an eye out for tornadoes."

"She's that powerful?"

"Unfortunately, yes. I'm probably lucky that she doesn't like to get her hands dirty. She always hired halfwits to kill me instead of doing the job properly herself."

I chose a different place to park the car from where I had hidden my motorcycle. I had anticipated the storm, so I pulled out two rain ponchos from the back seat.

Aleks chuckled. "I'll just shield to stay dry."

"Jerk." I pulled the poncho over my head.

"Good genes."

"How's your sight in pitch dark?" I asked holding out a pair of night-vision goggles. "You operate them like a magitek light switch. On and off."

He took them and we set off through the woods. The trail was a soggy mess, and the leafless trees did nothing to alleviate the downpour. Sounds of battle were louder, and the flashes of light and lightning made it easier to see where we were going but gave the woods a surreal feeling.

"How far?" Aleks asked.

"About fifteen hundred yards—fourteen hundred meters—to the wall. We're on the estate now. There's an escape tunnel outside the wall, but it supposedly can't be opened from this side. It's going to be a bitch to find, though."

"Supposedly can't be opened?"

"I wouldn't be much of a magitek if I couldn't operate a simple latch my daddy designed, now would I?"

"Do you think that's how he plans to get in?"

"I'd bet on it. But he has more than an hour's head start on us. He's probably inside already."

We slogged on. When lightning flashes illuminated the scene, Aleks looked disgustingly dry. I, on the other hand, was soaked to my knees. The rain poncho kept my body and head dry, but I was still uncomfortable.

After we had walked about twenty minutes, I said, "Slow down. We're getting close, and I don't want to miss it."

A couple of times, I thought I spied the rock I was looking for, but I was wrong. Finally, off through the trees, I saw it. Twenty feet off the trail, a large rock jutted up from the forest floor. It was about five feet in diameter and stuck up as high as my chest.

"This way," I told Aleks, and walked to the rock. I directed my magik at it and felt the latch trigger. "Now, hurry," I said. "It won't stay open long."

I dashed through the trees until I reached a fallen log. On the other side of the log was a small hollow under it.

"Follow me," I said, lying down on my stomach and sliding into the hollow. I had entered the space before me from outside only once, when Dad showed me the secret. I had snuck out that way a dozen times or more. Its disadvantage over the wall crossing I'd used when I killed Susan Reed was that it brought me into the tunnels under the estate. We would have to travel through almost the entire house to get to our target.

Aleks followed me. He kindled a dim light and looked around. "Where are we?" he asked.

"Still about five hundred meters from the wall. Come on."

From the room we were in, a steel ladder took us down into a larger tunnel, which was dimly lit by mage lights. I shrugged out of the poncho and struck out toward the mansion, wincing as my boots squished.

"Surely Courtney knows about these tunnels," Aleks said.

"She knows *of* the tunnels, but I doubt she's ever been down here. Courtney's a girly girl, and this is a long way to walk in high heels. If there was ever an emergency where she had to evacuate, she'd depend on her guardians to get her out. The problem is, all the Findlay guardians who were worth their salt are gone. They either died defending Olivia's retreat, or Courtney purged them because she didn't trust them, or they melted into the night. A lot of those have been my eyes and ears the past few months."

"Kirsten said that you snuck in here recently. Is this how you got in?"

"Nope. It's not how I got out, either. This is going to bring us right under the main family wing. From there we can either use the servants' passages or the escape stairs that will take us right into Granduncle George's suite. I'm betting that Grandaunt Denise is still living there, not Courtney. I'm going to depend on you to disable Denise without harming her in any way. You can do that, can't you?"

"Probably. What's her magik?"

"She's a hydromancer. A Butler. Aeromancy is her secondary talent, but she's not that strong. From the reports I've received, she's also not doing very well mentally. Uncle George's death had hit her hard, and she was never the sharpest knife in the drawer."

We passed through a place where the walls and the ceiling had an arched support brace.

"The wall is directly over us," I said. "Another four hundred meters to the house."

"How far down are we? I don't hear a thing from outside."

"About twenty feet from the surface to the top of the tunnel, and the tunnel walls are about three feet thick. This was supposed to be a bomb shelter, and a radiation fallout shelter as well."

"Okay, so, when we get inside, what's the plan?"

"Find Courtney and kill her."

CHAPTER 48

A staircase upward ended at a locked door. I used my magik to open the lock, and we stepped out into one of the servants' corridors. It was completely dark, as I knew it would be. Who wastes mage lights on the hired help?

We followed it for a couple of hundred feet. "All the locks in the mansion itself and in the main outbuildings are electronic keypads," I said. "When the electricity went out, they all opened. It's a safety feature."

We reached a door, and I cautiously pulled it open to reveal a mage light glowing in the ceiling. We passed through, and I led Aleks down a short hallway to the kitchen.

I was on familiar ground, but the deeper we got into the mansion, the more problems my self-confidence was having. A niggling little voice in the back of my head was telling me that what we were doing was crazy.

I sent out a call via my implant. *Dad, where are you?*

Busy, was the response. I hoped for more, but that was it.

We were faced with crossing through half of the building's ground floor to reach the main staircase in the entranceway or taking the servants' back stairs, where we were very likely liable to run into someone who didn't think we should be there. And even though the fighting was going on outside, I knew the guardians mostly used the servants' corridors to move around inside the house. There were definitely fighters on the roof using the magitek devices and heavy weaponry installed there.

I put the question to Aleks.

"In those servants' hallways," he said, "you'd have to be totally incompetent to miss someone, either with a bullet or with magik. And if they're even half-trained, they know enough to have an aeromancer lead a patrol. Escaping that kind of encounter won't be easy. Let's take the path that gives us the most freedom of movement."

To get to the main stairway, we had to go through the main butler's pantry into the family dining room. From there, I had a choice of the men's or women's parlors, although I figured it probably didn't matter. Both connected to the formal dining room.

Our luck didn't hold. The instant I set foot into the women's parlor, I heard a shout. Across the room from me in a chair sat a man with a rifle. He started to his feet, raising the gun to his shoulder. A bolt of energy buzzed past me and caught the guardian. He tottered, a gaping hole in his chest, and fell across the chair. From the room beyond, I heard voices raised and coming closer.

I motioned, and Aleks moved to the right and around a corner into an alcove the maids used when they were serving. I moved to the left. In the men's parlor, there was a bar I could have hidden behind. In the women's parlor, there was only a sideboard pushed up against the wall and much too heavy to move easily. My only choice was to hug the wall next to the door the sounds were coming through, and hope I could pull the trigger faster than the guards could.

The first guy who came in wasn't one for hesitation. He saw his buddy's body and sprayed the room with automatic weapon fire. He was two feet away from me, and I shot him. He staggered away and fell. Another rifle barrel poked into the room, and a bolt of energy from the maid's alcove hit the doorway.

"Shield!" I yelled and extended my electrical box into the doorway. When I triggered the fourth of its functions, it blanketed a twenty-foot radius around me with a sustained hundred thousand volts. I thought that Aleks was out of range but not by much. I let it run for a few seconds, then stepped through the door, and dashed for the protection of the sideboard in the formal dining room. It had an open shelf underneath it. I dived under and sprayed bullets from my Raider around the room. A couple more of Aleks's energy bolts shot into the room.

Cautiously, I switched off the lightning box. No one shot at me. In fact, there was no nearby sound.

Aleks crept in from the other room and moved to the wall on the other side of the door.

"I have the shield," he said, and I nodded, kneeling down.

He whipped around the corner, and I poked my pistol out behind him. When I didn't hear anything, I followed him. The reception area and the main staircase were empty of life. I nodded to Aleks and gestured toward the stairs. He leaped up and took them two at a time. He was halfway up when a guardian appeared at the top, aiming an assault rifle at him.

The explosive bullet from my Raider took out the guardian and part of the bannister in front of him. Aleks didn't slow down. When he reached the top, he looked both ways, then motioned for me to go up.

"Where now?" he asked when I joined him.

I went to the first doorway in front of me and slipped inside. Wending my way through the empty suite, I found the hidden panel next to the fireplace and triggered it. We went through, into a narrow hallway with a staircase leading up in one direction, and a narrow hallway leading to my left. We took it and came to a narrow doorway with a sliding panel set at eye level. I slid it aside and looked through the slit that was revealed.

The room beyond held a large bed, and I could see the closed door leading out into the rest of the suite. From the way it was decorated, I assumed it was a man's bedroom. The bed was made, and the room had an unused quality about it. The top of the dresser was almost bare except for a couple of pictures and an ornate box.

I pushed the door open and moved into the room, my Raider drawn and my concentrator in my other hand. A quick check showed there was no one in the bathroom, then I crossed to one of the three other doors. I opened it slowly until I could peek through into the next room, which turned out to be a butler's pantry that included a small kitchen and a bar. That was connected to what appeared to be a valet's room, and through it a dressing room. A second door in that led back to the main bedroom.

The third door opened into an alcove, beyond which was a large parlor. Considering there was a battle going on outside, I wasn't surprised there wasn't anyone in the room.

"Check out the other rooms in the suite," I whispered to Aleks. Motioning to one alcove on the other side of the room, I said, "That's Lady Denise's room. I'll check that."

CHAPTER 49

My Grandaunt Denise, wearing a nightgown, sat in a chair by the French doors leading to the terrace. A decanter and a snifter with brown liquid sat on a small table next to her. Magelights lit the room. As I watched, she reached out and picked up the glass.

"Come in, Dani," she said.

That was a little unsettling, since her back was to me and I couldn't see her face.

Denise chuckled. "You're not the only one with magik. Come in. There's a spectacular fireworks display going on outside."

I circled around until I could see her.

"You're looking well," she said. "Come sit down and have a drink with me."

"Thank you, no," I said. "I'm on duty."

"Ah. Come to arrest my daughter?" She sighed deeply. "I'm afraid she won't take that very well. Do be careful, Dani. She'll try to kill you. That's what she does to everyone who gets in her way."

"Do you know where she is?" I asked.

Denise waved in the direction of the door I had just come through. "On the far side of the parlor, there's a door. The staircase leads to the weather room on the roof." She chuckled. "Weather room. That's what George always called it. That's where storm mages do their magik."

Through the window in front of her, I saw tracer bullets arc across the estate wall toward the house. Lightning from a magitek generator arced back in response. With only glass separating us from the outside, the explosions and thunder were so loud I could hear her only in between them.

"Dani, can you do me a favor?" she asked.

"I think it depends, Aunt Denise."

"Make it quick. I don't want her to suffer."

"I'll do my best."

"I know you will. You were always such a good girl. Olivia bragged about you all the time. Even when you got in trouble, it was never very bad. She would tell me about it, and we would laugh. Is she all right?"

"Yes, ma'am. She's doing well. I don't know if you're aware, but she escaped to Ireland."

"I knew she got away. If you see her, give her my best."

My eyes got a little teary. "Are you all right?"

"Oh, yes. I miss George, of course, and I'm sad that Courtney turned out the way she did, but hopefully, when this is all over, I can get out of here. George and I bought a little place on Lake

Como years ago. I think I'd like to live out my time there. I'm tired, Dani. It's time for a new generation. Tell Olivia I said that. Tell her that she should turn it all over to Lucas. Our time is past."

My ears perked up. "Lucas? Have you seen him?"

"Yes, he was here a little while ago. I'm so glad he's back. I'm sure you and Oliva and your mother are very relieved."

"Did you tell him about the weather room?"

She chuckled. "No, but I'm sure I didn't have to. Lucas knows this house like the back of his hand."

I spun around and raced for the door.

"Aleks! This way," I called to him as I crossed the parlor. I yanked open the door Denise had indicated and found a spiral staircase. I started up, but my boots rang on the metal treads, so I had to slow down to a quieter pace. Aleks was right behind me.

The roof was three floors above us, and there weren't any exits from the staircase. By the time we reached the top, we had climbed seven stories from the tunnel, and my thighs had a greater appreciation for Findlay's servants.

We emerged into a large, round, glass-walled and glass-ceilinged room held together by metal framing. From that vantage point, I knew that in daylight—without the storm clouds—I would be able to see the Chesapeake Bay coastline twenty miles away.

Courtney stood on the far side of the room from us—the northwest side. My dad, Lucas James, faced her with about fifty feet separating them. Neither even glanced our way. Her face showed cruel rage. Dad's expression was one of determination.

Courtney lashed out with a bolt of lightning. My heart leaped into my throat, and I thought I would faint as the lightning seemed sure to hit Dad. But he waved his hand, and the bolt ricocheted to his left and up, striking the roof. I expected the roof to shatter, but it didn't, seeming to absorb the energy. The whole room—walls and ceiling—lit up, and then the light faded away.

A miniature tornado sprang up and rushed toward my father. The peripheral blast of wind knocked me off my feet. Using his concentrator, Dad carved the whirlwind up, and it fell apart.

Aleks and I watched for about a minute as they tossed magik at each other that would have destroyed a small city. I had no idea how long they had been at it, but neither of them showed any signs of damage or hesitation.

Courtney sent a strong gust of wind, and Dad staggered. It wasn't even aimed at Aleks or me, but we were buffeted by it and pushed back. She followed up her advantage with another lightning bolt. He managed to deflect it, but his response wasn't as strong.

She followed up by hurling a sharp spear of ice at him. His concentrator vaporized it. Another gust of wind kept him off balance, and then she launched another tornado. I huddled on the ground, feeling as though I was being beaten.

Rising to my knees, I shouted, "Courtney!" She half-turned toward me, and lightning shot out of the hand she extended in my direction. I dove to the floor and rolled, but the bolt of energy splashed harmlessly against a shield Aleks threw up in front of us.

Without thinking, I aimed and fired my Raider. The explosive bullet hit Courtney in the upper abdomen, practically blowing her in half. She was dead before she hit the floor.

All the wind and noise in the weather room ceased. The fighting outside and the storm continued.

Aleks slowly walked over to me and held out his hand. I took it and he pulled me up.

"I don't understand why she wasn't shielded," he said.

"She couldn't," Dad answered as he walked toward us. "She could shield when she used water or air, elements that were external to her. But she couldn't launch those lightning bolts from inside an airshield." He shook his head. "Why she kept using lightning, I don't know."

My dad and I had similar talents—magitek with a minor talent for electromancy. His was stronger than mine.

He got a faraway look on his face, then started to speak. His voice filled the room, and I could hear echoes of it from outside.

"Lady Findlay-Moncrieff is dead," he announced. "Cease fire, and throw down your weapons. Anyone who surrenders will be treated honorably. Anyone who continues to fight will be executed. I repeat, Lady Findlay-Moncrieff is dead. There is no one to pay you. This war is over."

He grinned at me. "Magitek intercom and loudspeaker system. George had me put it in so he could pipe music for Denise's parties. Now, if you could assist me in enforcing that? Help me disable those lightning projectors?"

He walked to the east side of the room, and I went to the west. Reaching out with my magik, I disabled the closest rooftop lightning projector, then proceeded to the next. Very shortly, the sounds of fighting died down.

The storm continued. I knew it would take a while for it to wind down. But without Courtney's magik, it would move off and dissipate.

CHAPTER 50

S he always wanted to be a princess, and on her wedding day, she definitely looked like one. I had seen bigger weddings, fancier weddings, but Kirsten was the most beautiful bride I'd ever seen. And she was radiant.

Mychal simply stumbled his way through the day looking gobsmacked.

Aileen couldn't stop crying, but she was smiling the whole time. Blair looked so incredibly uncomfortable that I took pity on him and took him around back and smoked a joint with him. After that, he just leaned against a wall with a bemused expression on his face and drank.

There had been a minor dustup about Kirsten's dress. It took Olivia stepping in to tell her that fire-engine-red wedding dresses 'are just *not* acceptable.' My mom wasn't any help, as she watched the whole thing laughing so hard tears ran down her face.

I did get some input on the bridesmaids' dresses. Mary Sue was pissed, but I out-voted her. No pink.

Aleks was more familiar with the Novak estate than I was, so he showed me around a bit. I also got to meet his parents and his uncle. They seemed like very nice people, and they invited me to the Family estate in Munich.

"Wow, you got to meet the parents!" Kirsten said when we had a moment together. "He must be getting serious."

"Bah. I'm the maid of honor. I've met more damned people today than I can count, let alone remember their names."

She laughed. "Admit it, you wouldn't say no if he asked you."

I shook my head. "I'm gonna miss you."

"We won't be gone for long, and I'm still going to have my shop two blocks from Police Headquarters. You're still gonna be stuck with me."

Soon afterwards, the bride and the groom took their leave, heading for their three-month honeymoon tour of Europe.

They looked so happy that it brought a tear to my eye. And in that moment, when I used my hankey to wipe it away, Kirsten struck. Something soft hit me in the face. I grabbed it in self-defense and found myself staring at her bouquet.

Looking up, I found her looking directly at me, a mischievous grin on her face. She stuck out her tongue, then she turned, took Mychal's hand, and they ran together toward their limousine.

I looked at the bouquet again, not knowing what to do with the damned thing. Aleks came up behind me—I knew it was him by his smell—slipped his arms around my waist, and nuzzled my hair.

"Danica James, will you marry me?" he whispered.

I turned around in his arms. "Are you crazy?"

He smiled. "So, is that a yes?"

I studied his face, then kissed him. "It's a maybe. I'll give you some time to sober up, and then we'll talk about it."

৩৵৩

If you enjoyed **Soul Harvest**, I hope you will take a few moments to leave a brief review on the site where you purchased your copy. It helps to share your experience with other readers. Potential readers depend on comments from people like you to help guide their purchasing decisions. Thank you for your time!

Get updates on new book releases, promotions, contests and giveaways! Sign up for my newsletter.